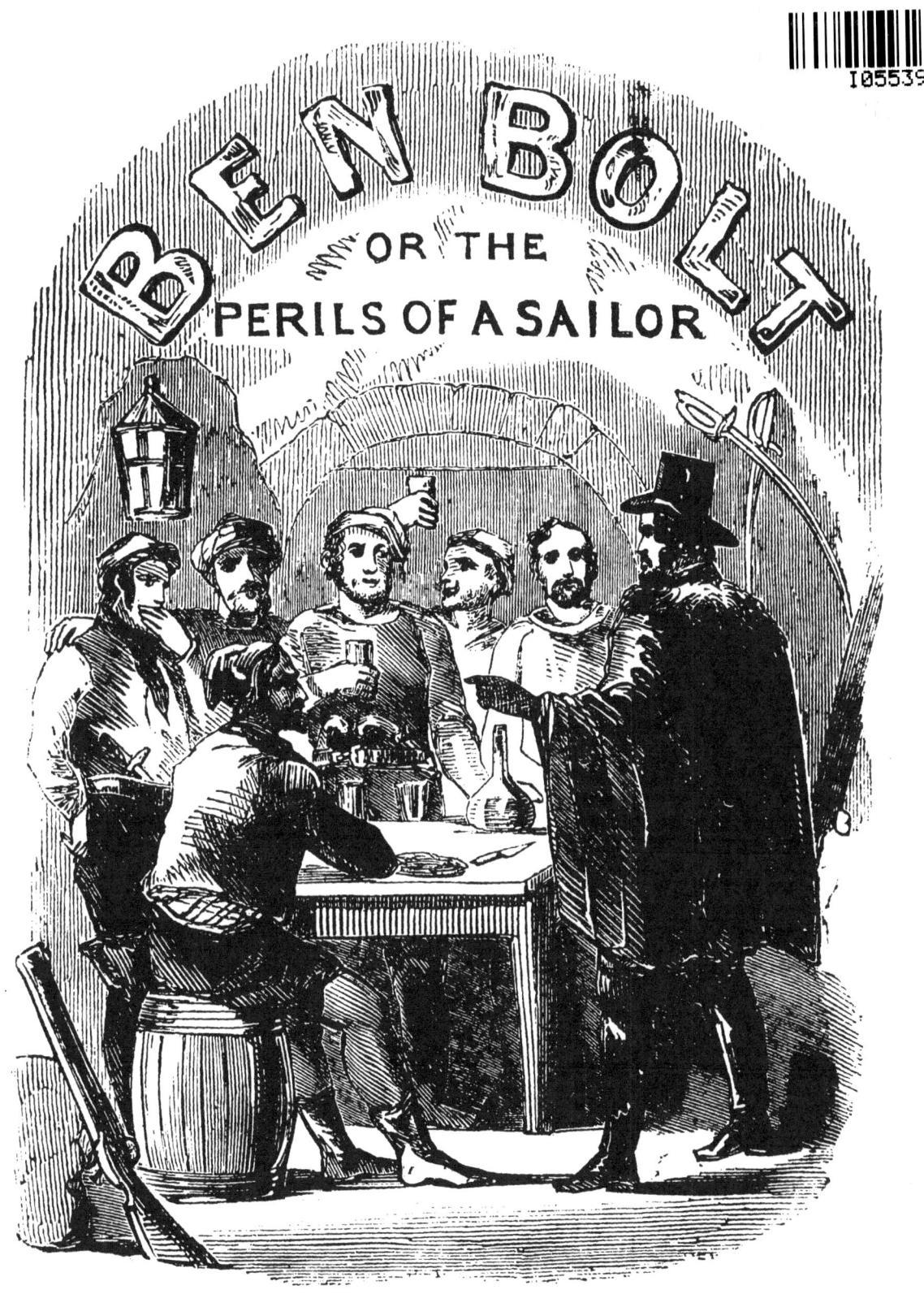

BEN BOLT

OR THE
PERILS OF A SAILOR

BY T. PREST, Esq.,

Author of " Gallant Tom," " The Death Ship," " The Smuggler King," &c., &c.

LONDON :—G. PURKESS, COMPTON STREET, SOHO.

BEN BOLT;

OR,

THE PERILS OF A SAILOR.

~~~~~~~~~~~

CHAPTER I.

THE VILLAGE FESTIVAL—ALICE MAITLAND—THE WIERD WOMAN'S WARNING.

It was a bright summer's day, and the fair face of nature never wore a more lovely or cheerful aspect; hill and dale, lake and rivulet, glistened 'neath the golden rays of the meridian sun; balmy perfumes filled the tranquil air, and peace and gladness reigned o'er all around.

Sad, indeed, must that heart have been which could not have bounded with joy in such an hour; insensible the soul which would not rise in wonder and admiration.

The scene to which we would direct the reader's especial attention, was one of the most romantic and animated description; it was on the outskirts of a neat little village, situated in one of the most pleasant parts of the Isle of Wight, and commanding one of the most picturesque marine views that the glowing fancy could well imagine.

On the brow of a lofty hill at a short distance, stood the stately and ancient Manor House, the family seat of Sir Raymond Perceval, and on a spacious lawn which stretched itself far before it, were assembled a happy group of rustic revellers, invited to feast and make merry on his natal day. The banquet over, the tables were cleared away, the musicians, hired for the occasion, struck up the most lively tunes, and each one present trod it gaily in the fantastic mazes of the dance; the baronet, and several of his distinguished guests looking on with mingled feelings of pleasure and admiration.

Among those assembled on this joyous occasion was a party of individuals that claim our particular attention, as they will have to act some of the most prominent characters in our tale. This party consisted of honest old Ben Bolt, a veteran seaman who had been for many years " laid up in port," in the neighbourhood; Ralph Maitland and his dame, together with their two lovely and innocent daughters, the admired of all who knew them—the ever-fascinating Alice and Rose.

Alice Maitland, " sweet Alice," as she was usually called, was scarcely eighteen years of age, which we should find, were we to attempt to give anything like an adequate description of the graces of her mind and person; suffice it to say that nature never formed a more lovely being, and that her bosom was the seat of the greatest purity and virtue. The beauty of Rose was of a different description to that of her sister, but she was equally charming in form and features, while her mind was as pure as innocence itself.

At the conclusion of one of the dances, Alice had retired with her sister to a remote corner of the lawn to rest herself, and to escape the too marked and familiar attentions of Sir Raymond, and the melancholy expression of her countenance showed too plainly that the feelings of her heart were little in accordance with the scene of gaiety before her; but the eye of the baronet still followed her, and there was a bold and sinister expression in his impassioned glances which was anything but pleasant to contemplate.

No. 1.

Sir Raymond Perceval was on the verge of fifty, but he aped all the manners of a much younger man, and his habits were wild and reckless in the extreme. There was an air of mystery about him too, which was calculated to excite unpleasant feelings of suspicion, and to create doubts as to his real character and secret motives; but of that more anon.

In person the baronet was tall and commanding; his features were manly and regularly formed, if not handsome; his address flattering and insinuating; but his dark piercing eyes spoke a language which ever raised a blush on the cheek of innocence and modesty, and caused it to shrink from him in doubt and timidity. On more than one occasion he had made such bold advances towards the gentle Alice that had confused and surprised her, and she, therefore, avoided him as much as possible, and it was not without the greatest reluctance she had been prevailed upon to join the present festivities.

Indeed the mind of poor Alice was ill at ease, for the noble-hearted adopted son of Ben Bolt, to whom her whole soul was fondly devoted, was far, far upon the sea; and so long had his absence been, that now the most dismal forebodings haunted her imagination, that she should never behold him again. These melancholy thoughts crowding upon her mind, she drooped under a depression of spirits which she could not conquer, and from which her affectionate sister in vain sought to arouse her.

As Alice viewed the broad calm waters of the deep, sparkling in the bright sunbeams, and the tall masts of the different gallant vessels anchored in the neighbouring harbour. the sadness of her feelings increased, and taking from her throbbing bosom a miniature likeness of poor Ben—the youth whom she so fondly loved—and pressing it fervently to her lips, her tears fell fast upon it, and deep sighs of the keenest emotion swelled her gentle breast. How glad would she have been to be permitted to retire, and, in the silence and solitude of her own chamber, to seek that consolation of which she stood so much in need.

Truth to tell, Rose Maitland was in scarcely a less gloomy state of mind than her sister, though naturally possessed of greater vivacity of spirits, for she also mourned the long absence of her youthful lover, Harry Helm, the schoolfellow, friend, and shipmate of Ben Bolt, and more than two years having elapsed since, in the same vessel, they had quitted their native shores, and war raging in all its dreadful fury, the beauteous sisters had ample reasons to entertain the most serious apprehensions for their safety, At length old Ben Bolt and Mrs. Maitland approached the place where Alice and Rose were sitting, and the former, in his usual bluff manner addressing himself to our heroine said :—

" Why Alice, lass, you and your sister have parted company with the other craft just at the time when pleasure is aboard, and we have piped all hands for fun and jollity. Dash my pigtail! girl, you look as dull as a tar in the bilboes, or as if you had just shipped a heavy sea of trouble. Come, come, no hoisting signals of distress, when the wind blows fair, and there are no breakers ahead."

" Alas! my kind friend," said Alice; " how little are my feelings in unison with the present cheerful scene; spite of all my efforts to subdue them, gloomy thoughts and fears weigh heavily on my heart. Two years and a half this very day;" she added, with a sigh yet more painful than had before agitated her breast; " two years and a half this very day, since the gallant Dauntless quitted these shores, with those so fondly loved on board of her, and for some months no tidings of her fate have been heard. Dear Ben, how fatally have the sad presentiments that crossed my mind on the day we parted, been realized; shall we never meet again ?"

" And poor dear Harry, too ;" ejaculated Rose, throwing her fair arms around the neck of her sister, and pearly tears of heartfelt emotion trembling in her beautiful eyes.

" Nay, nay, my dear children ;" said their father, soothingly ; " you must not give way to these sad thoughts, for it grieves me to see you do so; hope for the best, hope for the best, and all will yet be well."

" Aye, cheerly, cheerly, my fair and gentle craft;" observed old Ben, " and depend upon it the Great Captain aloft will protect your lovers from the shoals and the rocks, and will not suffer them to be cast away upon a lee-shore; for two braver or nobler lads, or better seamen never manned the yards than my adopted son and proty-gee (don't you call it ?) Ben Bolt, and his sworn friend and shipmate, Harry Helm."

"Heaven bless them!" ejaculated Mrs. Maitland, emphatically.

"Right, right, my worthy old dame;" responded the veteran, supplying his mouth with a fresh quid of enormous size; "and, God knows that, if the dear boy whom I have called Ben Bolt, after myself, had been my own son, I could not have loved him better than I do; and I trust I have done a father's duty by him."

"You have indeed, excellent old man;" cried Alice, tears of gratitude sparkling in her eyes; "and may the Almighty shower his choicest blessings upon your head for it. Oh, Ben! dearest Ben, art thou indeed lost to us for ever?"

"Avast, avast, my poor lass;" returned old Ben; "not so; depend upon it, he will weather every storm, and will again, ere long, be safely moored in the arms of the girl he so fondly loves. Ah! and I now remember that it is just twenty-one years this very day, since Providence rendered me the fortunate means of rescuing the dear boy from a fate which otherwise seemed inevitable."

"Then the young mariner known as Ben Bolt, and about whose fate the fair Alice expressed so much anxiety, is not your son?" asked Sir Raymond Perceval, who unobserved had approached the spot where they were standing, and had been an attentive and deeply interested listener to the latter part of the conversation which had passed between them. Our heroine started confusedly at the sound of his voice, and she thought she beheld a malicious expression pass over his countenance which made her involuntarily shudder.

"Oh, no, your honour," answered the old seaman, bowing; "there is something too noble about his character for the son of such a rough old tar as me; hows'ever, I have tried to be both father and mother to him; he has been a gift to me, and I consider him the most precious gift that Providence could have sent me. God bless him! and I only hope that he will soon again cast anchor ashore."

"Amen!" solemnly and fervently exclaimed Alice.

A slight frown for a moment contracted the dark brows of the baronet, and he fixed an earnest and peculiar look upon our heroine, but quickly seeming to recollect himself he said, addressing the question to Ben :—

"Did you not know the parents of this youth then?"

"No, your honour;" replied the old man.

"How then did he come under your protection?" interrogated Sir Raymond.

"Why," returned old Ben; "if your honour wishes to know, I will give you the particulars in a few words, for they are all entered in the log-book of my memory. You see, your honour, it is now about twenty-one years ago, aye, twenty-one years this very day, that I was serving on board the Alligator, Hingyman, homeward bound, Captain Beaufort skipper, and we had just weathered a stiff gale, which had been blowing great guns from the N.N.E., and we were not more than a league from the shore, when the man upon the watch suddenly descried through the hazy mist a dark object on the surface of the waters drifting towards us, which, on closer inspection turned out to be a boat, stretched at the bottom of which was something which appeared to be a human form, helpless and inanimate, if not dead. By the captain's orders we hove too, and I and two more then put off to the boat, which we soon reached, and found it to contain the form of a female of handsome features, elegantly dressed, bound hand and foot in the boat, with a sweet little infant clinging to her breast. Poor thing! there had been some foul work to bring her into that dreadful situation, for the blood still flowed from a deep wound in her side, though she was quite dead. Ah, your honour, how I shuddered with horror at that dreadful sight, and—"

"Proceed, proceed," interrupted the baronet, impatiently, and his lip quivered and his countenance underwent a remarkable change; "and this child is he who has since been known as the young seaman, Ben Bolt?"

"True, your honour."

Sir Raymond muttered some unintelligible words between his teeth, and averted his looks; but in a moment or two he regained his composure and self-possession, and urged Ben to complete his narrative.

"Well, your honour;" remarked the old man. "I have not much more to tell. My heart yearned towards the poor child from the first moment I saw him. He was taken on board, and placed under the motherly care of one of the female passengers. The ship arrived in England, and, at my earnest request, the child was entrusted to me by the captain. I had no children of my own, and my poor wife, heaven rest her soul! received the little stranger with the deepest sympathy, the captain promising ever to be a friend to it; but he died on his next voyage, poor fellow, and so the child was left entirely to the care and protection of myself and my wife. I adopted him as my son, and had him baptised after me. When not half a handspike high, his heart yearned for the sea, the young dog. I encouraged his inclination, and now I'll be bound to say there is not a braver or better seaman in his Majesty's service, or a more generous-hearted, noble-minded youth than young Ben Bolt, the son of the deep!"

Alice clasped her hands vehemently together, and she breathed an earnest prayer to heaven for the preservation and speedy return of her lover. Sir Raymond fixed a keen and penetrating glance upon her, and then, once more averting his looks, seemed to commune with himself in an evident state of excitement, but at length said: "This is a strange story you have been relating, friend Bolt, and is the young man himself acquainted with the particulars?"

"To be sure he is, your honour, for it would have been wrong of me to have kept him in ignorance of 'em."

"And you discovered nothing that might lead you to a knowledge of his origin?"

"Nothing but a small gold locket, suspended from the unfortunate woman's neck, which contained a portion of dark hair," answered old Ben;" "and was marked with the initials A. S."

"Ah!" ejaculated Sir Raymond, in an under tone, and he again seemed to reflect seriously for a minute or two.

"But pshaw!" he said at length; "this dismal subject is calculated to give one the horrors, and but ill accords with the present joyous occasion. Fair Alice, you have already withdrawn yourself too long from the sports, and our friends, no doubt, are most anxious for your return."

"Pardon me, Sir Raymond;" replied our heroine, in a timid voice, and feeling a certain dread and foreboding of she scarcely knew what, as she noticed the warm and eager looks which the baronet fixed upon her; "but I do not feel at all well, the evening is advancing, and I—I would much rather now return home, and—"

"Return home?" repeated Sir Raymond, interrupting her;—"unreasonable; I cannot listen to such a thing for a moment, and what is more, I must claim the honour of your hand in the next dance."

"Oh, Sir Raymond!" said the agitated maiden, blushing deeply, and trembling violently. "Spare me, I beseech you. I—I—"

"Nay, nay," rejoined Sir Raymond, taking her hand and fixing upon her one of his most insinuating smiles; I positively must not be refused; plead for me, fair Rose,—plead for me, my kind friends."

Alice looked imploringly at her parents, and her heart palpitated violently against her side. She thought of her lover, and she felt a sensation of dread, mingled with disgust, which she had never experienced before.

"Nay, my dear child," answered her father, "it would appear ungracious to decline Sir Raymond's condescending invitation. Arouse yourself from this lassitude of feeling, and enter with renewed vivacity into those innocent sports so suited to youth, and so much in keeping with the present auspicious occasion."

"Aye, aye," shouted old Ben, "all hands on deck for a dance. Splice my timbers, if I haven't a good mind to shake a toe with the best of ye, only as how, yer see, my old hull has been tossed about in so many rough gales, that it is not now exactly in first-rate sailing condition. Come, come, Alice, my pretty lass, overboard with the blue devils say I, and trip it lightly as a little fairy, as you are."

A look of exultation overspread the features of Sir Raymond as he again took the hand of our heroine, and followed by Ben, her parents, and Rose, led her forth. Poor Alice could scarcely refrain from tears, and her mind was so bewildered and agitated that she scarcely knew what she was about. The music struck up one of the most sprightly tunes, and notwithstanding the state of her feelings, never had the gentle Alice moved with more simple ease and grace in the dance. Everybody was wrapped in astonishment, and gave vent to their feelings of admiration in loud demonstrations of applause.

Suddenly, however, the sky, which had hitherto been so clear and brilliant, became overshadowed with dark and ponderous clouds;—a terrific peal of thunder reverberated through the heavens, which had scarcely rolled away in the distance, when a loud and simultaneous exclamation of mingled astonishment and consternation escaped from the revellers, and all eyes were directed towards a strange and mysterious object that had seemed to rise suddenly out of the earth, and stood upon a slight elevation in the midst of the alarmed and wondering group, and immediately before Sir Raymond Perceval and the trembling Alice Maitland.

The strange being who thus arrested universal attention, appeared to be scarcely human, and it was only the patched and ragged garments that scarcely covered its tall and bony form, denoted it to be something in the shape of woman, and over whose head a hundred winters seemed to have spent their inclement fury. In one thin hand she held a long staff, formed out of the branch of a tree, and, with the other arm extended, she pointed menacingly towards the baronet. Her gray dingy hair hung wild and dishevelled over her shoulders; her features were large and haggard, her skin brown and shrivelled, and her large black eyes, which glistened with a supernatural lustre, were fixed sternly and intently upon Sir Raymond, who seemed to be completely paralysed to the spot, while poor Alice quitted his side, and clung with terror to Rose and her parents.

Still darker were the clouds that obscured the horizon, and again a deafening peal of thunder shook the heavenly concave.

" The wierd woman ! the wierd woman !" now in trembling accents escaped from several lips; " Heaven help us, for some terrible calamity is at hand !'

" Aye, dolts !' cried the hag, in a hoarse discordant voice; " there is evil weaving in the web of fate, and woe to them on whom its fury is destined to descend. Guilty Sir Raymond,—" she added, approaching him nearer, and with peculiar emphasis in her tones ;—" guilty Sir Raymond, darest thou to contaminate the hand of purity and innocence with thy touch ? Tremble, villain, for the hour of retribution will yet arrive !''

" Croaking idiot !" exclaimed Sir Raymond passionately, " how darest thou obtrude thyself upon my presence ? Begone, or fear my vengeance !"

'*Thy* vengeance !'' repeated the mysterious woman, with an unnatural laugh of scorn and malicious triumph ; " fool thou little knowest her whom thou thus venturest to threaten, or thou wouldst tremble to give vent to thine enfuriated feelings. There is blood upon thine hands, there is blood upon thine hands, which calls aloud to high heaven for justice and revenge. Tremble ! tremble !—And thou, poor innocent maiden," she added, softening her voice, and turning to our heroine with something like an expression of compassion ; oh, beware, beware, for the storm is gathering, and when the clouds shall burst even thy guileless nature shall not shield thee from their fury. Think of he whose heart still faithfully throbs for thee, and beware, oh, beware of the tempter !''

" Damned wretch !" cried Sir Raymond, furiously. " I will have no more ; thus do I punish thee for thy bold presumption."

As he gave utterance to these words, he rushed desperately and determinedly towards her, but in an instant he was felled to the earth by a heavy blow from the wierd woman's staff, at the same time she uttered a wild and unearthly laugh of exultation and derision ; another fearful crash of thunder followed, and when the petrified persons present looked around, the mysterious being had disappeared, no one knew how or whither.

The terrified Alice was led away from the spot by her parents and Rose, the astonished guests looked at each other for a few moments with feelings of the most indescribable awe and consternation, then quickly dispersed, and Sir Raymond Perceval was left alone, stretched insensible upon the earth.

CHAPTER II.

THE REMORSE OF CONSCIENCE—SUBTERRANEAN RETREAT OF THE PIRATES—VILLANOUS DESIGNS.

Completely stunned from the effects of the violent blow which the wierd woman had dealt him, Sir Raymond remained in a state of stupor for several minutes after the startling and extraordinary adventure recorded in the preceding chapter, and when he did recover his senses, and looked inquiringly and anxiously around him, he discovered for the first time that he was alone, his guests and attendants having quitted the place in dismay. He muttered, cursed between his teeth at the unexpected and singular interruption that had taken place, but the words of the mysterious woman flashed vividly on his recollection, and conscience, that busy monitor to the guilty mind, in spite of his sturdy and reckless nature, made him quail beneath their influence. At length, endeavouring in some degree to collect himself, he slowly entered his mansion, which he found lonely and deserted by the guests who lately had been assembled there, and made his way to his own private sitting-room, to brood sullenly over the strange events of the day, and the guilty deeds of the past.

The Manor House was a fine gothic building which had come into the possession of the family of the Percevals in the early part of the reign of Henry the Seventh; but it had undergone so many alterations and improvements in different ages, according to the taste of its proprietors, that very little of the original structure remained.

Its external appearance was venerable and imposing in the extreme, with its ancient towers and lofty turrets; its gothic casements and ivy-mantled walls; and its halls and galleries, and numerous apartments were spacious and furnished with all the elegance of modern times.

Like most old buildings, the Manor House had its legends attached to it, in relating which the domestics and peasantry on the estate frequently amused and alarmed themselves on many a cold and dreary winter's night, over a blazing fire, when the wind howled and bellowed without, and the tempest increased in violence every minute.

Strange and dismal stories were also told of long, winding, and intricate subterranean passages, and gloomy dungeons, and of the awful crimes that in former ages had been perpetrated therein. The ignorant and superstitious placed the most implicit confidence in those idle tales, and would almost as soon have faced death in its most frightful form as to have ventured to penetrate those unhallowed precincts.

The Manor House, and the valuable estates attached to it, had come into the possession of the present baronet on the demise of his father, about seven years previous to the period at which our eventful story commenced. Sir Raymond had resided on the Continent, or amid the giddy scenes of the gay metropolis, for many years, only visiting his parents at lengthened intervals, and at such times appearing to be under a restraint which was anything but agreeable to his tastes and inclinations; and even now he was frequently absent from the manor for months together, and no one knew whither he was gone, with the exception of two or three confidential servants, who accompanied him.

Sir Raymond had never been married, though his bold and licentious habits had gained him an unenviable notoriety among the fair sex, and parents and guardians looked upon him with dread and suspicion. The transcendant charms of the fair and gentle Alice Maitland had completely ravished his senses, and he took every opportunity of paying her the most marked attentions, and of convincing her how great was the admiration she had excited in his breast; but the lovely and innocent girl could not help viewing him with feelings of fear and repugnance, and which the remarkable adventure related in the first chapter rather served to increase than abate.

Notwithstanding that the baronet was most profuse in his liberality, and complaisant to all, there was a certain tone of mystery about him, and his manners were at times so forbidding and reserved that he was little calculated to inspire implicit confidence, or to obtain that universal respect he might otherwise have done.

And now, before we proceed further with the chain of our narrative, it may be deemed necessary to mention a few particulars respecting that singular and mysterious individual who has been introduced to the reader by the name of the Wierd Woman!

On the summit of a craggy steep, which hung far over the sea, stood the ruins of what had once been a powerful castle, but of whose former strength and grandeur but few traces now remained. Its black and crumbling walls seemed scarcely capable of affording even temporary shelter to a human being, and it was shunned with a feeling of superstitious awe and dread by every one who resided in the vicinity. Here, then, had the wretched creature of whom we are writing taken up her miserable abode, and there was no person who would think of disturbing her in her lonely retreat.

Old Maude (for by that name she was sometimes called) had been an inmate of these gloomy ruins from the earliest memory of "the oldest inhabitant." Whence she had come, her real character, or by what means she existed, was a mystery which no one could penetrate. She was evidently of great age, by some she was supposed to be no more than a poor wretched maniac, but the more ignorant and superstitious attached a supernatural importance to her character, and looked upon her with feelings of the most uncontrolable fear whenever she made her appearance before them, which she always did at times when she was least expected, and so sudden and unaccountably, that it increased their terrors, and involved them in still greater wonder and perplexity. Her wild prognostications were firmly believed in, and listened to with fear and trembling, and the presence of old Maude on any particular occasion, was always looked upon as the harbinger of some approaching evil, and dreaded accordingly. No one would have been bold enough to attempt to offend or molest her, or venture to oppose her in any shape or form, for fear of incurring her terrible malediction, which they felt certain could not fail to bring destruction on their own heads, and on all those who were in any way connected with them.

Such was *The Wierd Woman of the Ruins*, the dreaded of all; but to return to Sir Raymond Perceval.

On entering his room, he secured the door, to prevent the sudden intrusion of any one, and throwing himself dejectedly in a chair, abandoned himself to the most gloomy and torturing thought. His pale features, quivering lips, convulsive working of the muscles, and contracted eye-brows, told in language too plain to be misunderstood, the agitation of the mind within; and the dismal character of the room he was in (for it was situated in one of the most ancient parts of the building, and its furniture was old and ponderous) did not tend to alleviate his gloomy and painful reflections.

The storm now raged in earnest, frequent peals of thunder seemed to shake the house to its foundation; the flashes of lightning every minute became more vivid, and the rain rattled against the casements with a hollow, melancholy sound. Darkness too, had set in unusually early for the time of year, and nothing could surpass the cheerlessness and misery of the hour; but it was in perfect unison with the state of Sir Raymond's mind at that moment. There the still, but overwhelming voice of conscience was at work, and would be heard even above the tumult of the tempest.

For some time the wretched baronet thus sat in moody silence, brooding over the past and the events of the last few hours, but suddenly starting to his feet, and folding his arms across his chest, he paced the room with hasty and disordered steps.

"What infernal hag is she," he said at length, in a hoarse voice, which shewed the inward tortures of his guilty soul; "what infernal hag is she, who thus with bold front and threatening aspect, thus comes to remind me of the dark deeds of the past, which I would that I could long since have buried in oblivion, and to warn me of the future? Or, have my senses forsaken me, and am I now labouring under some frightful delusion? Psha! I have become a very child, thus to abandon myself to such weak and idle fears. '*There is blood upon thine hands!*'—Yes, yes;" he added, with a shudder, after a brief pause, during which he glanced timidly around the room; as though he was fearful of encountering some grim and ghastly object; "the wierd woman spoke the truth; these hands are indeed stained with blood; the blood of the pure, the good, and the innocent, and conscience, in spite of all my efforts to the contrary, weighs down my guilty soul with misery and despair. It was a fearful, a monstrous deed, and neither time nor circumstance can possibly obliterate it from my memory. The narrative of the old seaman too, this day, has recalled it still more vividly to my brain. The youth then to whom the affections of the lovely Alice are so ardently, so fondly devoted, is the offspring of that unfortunate woman who so brutally perished by my hands, and should he ever return, and by some strange and unforeseen circumstance become acquainted with the damning truth, I—but no? fool that I am, I torture myself with vague apprehensions that can never be realized. Let me arouse myself from this dismal state of mind, and endeavour to be firm, for if I do not by my own folly betray myself, suspicion can never possibly light on me. Courage, courage, and I may yet be able to set detection at defiance."

Sir Raymond paused, and became somewhat re-assured as he gave utterance to these words; but still his mind was ill at ease, and he pondered again and again upon the startling and warning words to which the wierd woman had given utterance. It was in vain for him to attempt to despise them, for he could not deny them to be the truth; and he was lost in wonder and perplexity to imagine by what means she had been able

No. 2.

to penetrate his secrets, or to guess who she was. Once more he threw himself on a seat, and abandoned himself to the indulgence of his own gloomy thoughts.

The storm increased, and it was fearful to listen to the fierce raging of the warning elements. Peals of thunder roared through the heavens in rapid succession, the lurid lightning gleamed around, threatening destruction to all those unfortunate beings who were exposed to its fury, and the rain descended in overwhelming torrents, laying waste everything beneath it.

"It is an awful night;" said the baronet, as he again looked fearfully around him, and partly arousing himself from the deep lethargy that had before steeped his senses; "even such a night as this it was, when—but away with thoughts that only drive me on to madness. Luke Harden and his guilty associates are no doubt now assembled in their secret haunt, and I must seek their counsel and advice. It is fortunate for me that I am connected with such determined and reckless fellows; I have already experienced the value of their services on more than one or two occasions, and no doubt shall find them useful to me in the furtherance of my future designs."

He took a lighted lamp from the table as he thus spoke, and advanced towards the further end of the room, where an ancient painting descended from the ceiling to the floor. He pressed hard upon a certain portion of the frame-work of this, which communicated with a secret spring, the picture then glided easily back, and discovered an opening big enough for the admission of a person's body, and which led to a winding flight of stairs. These Sir Raymond slowly and cautiously descended, and at length alighted in a kind of small paved court, which received a slight portion of light and air from a small crevice in the wall. The baronet now took a small bunch of keys from his pocket, and unlocked a low wooden door on the opposite side, which revealed a dark narrow passage, apparently of great length, winding and circuitous, but which the feeble light remitted by the lamp he carried could not penetrate. Sir Raymond held the lamp above his head, the better to accelerate his view, and as he began to traverse it he could not help shuddering, as though he was fearful of encountering some frightful object, such as his feverish imagination was likely to conjure up.

This subterranean passage was evidently the work of an age long past, and the walls were black, and dripping with unwholesome dew. The wind whistled in hollow moaning gusts along it, and Sir Raymond had frequently a difficulty in preserving the light. As he advanced further, the sound of several coarse voices, apparently in uproarious mirth, saluted his ears, and he paused to listen.

"They are there," he said, "and it is quite evident that no anxiety of mind depresses their spirits. They are reckless, dare-devil rascals; bolder or more determined never ploughed the ocean's breast, or hoisted the black flag. How little does any one suspect that beneath the walls of the old Manor House, is the secret haunt of the pirate, Luke Harden and his daring crew, and that the proud Sir Raymond Perceval has for years been their friend and associate."

A smile of satisfaction passed over the baronet's features as he gave utterance to these words, and he again walked on. He had not proceeded many paces, when a ray of light streamed across his path, which proceeded from the interstices of a door at the further extremity of the passage, and which evidently opened upon some apartment or cavern beyond. The baronet paused at the door for a minute or two before he ventured to knock. All was again silent for a short time, when suddenly a rather musical voice burst forth into the words of the following song, at the end of each verse the whole of the individuals present apparently joining in the chorus.

SONG OF THE PIRATES.

O'er the dark blue surging wave,
Oft the shipwreck'd seaman's grave;
Though the tempest loud does blow,
Dauntless on our course we go.

CHORUS.
In storm or calm, we plough the sea,
For daring buccaneers are we.

Let lightnings fire the murky air,
The hardy pirate knows no fear;
Still so boldly on his way,
Anxious for his destined prey.
CHORUS.
In storm or calm, we plough the sea,
For daring buccaneers are we.

Loud demonstrations of applause followed this vocal display, which having subsided, Sir Raymond knocked with his fist three times on the door, which signal seemed to be well understood, for it was immediately opened by a tall muscular man, with dark sunburnt features and huge black whiskers, and the baronet on entering the place was received with a loud tumultuous welcome by the persons present. The scene which presented itself was of rather a wild and remarkable description. It was a spacious, lofty, vaulted apartment, cavern,—or, rather, an excavation in the solid rock—and from an opening at the further end, a few feet from the ground, and which was ascended to by a step ladder, the sky was visible; and from the dashing sound of the waves, no doubt immediately beneath it was the sands or beach. This opening the pirates had a means of blocking up and concealing, should any danger happen to threaten. The walls were hung with arms of different descriptions, and beneath them were piled numerous sea-chests, powder-casks, kegs, &c. In the centre of this cavernous abode. was a long, rudely constructed table, and round which the pirates were carousing, Luke Harden (who was a remarkably tall, powerful, and ruffianly-looking fellow, with ferocious and determined features) being at the head, on a seat rather more elevated than any of his lawless associates. The place was lighted by three large lamps, suspended by chains from the roof.

On the entrance of the baronet, Luke Harden left his seat, advanced towards him, and extending his hand with the utmost familiarity, said :—

" Welcome, Sir Raymond; we did not expect to see you to-night, supposing that, on the occasion of the festivities at the manor, you would be otherwise engaged. What, has the storm dampened the ardour of the spirits of your guests, and caused them to weigh anchor rather sooner than they otherwise would ?"

Sir Raymond returned no immediate answer to this, but drew Harden aside into a remote corner, in order that he might commune with him without being overheard by the rest of the pirates.

" Luke," he said, after a brief pause, " I have had that occur to me to day that annoys me sadly, and upon which I wish to have your serious advice."

" Indeed ?" observed Luke; " why, what's in the wind now ?—Your spirits seem to have sprung a leak."

" Seriously speaking, I am rather excited, and I think you will acknowledge that I have good cause to be so, when you hear the particulars."

" Explain yourself, Sir Raymond ?"

" A moment's patience and I will do so," answered the latter. " In the first place, I have heard from the lips of old Ben Bolt sufficient to convince me that the youthful seaman who goes in his name, is no other than the son of her who perished by my hands."

" And whom with her infant we consigned to the crazy boat," added Luke Harden; " and whom we hoped would have been swallowed up by the waves. It was a foul deed, Sir Raymond."

" It was—it was;" hastily returned the latter, with a look of the most painful emotion; " but it is useless to repent it now. The boat, it seems, was discovered by a trading vessel called the Alligator, of which this old man was one of the crew; the child lived, was adopted by Ben Bolt, and it is he who possesses the heart of the beauteous Alice Maitland."

" It is strange," observed Harden; " but still I do not see why you should let that circumstance trouble you; the boy has no means of discovering his origin, or by whose hands his mother perished; besides, should he ever return—which I do not think is very probable, the Dauntless having most likely gone to Davy Jones's ere now—we may easily secure his person, and there will be an end to all your fears."

" True," coincided the baronet; " but there is something else that excites my apprehensions."

"What mean you?"

"That mysterious being, old Maud."

"What, the Wierd Woman of the Ruins, as she is called ?"

"The same."

"And what of her, Sir Raymond ?" investigated Luke.

"She knows my secret," replied the baronet.

"Impossible!"

"It is true."

"Explain yourself; you astonish me," said the pirate.

Sir Raymond did so in as few words as possible, and Harden listened to him with much attention, and when he had concluded, said :—

"Pshaw! Sir Raymond, you surprise me to hear you talk; why should you attach any importance to the ravings of such an old idiot as Maud ? But should she continue to annoy you, you have the readiest means of silencing her for ever, and setting all your doubts and apprehensions at rest."

"True, true," answered Sir Raymond; "yet would I fain avoid the shedding of more human blood. My hands are too deeply stained already. Heartless monster that I must have been that I could turn a deaf ear to the piteous supplications of the unfortunate Emmeline for mercy! Oh, it was a hideous crime, and heaven in the loud voice of the roaring thunder seemed to utter its curses on my head. Methinks that now I see her, when my remorseless dagger had pierced her side, as she turned her dying eyes with a ghastly expression upon me, and—"

"Hold, hold!" interrupted the ruffian, Luke Harden, impatiently; "you unman yourself, Sir Raymond Perceval; give not way to such coward thoughts as those. Let us change the subject. The beauteous Alice Maitland is the object of your most ardent admiration and desire?"

"True," exclaimed the baronet, his eyes sparkling as he spoke, from the influence of the guilty passions that had taken possession of his breast. "I love her—to distraction love her—and what sacrifice is there that I would not willingly make to possess her; but it is quite evident that she views me with fear and repugnance."

"And what matters that if you are only determined?" demanded the pirate; "it would be no difficult task for you to get her in your power, and she would be secure enough here, or on board our gallant barque, the Bloodhound."

"Ah!" ejaculated Sir Raymond, eagerly, a sudden change coming o'er the expression of his features; "you inspire me with fresh hopes, Harden, and I thank you for it. We will talk further of this business anon. Hold yourself in readiness to act according to my instructions at a minute's notice."

"Aye, aye;" returned Luke; "you shall have no reason to complain of me or my crew. The bold hearts of the lads of the Bloodhound are strangers to fear. We are at your service whenever you may require us."

"Well spoken, Luke," remarked Sir Raymond; "your hand. The Bloodhound, under false colours, is now anchored only a short distance from hence, is she not?'

"She is," answered Harden; "and the secure disguise which I and my men have assumed, whenever we venture forth from this retreat, or go on board our vessel, has completely deceived the land-sharks. Ha, ha, ha! they believe me to be a fair trader, and that the name of the ship is The Water Nymph."

"Aye, Harden," said his companion; "you have managed the business admirably, I must say, and I give you full credit for it. I expect before long that I shall have occasion to take another voyage with you."

"Be it so,' replied Luke; "I shall be most proud and happy of your company; and, truth to say, I do not care how soon I am on salt water once more, for I am quite tired of leading this indolent life.'

"Well, then," observed Sir Raymond; ' I have now, I believe, explained everything to you, and we understand each other perfectly?"

"Certainly," answered Hardman.

"Enough," said the baronet; "I am satisfied; and for the present I leave you. Good night."

"Good night," responded Luke, and having again shook the hand of Sir Raymond, familiarly, the latter took up his lamp, and, quitting the room, once more retraced his steps towards his own apartment, reflecting upon all that had passed between him and the pirate, and feeling somewhat more easy in his mind.

The storm still raged with unabated violence, and when the guilty Sir Raymond again found himself alone, he once more resigned himself to the same dismal thoughts that had before occupied and distracted his brain.

CHAPTER III.

THE FEARS OF ALICE—MAUD OF THE RUINS AGAIN—THREATENED DANGER.

We have described the agitation of Alice Maitland at the scene which took place on the appearance of the wierd woman, and the precipitation and dismay with which she and her parents quitted the place, surprised and shocked at what they had heard and seen, and completely lost in the mystery which the circumstances had created. The fearful words which old Maud had uttered respecting Sir Raymond had made a powerful impression on her mind; and the warning she had given to herself filled her breast with the most painful doubt and apprehension; at the same time she felt hurt and disgusted at the boldness of the baronet's behaviour towards her, and she could not but entertain the most serious forebodings as to the danger which might threaten her from him. She deeply regretted that she had been prevailed upon to join the festivities at the manor at all, and trembled to anticipate the dreadful consequences of which it might be productive.

Little conversation took place between Alice and her friends on the way home, and they arrived there just as the storm which had been threatening for some time commenced with the greatest violence; but Alice, on entering the room, sank in a chair, and was too much absorbed in her own thoughts to pay much attention to the rude voice of the tempest. From this melancholy state of torpor her parents tried to arouse her, but with very little or no effect; and, indeed, the strange observations of Maud, who had indirectly accused the baronet of murder, and her wild predictions regarding their lovely daughter, had made almost as powerful and painful an impression on their minds as her own.

As Alice now listened to the loud tumult of the warring elements, which ever and anon was sufficient to shake even the stoutest heart with terror, her thoughts reverted to her lover, and as she reflected upon the uncertainty of his fate,—the dangers to which he might this night be exposed, if he still survived, and the improbability that they would ever meet again, scalding tears of the most poignant anguish chased each other down her pale cheeks, convulsive sobs at intervals escaped her bosom, and the poor girl was, in fact, wrought up to such a pitch of excitement, that she felt as if her heart would break.

The cottage of Ralph Maitland was a commodious four-roomed dwelling, which had been bequeathed to him, together with a small annuity, by an only and affectionate brother, who died some few years prior to the commencement of our tale, and this little property, together with what he realised by farming pursuits, rendered the circumstances of the humble family tolerable comfortable, if not exactly affluent. But they possessed those blessings that far surpassed all that the most unbounded riches could bestow, namely, peace, virtue, and sweet content. The beauteous Alice, and her equally captivating, and more lively sister Rose, were the pride and comfort of their parents' declining years, and never had they given them cause for a single pang of regret, or done that which could call for a word of reproach from their lips.

A pretty, attractive little residence was Woodbine Cottage, with the honeysuckles climbing its casements, and its neat little gardens behind and before, so tastefully arranged by the skill and attention of the fair sisters, while every room, with its handsome, though humble furniture, was kept in that clean and compact order which was quite refreshing to look upon. Indeed, the village of Mayland, as we shall call it, was an interesting place altogether, situated as it was so near the sea-side, and commanding at the back, and to the right and left, extensive views of the most fertile, romantic, and diversified description that could well be imagined.

The dwelling of honest old Ben Bolt, adjoined that of the Maitlands', and like it, was remarkable for its neatness and simplicity. Then a few doors off was the village barber's, the proprietor of which, Jemmy Jingle, was an honest, simple, good-humoured, but eccentric young man, who prided himself upon being a poet, and could take credit to himself for stringing together some of the most remarkable and wretched doggrel that was ever perpetrated by morbid brain ; and whose time was fully occupied between shaving, versifying, and making love to a buxom lass, yclept Miss Sally Simper, who was one of the domestics at the Manor House. Then there was the village ale-house, "The Jolly Topers," kept by old Matty Muggins, a thirsty soul ; with its rustic seats and tables in front, its fine old tree, stretching its leafy limbs over the roof of the hostelrie ; and its swinging sign-board, with the red-faced portrait of a grog-blossomed tar, and having underneath the following very enticing, lines :—

> " All those who would blue devils cure,
>   Will never pass Mat Muggins' *dore*,
>   For Matty Muggins he lives here,
>   And sells the very best of fare."

Nor must we forget the unpretending little school house—

> " And the master so kind and so true ;
>   And the little nook, by the clear running brook,
>   Where you gather'd the flowers as they grew."

Such is a brief description of the village of Mayland, one of the principal scenes of our tale.

Notwithstanding that the lurid lightning continued to dart its fury in at the casement, and the voice of the thunder increased in might, Alice remained seated in the parlour of the cottage, in the same pensive attitude, and seemed completely lost to everything but her own torturing meditations.

"Come, Alice, my children, and you, my dear Rose," said their father ; " do not remain any longer there, exposed to all the terrors of the storm, which are so little suited to the present depressed state of your spirits ; retire my girls, and in sweet slumbers endeavour to forget the strange events of the day."

"No, my dear father," replied Alice, in a melancholy tone of voice ; "indeed I am but ill-disposed for rest on such a fearful night as this ; suffer me to remain here for awhile to collect my thoughts, and Rose no doubt will keep me company. Dear, dear Ben, if you are still living what must be the horrors you are this night enduring."

"And alas, my beloved Harry !' sighed her sister, "how vividly does my perturbed imagination picture to me the terrors of his situation. May all merciful heaven watch over and protect them both. Oh, why should the cruel waves separate us from those we so fondly love ?"

"Avast, avast heaving, my poor lasses," ejaculated old Ben ; "and take in a reef ; you must not yet founder in the sea of despair ; you will weather the storms of adversity yet, never fear, and ere long, when the wind veers, all will again be calm and sunshine, and you will find safe anchorage, with your lovers, in the haven of happiness. But good night, my friends, 'tis time I set sail for home, and turned into my hammock. Good night, good night."

And cordially shaking a hand of each, Ben Bolt quitted the cottage. Finding that it was useless to endeavour to oppose the whim of Alice, Mr. and Mrs. Maitland embraced their daughters affectionately and then retired to their chamber.

Alice and her sister sat for some time in dismal silence, while the tempest raged without ; but though their tongues were silent, their brains were busy at work, and their bosoms were racked in the most torturing and insupportable manner. Between the pauses of the blast, they were interrupted by hearing a gentle knock at the cottage door, which having been opened by Rose, they were surprised to see Jemmy Jingle enter, completely wet to the skin.

"La ! Mr. Jingle," said Rose, "whatever in the name of goodness brings you from home on such a stormy night as this ?"

"Why, you see, Miss Rose," answered Jemmy, after the hubbub on the lawn," with that old witch, and which put such an unceremonious stoppage to our festivities, I entered the Manor House with my dear Sally to have a bit of chat with her, and in hopes that the storm would pass over ; but seeing there were no likelihoods of that, and it getting late, I was forced to depart. So seeing a light in your cottage window, I could not help calling in to bid you good night."

Alice and her sister thanked him, and the garrulous Jemmy thus continued :—

"It was cursed provoking that frightful old woman appearing at the time she did, for I was just about to make such a display as a poet, as I flatter myself would have immortalised me. I had written some lines for the occasion, that should have gained me a marble statty at least, or else there is no reward for real genius in the world. I ll read them to you, if you have no objection, for they are very pretty,—splendacious !"—

With these words Jemmy Jingle took a sheet of paper from his pocket, and commenced reading as follows:

" The *hoderous* flowers their *hoderous hoder*—sheds,—

" Beautiful line !" said Jemmy; "what I admire it most for is that there's no tortology, as they calls it, about it."

"Very pretty indeed," archly said Rose, with a smile,—

" The *odious* flowers, their *odious—*

"Shades of the muses !" interrupted Jemmy;—"hear this;—Odious too ! Ah, Miss Rose, you are something like my Sally Simper, you have a heart for love, but no soul for poetry. As for me I am not too modest to say that I'm a living wonder, I'm a natural—"

" Well, Mr. Jingle," said Rose, again smiling, " if you are a natural, and a little bit *soft*, you cannot help it. I suppose you was born so."

" Ah, Rose, you little gipsy ;" said the poetical barber, " I see you are quizzing me, however, I must read the lines to you."

> " The hoderous flowers their hoderous odour sheds,
> The buttercups and daisies rears their heads;
> Lillies and daffy-down-dillys their charms display,
> To welcome in Sir Raymond's natal day."

" There's lines, Miss ! in years of *maturity*, my name will be classed among the rest of the great poets, and my statty in marble *fool*-length, will be mounted on the *pebblestones* of fame !'

"Pebblestones !" repeated Rose; " the *pedestal* of fame, you mean, Jemmy."

" Well, well," returned Jingle, " its all the same. Pebblestone's the Latin for pedestal, you know, and is much more expressive. But la! I cannot help thinking of old Maud of the Ruins, and what she said."

" She is indeed a fearful and mysterious woman ;" remarked Alice, " and never shall I forget the ominous words she uttered."

" Oh, as for that, my dear Miss Alice," returned Jingle, " I should not let them trouble me at all, for she is only a poor idiot, that's very clear, and she knows not what she says. For my own part I am resolved the next time I see her not to mince the matter with her, but to insist upon an explanation, and—God bless my soul! Heaven preserve us !" he added in a trembling voice, and casting his eyes fearfully towards the window ; " what was that ?"

At that moment a tremendous crash, followed by a wailing sort of cry, was heard outside, which made them all start and look with alarm towards the window; but nothing was to be seen but the blazing lightning, and no other sounds were to be heard but the howling of the tempest.

" It must have been only fancy," said Jingle, after a pause, and endeavouring to compose himself. " But I must be going, so good night, ladies; good night, and may all good angels watch over your slumbers."

Thus saying, Jemmy Jingle, having first cast an anxious glance out at the window, hurried from the cottage, and again left the sisters to themselves.

" What could be the meaning of that fearful sound ?" said our heroine; " did you hear it, Rose ?"

" I did,' answered the latter, " but do not believe that it proceeded from anything else but the storm. Come, my dear Alice, you must try to arouse yourself from this gloomy state of feeling. Let us retire to rest."

" Rest !" repeated Alice, " I am certain there is none for me; my thoughts are with that beloved being who is far, far away, and perhaps at this awful hour exposed to the most imminent danger."

" Oh, let us pray to heaven," ejaculated her sister, " to watch over and protect those whom we so fondly love from the terrors you apprehend.   As for the wierd woman—'

She was prevented from finishing the sentence, by again hearing a mournful cry outside, which was followed by a crash and a loud clap of thunder, and simultaneously directing their eyes towards the casement, by the glare of the lightning they were terrified to behold the hideous features of old Maud of the Ruins staring full upon them.

Alice could not repress a faint scream, and clung to her sister, who was more firm than herself, and the next moment the casement was thrown wide open, and Maud pointing significantly with her long bony hand, directed their attention towards her, as in a harsh, grating voice she said :—

" The tempest howls—lightnings dart their forked fury, thunder shakes the vaulted roof of heaven, and the wild sea-mew, as it wanders through the blast, utters its wailing cry, sad omen of coming danger ; but Maud of the Ruins heeds it not, she braves the bellowing wind ; the lurid lightning's fires ; the loud roar of the heavenly lion—all—she boldly braves to perform her mission.   You tremble, maidens, and your cheeks are blanched with terror ; but fear not—I will not harm ye ; innocence and virtue are still sacred to the wretched being before you."

As the singular being thus spoke, the expression of her dark features became less severe, and Alice and her sister felt somewhat more encouraged.

" Mysterious woman," interrogated our heroine, " who are you, and why do you thus appear before us ?"

" To warn you of the danger that threatens you ; the evil spirit that is abroad to disturb your peace.   Come nearer, maidens ; come nearer."

They did so, and after a brief pause, Maud, fixing her eyes stedfastly upon them, ejaculated in solemn accents :—

" Faster ! faster the storm-clouds gather, and deeper become the designs, the black designs of villany to lure and work the destruction of the children of innocence and inexperience.   Oh, beware that they succeed not.   Alice Maitland, as you value peace and virtue—as you remain faithful to him who still lives to love you—though even this night ; nay, this very hour, a frightful death threatens him—beware of the insidious serpent who has oft-times crossed your path ; beware of the man of blood—beware of Sir Raymond Perceval !"

" Sir Raymond Perceval !" repeated our astonished heroine ; " your words are ambiguous ; oh, why should I fear him ?"

" Slight not my warning, maiden,' replied Maud ; " for ere long you will discover its import.   Shun him, I say again, as you would a demon.   But I am forbidden to reveal more at present ; farewell till we meet again, and remember !"

And before either the astonished Alice or her sister could question her further, Maud hastily shut to the casement, and immediately, as if by magic, vanished from their sight, leaving them to recover themselves in the best manner they could.

————

CHAPTER IV.

THE DREAM—SIR RAYMOND PERCEVAL AND ALICE—THE INSULT AND THE INTERRUPTION.

It was some time after the departure of Maud before either of the sisters could recover themselves sufficiently from the surprise and confusion into which their second interview with the mysterious sybil had naturally thrown them to speak ; and they stood in the same attitude, with their eyes earnestly fixed upon the casement, as if they still gazed upon the frightful visage of that inscrutable being.

" She is gone," at length observed Rose ; " strange woman as she is, what can possibly be her real character and motives ?"

" Alas ! I know not," answered our heroine ; " but the words she uttered, and her solemn and emphatic manner, have filled me with an indescribable and unconquerable feeling of dread.   I tremble for the future, for much I fear that some terrible calamity is about to befall us."

" Nay, my dear sister," said Rose. " try and subdue all such fearful forebodings; you must really not allow such sad thoughts to disturb your mind."

" Would that I could indeed conquer them," returned Alice ; " but, alas ! they

ALICE RESCUED BY BEN BOLT.

resists all my efforts to do so. 'Tis certain that old Maud is no common woman, and it is impossible to disregard her solemn injunctions. You remember the lines that are said of her, Rose ?"

" Yes," replied the latter; " they are these, I believe—

" Whenever Wild Maud doth appear,
  In day's bright sun, or midnight drear,
  Be sure that danger hovers near !"

" But that is only an idle superstition, Alice;" she continued; " and as such, unworthy of consideration. Come, it is late; the strange and exciting events of the day have fati gued us, and we had better, in repose, seek that refreshment of which we stand so much in need."

" May heaven in its infinite mercy, watch over us !" ejaculated Alice, solemnly; and, clasping her hands vehemently together; " and shield us, and all those so dear to us, from those dangers I so fearfully anticipate."

No. 3.

" Amen !" fervently responded Rose ; and having affectionately embraced her sister, they slowly quitted the room, having first closed the window-shutters, and retired to their chamber.

The storm abated; the thunder no longer shook the vault of heaven ; the flashes of lightning became less frequent, and then entirely ceased; but the rain still continued to descend with considerable violence, and appeared likely not to terminate during the night.

On reaching their chamber, which adjoined that of their parents, the lovely sisters, having offered up their usual evening prayer to the Supreme, Rose immediately sought her couch, and having tranquillised her feelings, soon forgot the stirring events of the day in sleep; but Alice threw herself on a seat, and pondered seriously over all that had occurred, and augured the worst results from it.   There was an air of probability about the prognostications of the wierd woman which made a lasting impression upon the mind of Alice ; and the bold conduct of Sir Raymond Perceval towards her that day, and his general character, which he had been unable to conceal from her penetrating observation, gave greater weight to the warning words of Maud, and increased the prejudice of our heroine towards him.   The words she had uttered respecting her lover also recurred most vividly to her memory, and conjured up a variety of conflicting doubts and fears in her breast.   Again she took the treasured miniature from her bosom, and her tears fell fast as she gazed upon the beloved features of her sailor-love.

At length, worn-out with thinking, she retired to rest, and sleep soon descended upon her eye-lids.   But busy imagination was still at work, and her slumbers were disturbed by troublesome dreams.

At one time she imagined that she was, with her lover, exposed to the open sea on a raft, which threatened every moment to go to pieces.   It was night, and impenetrable was the darkness that reigned around.   The cold was most piercing ; the wind blew a perfect hurricane ; the roaring waves rolled mountains high, and every moment their awful fate seemed to be the more inevitable.   Still they were driven wildly on, at the mercy of the angry billows, and the fierce wind, as it howled around them, sounded their solemn death-knell.

And how fearful and despairing were the looks of her lover, as he gazed in silent anguish upon her, and held her still closer to his bosom, to shelter her from the blast, and overwhelming waves that dashed over them.   Another moment, and she imagined that they were struggling together in the deep, and gasping for life.

Suddenly a tremendous wave tore them asunder, and calling frantically on her name, she beheld her lover sink to rise no more.

Her brain swam round, and for a moment her senses seemed to leave her ; but soon her recollection returned, and then how changed and fearful was the situation she found herself in.   She was on a wild and barren rock, exposed to all the fury of the elemental wrath, the forked lightning playing around her, and she was struggling violently in the hated embrace of Sir Raymond Perceval.   With what fiendish expression did his eyes glare upon her, and how awful were the words that escaped his lips, as he held her more closely in his arms, and tried to pollute her blushing cheeks with his odious kisses.   In vain she struggled to release herself, and screamed for help ; her strength was nearly exhausted when the spell of sleep was broken, and she awoke.

The perspiration stood in large drops upon her forehead with the excitement of her dream.   She pressed her hands upon her aching temples, and her brain was so confused and bewildered that for a few moments she could scarcely persuade herself that what had been presented to her perturbed imagination had not occurred to her in reality.

It was quite dark, and a death-like silence reigned around, which rendered the moment still more solemn and impressive.   Alice cast her eyes timidly around the room, and almost fancied she saw the form of the baronet gliding stealthily by in the obscurity of the farther end of the chamber ; and so powerful was this impression, that she was half inclined to call aloud for help.   But in a few minutes she recovered herself and endeavoured to be more firm.

Rose still slept soundly, and no torturing visions, such as had occurred to Alice seemed to disturb her rest.   Our heroine could not but envy her tranquillity, and at the same time she heartily prayed for morning.   At length, however, she conquered her feelings in a great measure, and succeeded in composing her mind once more to rest, and continued to sleep soundly and calmly till the morning's sun beamed in at her chamber window. Her sister also awoke at the same time, and they arose, and having returned their thanks to heaven for its protection from evil throughout the night, they dressed themselves, and it being yet too early for their parents to be about, they took their seats at the window, and tried to divert their minds at the prospect beyond.

It was a beautiful morning, but the storm of the previous night had left many sad traces of its ravages, though all else around was bright and cheerful. The situation of the chamber was such as to command a most extensive view of a very diversified and picturesque description; and here the eyes of the lover of the beautiful and wondrous works of nature could luxuriate to the fullest extent. But the mind of our heroine at this time was not free to enjoy it; and the remarkable events of the previous day, and the painful vision which had occurred to her imagination in the course of the night were the principal subjects that engrossed her thoughts, and rendered her restless and fearful. From this morbid state of feeling Rose sought all that she could to arouse her, but she succeeded only indifferently; and at length hearing the voices of their parents below, they descended to the parlour and joined them. In the course of the morning repast Alice related to her father and mother all that had occurred to them when they were left alone, and Mr. Maitland and his wife listened to her with some degree of surprise and uneasiness.

"And yet, after all," said Mrs. Maitland, after a few minutes' reflection; " I cannot believe that the predictions of old Maud are worthy of any serious consideration. Her intellects are evidently deranged, poor creature, or she would never lead the wretched, lonely life she does. Banish her from your thoughts, Alice; or only treat her with pity, instead of viewing her with dread."

" But Sir Raymond Perceval, my dear father;" ejaculated our heroine, with an involuntary shudder.

" Why," answered the former; " I must say, from all that I have seen and heard of the baronet, I certainly do not much admire his character, and it will be as well for us to be on our guard against him. But he surely will not dare to raise any unholy thoughts towards you, my child, or presume to insult you with his bold advances."

" Alas!" sighed Alice, " I know not what to think, but only hope that he will cross my path as seldom as possible. I fear that he is a man of crime, and that the fearful charge which old Maud has brought against him is not altogether unfounded."

" Nay, nay, my love," remarked her mother, " we must not judge Sir Raymond too harshly, and we must be careful that we are not too much and too unjustly prejudiced against him, by the dark and calumnious insinuation of this singular woman. For my own part, I place but little confidence in anything she says, convinced as I am that her mind wanders and she knows not what she utters."

Alice shook her head doubtfully.

" Ah, my dear mother," she observed, ' if the brain of the poor creature is affected, there is a method in her madness which has made a most forcible impression on me. As for Sir Raymond Perceval, in spite of all my efforts to the contrary, I cannot even think of him without a sensation of dread, and I have a sad presentiment that he is destined to be the cause of much misery to us all."

" Come, come, my poor child, enough of this," said Mr. Maitland impatiently. " I see that at present your mind is not in a fit state to discuss this delicate subject; the strange behaviour of old Maud, and the wildness of her remarks, has distressed and bewildered you, and you are not just now prepared to judge of all the circumstances impartially and dispassionately. We will talk further about it at some future period, and, in the meantime, I trust that Providence, who ever watches over the good and innocent, will avert all those dangers which you so painfully apprehend."

To this wish Mrs. Maitland and Rose most fervently responded, and the topic of conversation was changed. Alice, however, was far from feeling satisfied, neither had her parents made use of any argument whatever, which was at all calculated to do away with the painful doubts and surmises that had taken such powerful possession of her mind. The wild predictions of the sybil, and the serious tone in which they were uttered, still seemed to ring in her ears, and had made such an impression upon her that nothing seemed likely to eradicate.

Mr. and Mrs. Maitland having some business to transact at Newport, shortly afterwards left the cottage, and the two sisters were left alone to the free indulgence of their own thoughts and conversation. In this manner more than an hour after the departure of their parents passed away, and the mind of our heroine was getting somewhat more composed, when they were suddenly interrupted by hearing a gentle knock at the door, which Rose opened, but her and her sister turned pale, and started back in amazement, alarm, and confusion, when Sir Raymond Perceval entered the room.

The baronet noticed their agitation, and seemed rather abashed at it.   He, however, bowed politely, and appeared to hesitate ere he ventured to address them.

"You will probably pardon this intrusion, ladies," he said at length, and regaining his confidence; "but as I was passing this way, I could not help calling to inquire after your health; and to ascertain whether or not you had suffered any ill effects from the storm of last night, and the unpleasant affair which brought our happy revels to such an abrupt and unexpected termination."

Rose, in a timid voice, thanked him for his polite consideration; but our heroine was too much agitated to make any reply, and trembling, as a secret misgiving crossed her mind, she averted her eyes from the too familiar and ardent gaze of the baronet.

"And how fares the sweet and gentle Alice this morning?" interrogated the libertine, in an insinuating voice, and approaching her nearer. "Not a word, my bashful little gipsy? Nay, this is unkind, and I really must lay an embargo on your too modest diffidence."

"Sir Raymond Perceval cannot feel surprised at the reserve of the humble Alice Maitland," she replied, pointedly; "especially when he perceives that her parents are from home."

"And which I cannot but hail as an excellent opportunity," he said, with increased confidence and avidity; and attempting to take her hand, which she, however, withdrew from him with a crimson blush and a look of repugnance.

"What bewitching innocence and simplicity!" he added, fixing upon her an intense look of admiration. "By the gods! to contemplate such heavenly charms as these is sufficient to ravish the senses, and to melt the very soul away in love and transport.

"Forbear, Sir Raymond Perceval," commanded Alice, with a look of offended modesty and indignation, "language such as I must not, will not listen to. You deceive yourself, sir, if you imagine that the hypocritical voice of flattery can have any other effect on me than to excite my utmost hatred, disgust, and contempt. Pardon me, Sir Raymond, but prudence tells me I should positively decline to prolong this interview in the absence of my parents."

The baronet was unprepared for such a reception as this, and he felt more confused and abashed. Rose could not but approve of the conduct of her sister, and looking upon Sir Raymond as she did with the strongest feelings of doubt and suspicion, she heartily wished that he would retire from the cottage as quick as possible.

"Why so distant, Alice?" said the baronet at length, after a pause, during which he had endeavoured to recover himself. "Indeed you wrong me, if you suppose me capable of pouring fulsome flattery in your ears, or entertaining a single thought to your prejudice. I fear that the words of old Maud of the Ruins have made too powerful an impression upon you, and excited in your breast unjust and unfounded suspicions against me."

"Ah!" replied Alice, "the observations of that mysterious woman were indeed solemn and impressive; nor can I slight the warning. Conscience will convince those interested, whether or not, in other respects, she spoke the truth."

A dark frown passed over the features of Sir Raymond as Alice gave utterance to these words; and he bit his lips, and cast his eyes to the ground.

"The croaking hag!" he passionately exclaimed at length, "and is it possible that you can pay any serious attention to the observations of that mad woman? But enough of this. I have a favour to ask you, Alice, which I trust your kindness and condescension will not suffer you to refuse me."

"I do not understand you, Sir Raymond," returned the damsel, in a timid voice, and fixing a keen and penetrating glance upon him.

"To be explicit then," observed the baronet, "would you grant me the honour of a few minutes' conversation with you alone? Your sister, probably, will have no objection to retire while—"

"Hold, Sir Raymond," interrupted Alice, in a resolute tone; "you can have nothing to say to me which it would not be proper for my sister to hear. Your request is a bold and a strange one, and I must therefore beg most positively to decline to comply with it."

"Perverse little beauty!" he ejaculated, in a tone of vexation and disappointment; "how cruel and unjust are the doubts and suspicions you seem to entertain towards me. But even at the risk of your displeasure, fair creature;" he added, forcibly taking her hand, which, in spite of her efforts to prevent him, he raised to his lips; " even at the risk of your displeasure, I cannot longer keep the torturing and important secret confined to my breast. Beauteous Alice, hear me, and bear with me while I avow in all the sincerity of my feelings, the ardent passion which your transcendant charms, and incomparable graces of mind, has excited in my heart, and—"

"Forbear, Sir Raymond," said the blushing and indignant maiden, "forbear to disgust my ears with an avowal so hateful to my feelings, as that which you have just made. Think not to delude the senses of the humble rustic maiden with your empty sophistry, and honeyed accents; you have torn aside the mask, and I now behold you in your natural deformity, and more fully appreciate the warning of Maud of the Ruins. Begone, dangerous man, leave me !"

"Scornful beauty!' exclaimed the libertine, resolutely clasping her fair form in his arms, and notwithstanding her resistance, polluting her lips again and again with his loathsome kisses;—' scornful beauty, I will not be rejected thus. Let this fond embrace be the prelude to future bliss too great to name."

"Oh, help! help!' screamed the terrified and disgusted Alice and her sister in a breath; and the former tried in vain to release herself from the rude embrace of the guilty Sir Raymond; when just at that critical moment, and when the senses of poor Alice were about to leave her, the room door was thrown open, and old Ben Bolt, carrying a stout stick, rushed into the place, to the rage and disappointment of the baronet, who muttering a bitter curse between his teeth, released his hold of our heroine, who flew for protection to the old seaman, trembling in every limb, and her face crimsoned with the blushes of shame and resentment.

"Holloa!" cried Ben, flourishing his stick with a menacing air. "Shiver my timbers! my pretty Alice yard-arm-and-yard-arm with an infernal pirate! Sheer off, you damned grampus—top your boom, or I will not leave you a sound timber to float with! Wheugh! helm-a-lee! Here's a pretty squall! If it ain't his honour that has hoisted the black flag, my name's not old Ben Bolt!"

"Why this bold intrusion?" sternly demanded Sir Raymond.

"Why, for the matter of that," returned Ben, with a sarcastic look, and giving his stick another threatening twist; " it strikes me as how that's the very question I ought to ax you, seeing as how you are sailing on a wrong tack, and this pretty craft would not have sounded signals of distress if it had been all fair and above-board. Hows'-ever, it's no use spinning a long yarn upon the subject; and what I would just advise your honour is, if you have any regard for your precious carcase, to slip your cable, and sheer off as quick as you can, for if I only pour one broadside into you, you will find that old Ben Bolt has still the courage and the ability to protect a lovely and innocent woman from the insults of a damned shark like you!"

"Daring fool!" said the enraged Sir Raymond; " you shall pay dearly for this. Beware!"

And scowling threateningly on Ben, the defeated baronet, scarce venturing to cast his eyes towards Alice or her sister, hastily quitted the cottage.

CHAPTER V.

THE OLD CASTLE RUINS—THE DEED OF BLOOD—THE RESOLUTION.

"Foiled! degraded—defeated!" furiously cried Sir Raymond Perceval, as he hurried on his way from the cottage; " the girl loathes and despises me then; and, fool that I was, I have betrayed my real thoughts and designs, and she will now be on her guard against me. I have been too precipitate, and had I acted with more due precaution, my plans might ultimately have succeeded. But shall I, because of this single defeat abandon all my hopes?" he added, after a few moments' reflection; " no, by all the infernal host I swear I will not. I have the means of securing her in my power at my command; Luke Harden and the other pirates will be faithful, and with their aid she cannot escape me. Yes, beauteous Alice, you shall yet be mine, in spite of the disgust and detestation with which you view me!'

With these guilty determinations he hurried on his way, intending to return to the Manor House; but his thoughts were so fully occupied that he noticed not the road he took, until suddenly looking up he found that he had wandered from the right path towards the sea beach, and that he was immediately beneath the cliffs, on the summit of one of which the ruins of the old castle in which Maud found a wretched retreat stood, and he beheld their black and crumbling walls frowning high above him.

A sudden thought struck him, and he resolved to penetrate the dreary place with the design to endeavour to obtain an interview with the sybil, and to seek an explanation of her ambiguous conduct towards him. He, therefore, began the steep ascent, which after some difficulty he accomplished, and stood within the ancient ruins.

Nothing could equal the gloom and loneliness around; but it perfectly accorded with the dismal state of mind which the guilty baronet was in at that time. It seemed scarcely possible that in such a dilapidated place any person could find the least shelter.

Sir Raymond, with much difficulty, scrambled his way over the heterogeneous masses of fallen fragments, and at length gained one wing of the building which had not suffered so much from the ravages of time as the other portion, and entering at a low gothic doorway, found himself in an old corridor, the pavement of which was much broken, and overgrown with dank weeds. He crossed this place to a door opposite, which opened on to a long passage, at the extremity of which was a winding flight of stone steps. These the baronet ascended, and at the top his further progress was stopped by a massive oaken door, which was fastened on the inside. He now paused and hesitated what to do; and while he did so, his ears were saluted with a strange rumbling sound, which convinced him that some one was inside. This aroused him into action, and determined to be satisfied, he knocked loudly at the door three times. All was hushed in profound silence for a minute or two after this, when Sir Raymond heard a footstep advancing, and the next moment the door was opened, and the wierd woman stood before him and confronted him; the expression of her features being even more harsh and forbidding than usual.

Maud walked back into the room, which had not a vestige of furniture, save an old, broken arm-chair, and motioned him with a commanding air to follow her. He did so, feeling at the same time anything but easy, and almost regretting that he had ventured to enter the ruins on such an uncertain and useless errand.

The old woman now fixed herself in an attitude in the centre of the room, and leaning on her staff scowled fearfully upon the baronet, but for a minute or two without offering to break the silence.

"Proud Sir Raymond Perceval—man of crime;" she said at length, in her usual harsh, discordant voice; "why venture ye to intrude upon the lonely haunt of Wild Maud of the Ruins?"

"Mysterious woman," answered Sir Raymond, "because I would question thee respecting thy motives for pursuing me with the hatred and enmity thou hast evinced towards me. I would penetrate the dark secret of thy real character."

"Wouldst thou know the power and real character of Maud," returned the sybil, "thou must watch her actions. To her all things are known, past, present, and future, nor canst thou hide from her piercing eye the most secret designs of thy guilty soul. Beware, beware, Sir Raymond Perceval; though for a time thou mayst appear to triumph, the hour of retribution will come at last, and thy doom is sealed."

"Croaking hag!" exclaimed the baronet, passionately; "vile impostor as thou art, what canst thou know of me or my deeds?"

"What know I of thee?" repeated Maud, at the same time glaring upon him with a fiendish look of malice; "fool! ask thine own conscience, where the dark deeds of the past are written in characters of blood!—aye, blood!—the blood of the good and the innocent. Remember the ill-starred Emeline, who, in all the pride of youth and beauty, perished by thy remorseless hands. Think of her whose earnest, whose heart-rending supplications for mercy, could not move thy relentless heart to pity and forbearance, think of her, and tremble, monster—tremble!"

"Cease, woman!" exclaimed Sir Raymond, furiously, while at the same time, tortured by remorse, fear, and the terrors of a guilty conscience, he quailed beneath the ominous import of Maud's words; and he shuddered at the recollection of the dreadful tale which she recalled in such vivid colours to his memory. "Cease woman," he repeated, in a voice still more hoarse with the powerful emotion of his feelings; "I will no longer listen to thy wild remarks and bold threats, the emanations of a disordered mind, or a feeling of malice and savage revenge, which you so unaccountably seem to bear towards me. Thou hast some sinister object in view against me which I cannot penetrate. But beware, lest thou shouldst exasperate my deadliest vengeance, and—"

"Thy vengeance!" interrupted the wierd woman, with a bitter laugh of scorn; "boasting fool, villain, murderer, seeking again the destruction of all that is lovely and innocent, thinkest thou to intimidate Maud of the Ruins with thy empty threats? Miscreant! she defies and despises thee, and will never cease to haunt and denounce thee till heaven's avenging wrath shall descend upon thy devoted head, and lightnings blast thee. In the day's bright sunshine—in the solemn midnight hour—the storm and the calm; and in the festive hour, when all other hearts are light and glad, thy blood-stained conscience shall realise to thy guilty soul all the torments of perdition; and the ghastly features of thy murdered victim shall ever be present to thy terrified imagination."

"Cursed fiend in human shape," cried the baronet, fiercely, and drawing a pistol from his bosom, which he levelled at Maud's head;—"I will hear no more;—at least I will rid me of so deadly a foe, and silence thee for ever! Die, damned hag, and with thee the secret of the dreadful crime of which thou hast so boldly accused me!"

With these words Sir Raymond discharged the contents of the pistol full at the head of the mysterious woman, and when the sound of the loud report had died away, a scornful laugh saluted his ears? He looked up, and with feelings of mingled fear and astonishment, found that Maud had disappeared, but in what manner, he was totally at a loss to imagine.

For a few moments he stood completely transfixed to the spot, alarmed and bewildered, and so sudden and extraordinary had been the circumstance, that it was not without the greatest difficulty he could believe the evidence of his senses. How the wierd woman could have avoided the fate he intended for her, he was at a loss to conceive, and there was something so strange and supernatural about the whole adventure, that his brain became the more perplexed and tortured the longer he reflected on it. He examined the flooring-boards minutely, but could discover no signs of a secret trap, nor could he perceive any other means by which old Maud could so suddenly have effected her escape, so that he became still further involved in mystery.

"Strange and fearful being," he muttered to himself; "by what unaccountable means does she accomplish her designs? Now were I prone to feelings of superstition, I might be disposed to believe that she had some dealings with the devil. Curses light upon her! I fear that I have yet some terrible danger to apprehend from her. Fool that I was to seek this interview, when it could only serve to disturb my mind? And why do I now tarry here? Let me begone, for the gloom of these old ruins are but little suited to the present state of my feelings."

Once more Sir Raymond cast an inquiring glance around the room, and then slowly retraced his steps, looking cautiously about him as he proceeded, and in a state of mind which we need not attempt to describe. He soon regained the lower part of the ruins, and descending the craggy steps, struck into a pathway which led direct towards the Manor House.

Rage and disappointment now held a predominant place in the bosom of the baronet, and he feared that he had acted with great rashness and imprudence in his conduct towards our heroine; and that it might, in all probability be the means of delaying the execution of his nefarious plans, and enable her and her friends to be upon their guard to frustrate them.

"But," he soliloquised, after a few moments' reflection, "let me but be wary and determined, and I may yet be able to baffle all their precautions. The beauteous Alice must and shall be mine, at all hazards; and I will lose neither time nor opportunity to render my triumph complete. Oh, how my heart throbs for the proud moment when I can call her mine, and all those matchless charms are made to yield to my power."

A smile of exultation passed over his features as he gave utterance to these words, and his prospect of success seemed all but certain.

By this time he had reached the Manor House, which he entered, and having made his way to his own private room, he threw himself on a seat, and endeavoured to collect his thoughts. For some time they were of the most torturing and conflicting nature. The interview he had had with old Maud served the more to perplex him, and to increase his fears; but still he exerted himself to the utmost to conquer them; and at last he succeeded much better than could have been anticipated. Anxious to have the further advice of Luke Harden, he quitted the room, and by the same secret and gloomy way which has been formerly described, he took his departure to the pirate's haunt.

On entering the cavern he found Luke alone, and he arose on his appearance and greeted him in his usual familiar manner.

"Well, Sir Raymond," he observed, "what brings you hither now? Has anything more particular occurred? I hope you have no bad news to communicate."

"To say the truth, Luke," answered the baronet, "what I have to tell you is none of the most agreeable or promising. In my anxiety to commence the operation of my designs, I fear I have been rather too precipitate."

"Indeed!" said Harden; "explain yourself."

Sir Raymond did so, and the pirate listened to him with due attention.

"You have certainly acted rather hastily and imprudently," Luke observed, after Sir Raymond had related the particulars; "however, you have broken the ice, and have only boldly to persevere to ensure success. The girl appears to view you with no very kindly feelings; however, do not despair, Sir Raymond, for, my word for it, you will soon find a way to subdue her obdurate spirit."

"Aye," returned the baronet; "I flatter myself that I shall; and her scornful resistance to my will, will only make me the more determined. But that mysterious woman, old Maud?"

"Ah," said Luke, "she certainly appears to be a dangerous woman, and I am at a loss to fathom her real character. She must be get rid of."

"Even so," coincided Sir Raymond; "I must acknowledge, after what I have seen of her, the feeling of deadly malice she evidently entertains towards me, and the threats she has so boldly uttered, she has inspired me with a feeling of dread, and I shall not rest satisfied until I have released myself from so dangerous an enemy. We must devise some means to do so, with as little delay as possible."

"Aye," returned Luke; "we shall find no difficulty in doing that; so you may set your mind at rest upon that point. As regards the girl Alice, you must act the part of the hypocrite towards her if you would hope to meet with success in the accomplishment of your designs. You have acted hastily, and in order to silence suspicion it is necessary that you should apologise to old Ralph Maitland for your recent conduct. You understand me?"

"I do," replied the baronet; "your advice is good, Luke, and fear not but I shall accomplish the business with my usual ability. My resolution is fixed, and in spite of all the difficulties and opposition which I shall no doubt have to encounter, by all my hopes, I swear that the lovely, but scornful Alice Maitland shall be mine."

"Boldly spoken, Sir Raymond," observed the pirate; "and you may rest satisfied that you can at any time command my assistance. The charms of Rose Maitland have also excited a powerful passion in my breast, and I have a strong inclination to get possession of her person."

"And what is to prevent you from doing so; if you make up your mind to it?" demanded Sir Raymond. "I admire your taste, Luke; Rose Maitland is a prize worth having. Be firm, then; and mark my word, she shall, before long, become the pirate's bride."

"Your hand, then," said Harden, "we are pledged to assist each other to the utmost in our mutual designs."

"We are," returned his guilty companion; "and success must crown our efforts. I will see Ralph Maitland without delay, and endeavour to appease the indignation he will no doubt feel when he is informed of the insult I have offered to his daughter. In the meantime we must keep a strict watch upon the movements of old Maud, or she may work us some evil before we are prepared for it. Curses light upon her tongue! which has already excited the suspicions of Alice and her friends against me."

"True," said Harden; "but let not that alarm you altogether, for she may yet be made to feel our power."

"But should the lover of Alice return," remarked the baronet; "and old Maud

THE DESTRUCTION OF THE SHIP BY FIRE.

should make him acquainted with the secret of his history, and denounce me as the destroyer of his father's peace—the murderer of his mother."

"Psha!" exclaimed Luke Harden, impatiently; "arouse yourself, Sir Raymond you must not allow such apprehensions as those to disturb your mind, for they will never be realised, depend upon it. Young Ben Bolt, as he is called—take my word for it—has been food for the sharks long ago; or, if he still lives and should return home, you will have nothing to fear from him, if you only act with anything like prudence and precaution."

"Well," answered Sir Raymond; " I will not fail to act as you advise, and hope for the best."

"A worthy reserve," observed Luke; " and depend upon it your wishes will not be disappointed."

After some more conversation, and further arranging their plans, they separated, and Sir Raymond quitted the cavern and returned to the house, pondering his nefarious designs in his guilty mind, and fully determined to accomplish them at every risk.

No. 4.

CHAPTER VI.

THE SCENE OF TERROR—THE SHIP ON FIRE—THE SAILOR'S RETURN.

We will not seek to pourtray the feelings of shame, disgust, and resentment, that filled the bosom of the gentle Alice, after the scene described in the previous chapter; and for some minutes after the abrupt departure of Sir Raymond from the cottage, she was unable to give vent to her emotions in words.

Honest old Ben, too, was bursting with indignation at what had taken place, for he regarded our heroine with the same feelings of respect and admiration as if she had been his own daughter, and would have risked his life in protecting her from insult.

"Poor lass—poor lass!" said the old man, in a kind voice; "and cannot even your innocence shield you from outrage? The infernal shark; I had as good a mind as ever I had in my life, to give him a sound drubbing; and if I had only laid my grappling-irons upon him, old as I am, I fancy he would have thought he was being overhauled by the devil before his time. It was lucky I happened to be cruising this way, and came athwart his hawse, or there is no knowing how far his boldness might have led him to go.'

"True, my kind friend;" replied Alice, "and I can never be sufficiently grateful to you for the protection you have afforded me."

"Avast! avast, there, my dear girl;" returned the veteran; "I require no thanks, for I have done no more than my duty. He must indeed be a cowardly lubber who would not willingly shed his life's blood in the defence of a lovely and innocent woman when borne down by a rascally pirate."

"But I fear that your noble conduct, Mr. Bolt;" remarked Alice, "will bring down the vengeance of Sir Raymond upon your head."

"*His* vengeance!" repeated the old man, vehemently; "he be damned—I ax your pardon for swearing, my lass. Old Ben Bolt is not to be frightened by any such a swab as he is, notwithstanding his rank. He will find me more than a match for him, I'll warrant, should he ever venture to attack me. If poor Ben, your lover, had happened to be at hand, it strikes me Sir Raymond would have had to pay dearly for his daring."

"Alas!" sighed Alice, and a tear trembled in her eye as she spoke;—"dear faithful, noble-hearted Ben, where art thou now? Shall it never again be my fate to behold thee?"

"Oh, yes, my pretty Alice," answered the old seaman, "belay your fears and still hold to the anchor of Hope. Something convinces me that the dear boy will soon again return safe and sound, and be moored alongside of her he so fondly loves, and whose heart throbs so faithfully towards him."

"Heaven grant that your predictions may be verified," ejaculated our heroine, fervently; "but alas! it is so long since he quitted these shores, and no tidings have been heard of the ship in which he and his friend sailed, that I tremble for his fate. And yet old Maud prognosticated that he would be restored to us."

"Ah!" cried old Ben, "said she indeed so? Shiver my timbers then, if I do not believe her, and shall ever in future consider her as good as a witch for the prophecy. Ah, poor Ben, no doubt he has encountered many perils and dangers since he has been away; but I trust that he will be able to brave the battle and the breeze, and soon again cast anchor on old England's shores."

Most sincerely and ardently did Alice and her sister respond to this prayer, and, whether or not it was the effect of the old man's observations, and the confident tones he assumed when speaking of his adopted son, we cannot say, but it is certain that a sudden feeling of hope animated their bosoms, and imparted sweet consolation to their minds; which Ben immediately perceiving, did not fail to encourage all in his power.

"Ah, my dear girls," he answered, "how does it glad my old heart to see bright sunshine again lighting up your pretty faces, after the dark clouds that lately obscured them. Put your trust in Providence and fear not that it will fail to watch over the life of the hardy mariner, who boldly exposes himself to all the perils of the deep, in the service of his king and country. Squalls may arise, and the fierce tempest for a time threaten him, but poor Jack shall at length meet with his reward; the favouring gale filling the swelling sails of the gallant ship that bears him, shall waft him happily to his native land, where he shall find faithful and affectionate hearts waiting to greet him, and joyful tongues to sing the 'Sailor's Welcome Home.'"

"Good old man!" ejaculated Rose, raising the hardy hand of the veteran to her ruby lips, and a tear of heartfelt gratitude and increased hope glistening in her eye; "how cheering is the picture which your vivid fancy has pourtrayed. A sweet feeling of confidence does indeed begin to dawn upon my mind, and long as they have been departed from us, and without our being able to obtain any tidings of them, I trust that the time is not far distant when poor Harry and Ben will both be restored to us."

"Still encourage those thoughts, my lass," said Ben, "and depend upon it all will be well. Harry Helm I know loves you as fondly and faithfully as my Ben loves your sister, and the lad is well worthy of you. I respect and honour him, for he possesses a noble spirit, and is a sailor every inch of him. He and Ben were playmates, school-fellows together, and have been sworn friends from their earliest days of childhood; and show me the lubber who will venture to say a word against either of them, and he will find old Ben Bolt on board his craft in less time than the bo'sun could pipe all hands."

Alice and her sister could not refrain from smiling at the honest fervour of the old man, and they suffered him to take their hands, and raise them respectfully to his lips.

"Oh, won't that be a happy and jovial day that witnesses the return of Ben Bolt and Harry Helm?" he remarked, "no more signals of distress then; but we will toss dull care overboard, and send the blue devils to old Davy. There shall not be a sad heart in the village of Mayland; all their messmates shall be invited to join the sports; there shall be oceans of grog, and mountains of baccy, and whole cargoes of the best provisions that money can purchase. And then won't we set the fiddlers to work; and only to think how we shall jig it, to be sure. Lor', lor',—I declare if it does not set my old heart going at the rate of fifty knots an hour only to fancy it."

"Ah, Mr. Bolt," returned Alice, a sad misgiving, in spite of her efforts to subdue it, again starting over her; "and yet we must not be too sanguine, lest we should be doomed to some bitter disappointment, which it would be almost too painful for us to bear."

"Avast, avast! Alice, my pretty one," cried Ben, "you must send all such sad thoughts as those adrift, for, my word for it, they will not be realised."

"Alas!' sighed our heroine, "I would fain endeavour to think and to feel as you advise me, but the bold and infamous conduct of Sir Raymond Perceval tortures and alarms me. I fear he has some dark designs against our peace in contemplation, and I much mistake his real character if he will be induced to abandon them."

"He will not surely dare to persist in his guilty projects," observed Ben, with a look of indignation. "Shiver my timbers, if I thought that he would, may I never go aloft if I wouldn't scuttle his vessel, and blow him to the devil in the cracking of a biscuit, though I am but a superannuated old tar, and he is the proud and haughty Sir Raymond Perceval, the lord of the manor, and basking in wealth and power."

Alice was about to make some reply, when the cottage door was opened, and Mr. and Mrs. Maitland entered the room. The two lovely sisters flew to their arms and welcomed their return with the most unfeigned affection; and their parents quickly perceived from the unusual agitation of their manner, and that of Ben, that something had occurred to disturb them, and anxiously inquired into the cause. They were not kept long in suspense, but were quickly made acquainted with the particulars of Sir Raymond's daring conduct, and the resentment, not unmingled with alarm, which filled their breasts may be readily imagined.

"The libertine, the unprincipled villain!' exclaimed Mr. Maitland, his bosom still swelling with rage, "thus to presume to call the blush of shame upon the cheeks of my innocent girls, and to commit such an unpardonable outrage, in the absence of their parents. He now stands unmasked, and proves the value and importance of the warning of old Maud of the Ruins."

"True;" returned our heroine. "Oh, my dear father, much I fear that we have every danger to apprehend; alas! what can protect your child from the diabolical designs of such a man as Sir Raymond Perceval?"

"Protect you, Alice;" replied her father, "and think you that your parent will fail to do so even with his life? 'Tis not his wealth or rank that can intimidate me, when my daughter's innocence is assailed; and humble though we are, and much as he may affect to despise us, mark my words, he may yet have bitter cause to repent of the baseness of his conduct."

"Well spoken, Ralph, my old friend," said Ben, approvingly, " and while I have a timber to float with, damme if I do not stand by you and yours, back and edge, in every danger. Oh, we are not all to be taken aback by a mere capful of wind, and if we do not soon make this rascally pirate lower his flag to us, and cry peccavi, why rank me no better than a powder-monkey, and say that I do not know a mainmast from a jibboom."

"My honest friend," remarked Mr. Maitland, grasping his hand in the most cordial manner; "I well know the warm and excellent feeling you entertain towards me and my family, and believe me that I most gratefully appreciate it. But Alice thinks right, when she would have us not to treat the observations of the wierd woman with indifference. It is evident that she is well acquainted with the real character of Sir Raymond Perceval, and it is necessary that we should be completely on our guard against him, to prevent his having an opportunity of putting his nefarious schemes into execution against us."

"Certainly," coincided Ben; " we must not suffer him to get the weather guage of us,—and should he venture again to open fire, then clear the decks for action say I, and give it him as hot as he can sup it. But courage, my friends, and depend upon it that you will be able to set all the infernal sharks who may seek to prey upon you at defiance. Good day—good day; and should the enemy again heave in sight, you will always find old Ben Bolt within hail."

With these words Ben departed, and they were left to discuss the disagreeable subject together. Mr. Maitland and his wife now plainly saw what they had to apprehend from the baronet, and they saw the necessity of adopting some means that were calculated to thwart his plans, which, however he might act the hypocrite, they had no doubt he would still attempt to put into execution, whenever an opportunity might happen to present itself. In this manner the day passed away, without anything worth recording taking place, and Alice and her sister retired at an early hour to their chamber, but not to rest; for that, at present, they did not feel at all disposed, and they sat near the window continuing to converse upon the painful and alarming circumstances which continued so fully to engross their thoughts. Notwithstanding all her endeavours to banish them, the most fearful doubts and misgivings continued to haunt the imagination of our heroine, and from this melancholy train of thoughts Rose in vain tried to arouse her.

"Strange fancies haunt my brain," she remarked; "I know not how it is, but I feel as if this night something of a remarkable and exciting nature was about to happen to us."

"Give not way to such torturing ideas, my dear Alice," said her sister; " for indeed I do believe them to be groundless. The events of yesterday and to-day have saddened your thoughts, and excited fears in your breast which I trust to heaven will not be realised."

" And have I not met with sufficient to alarm me, and create suspicions in my mind calculated to distract and perplex it. May the Almighty watch over us, and avert those evils which I anticipate!"

Rose could not but sincerely entertain a similar wish, but she returned no answer, and they remained silent a few minutes.

The night turned out anything but fine, though the day had been mild and serene. It was particularly dark for the time of the year, and there was a certain tone in the weather which was certainly calculated to inspire anything but cheerful thoughts. The wind ever anon moaned sullenly among the foliage of the trees, and on leaden weight seemed to hang upon the air, which was peculiarly oppressive. The moon had not yet shown her silvery face from behind the dark clouds that hung upon the horizon, and there was not a star to be seen.

" How solemn is the gloom which reigns on all around," observed Alice; " it seems to be the dismal omen of some approaching calamity."

" Dissipate those melancholy thoughts, Alice," again remonstrated her sister, " which only serve to keep you in a continual state of agitation, and let us retire to rest."

" No, Rose," returned our heroine; " indeed I do not feel at all inclined for sleep;

and I feel convinced that some extraordinary event is about to take place which will be of the utmost importance to us."

"Strange surmises!" ejaculated Rose; "whatever can give rise to them in your breast?"

"I know not," answered Alice; "but do not affect to despise them; for their may be much more in them than you seem to imagine. Oh, Ben—dear Ben—with what fond anxiety does your dear image now occur to my thoughts. If you are still alive, to what fearful dangers may you at this moment be exposed!"

She clasped her hands together as these dismal and painful ideas occurred to her, and breathed a silent prayer to heaven for the safety of that beloved being from whom she had been so long separated, and in this she was fervently joined by Rose.

Suddenly, however, they were aroused from this state of feeling, and started to their feet as the loud report of a gun boomed on the silent air from the direction of the ocean; and which was quickly succeeded by another and another, and excited a mingled feeling of pity and alarm in the bosoms of the fair sisters.

"These are doubtless signals of distress from some unfortunate vessel;" said Alice, gazing eagerly and timidly towards the deep; "God help those poor creatures who are thus surrounded by danger. Gracious Heaven! behold, Rose; behold! that fearful light! What means it?"

The broad and lurid reflection of some fierce, raging conflagration now shot up into the clouds, and illumined every object for miles around with a frightful glare, and Alice and her sister could not help shuddering with an uncontrouable feeling of horror as they beheld it. At that moment there was a hasty knock at their chamber door, and on it being opened, Mr Maitland, apparently in a state of great agitation entered.

"Some hapless ship is evidently on fire from stem to stern;" he said, in a voice of compassion;" alas! it is a fearful sight to gaze upon. God help the poor creatures whom this terrible catastrophe has overtaken!"

"Oh, may they not yet be saved from so dreadful a fate?" said the agitated Alice. "Even at this moment poor Ben may be exposed to a similar frightful destiny, and no one at hand to attempt to rescue him!"

Her heart sickened at the thought, and strange and awful fears and forebodings distracted her brain.

"They will not be allowed to perish, without an attempt being made to save them;" replied her father; "no doubt boats from the different ships in the harbour will put off to their assistance. I will immediately go to the scene of danger, and ascertain the particulars;—in the meantime, my dear children, offer up your prayers to heaven for the preservation of the unfortunate sufferers."

With these words Mr. Maitland, having embraced his daughters, hastily quitted the cottage, and joined by old Ben Bolt, who had also been alarmed by the conflagration, made his way to the sea beach.

When he was gone, Alice and her sister sank on their knees and clasping their hands vehemently together, fervently supplicated the merciful interposition of Omnipotence to reserve from their impending fate the unfortunate individuals who were on board the burning vessel. They then once more arose, and watched the progress of the devouring element with the most intense anxiety.

Higher and higher the fierce flames shot up into the sky, and it seemed totally impossible for human hands to stop their destructive fury. The tender hearts of the gentle and compassionate sisters were wrung with horror as they gazed upon the frightful scene, which every moment became the more terrific, and again their prayers ascended to heaven for those poor creatures with whom they so deeply sympathised.

"Alas!" sighed our heroine, "the remorseless flames seem to have got too powerful a hold, and I fear that all on board must perish. And what awful presentiments are those that still continue to haunt my brain?—Oh, Ben! Ben!"

"For heaven's sake, Alice, do not distract me with such fearful thoughts," said Rose.

She could utter no more, for at that moment the attention of them both was attracted by some tall object, which was standing in the lurid glare of the fire's reflection at some short distance from the cottage, but still it was impossible for them clearly to distinguish it. It approached nearer until it stood immediately beneath, and looking up, Alice and her sister could not help uttering a mingled cry of fear and astonishment when they recognised the forbidding features of the mysterious old Maud of the Ruins,

They gazed eagerly and anxiously upon her, and then waving her long, bony hand towards them as if to command attention, while with the other she pointed in the direction of the scene of conflagration, in clear and distinct tones, not a word of which the stillness of the night would allow to escape them, she said :

"This night is big with fate. Behold how the fierce flames consume the hapless vessel which contains the long anxiously looked for, the noble and the generous. Ill-starred maidens, do not your hearts tremble in this dreadful hour of peril, and fearful forebodings cross your mind ? Hark ! hear you not that wailing cry rising on the dreary night air ? They come ! they come ! midst horror and death they come; but oh, beware ! beware ! for great and terrible are the troubles that are yet in store for you."

As the wierd woman gave utterance to these last remarkable words, before Alice or Rose could recover from the astonishment into which her sudden and unexpected appearance at such a moment had thrown them, she turned away from the spot, and was almost immediately hidden from their sight.

The sisters clasped their hands together, and gazed anxiously after her in complete bewilderment, while a nameless feeling of dread came over them, which they found it impossible to subdue.

"God of heaven !" at length gasped forth our trembling heroine, and her face at the same time ghastly pale; "what meant she by those mysterious words ; and why did again appear before us in such a critical hour as this? My mind is filled with an indescribable horror, and I know not what to think. This night is big with fate," she said. "Oh, what strange event is before us !"

"Be calm, my dear Alice," returned Rose ; "and let us hope for the best."

"Ah ! see !" exclaimed Alice, pointing in the direction of the fatal spot; "the devouring element rages yet more fiercely, and may the Almighty help those who are exposed to its destructive fury ! They cannot be saved ! they cannot be saved ! Would that I had accompanied our dear father to the fatal spot."

"Nay, my dear sister, you talk wildly," observed Rose ; "what good could you possibly have done by being present at so appalling a scene? All that human aid can do to rescue them from their dreadful fate will be done. Come, let us rejoin our mother below till our father and old Ben return."

Alice sighed deeply as she cast her eyes once more towards the scene of death, and then, without making use of another observation, suffered her sister to lead her from the room.

In the meantime Ralph Maitland and old Ben, with the deepest feelings of sympathy excited in their breasts, as they gazed on the fearful signs of devastation that were so rapidly and irresistibly progressing, made their way towards the cliffs, from which they expected to obtain a better view of the awful sight ; and as they approached nearer they could hear the shouts of the people ashore, as they gave their hurried instructions to each other in the rendering of such assistance as might be necessary ; or expressed their fears and pity for those poor souls who were exposed to such imminent and frightful danger.

"Poor creatures !" said Ben; "what a terrible situation is theirs to be placed in. See how the huge flames mount aloft, roaring, hissing, and crackling like fiery serpents. Ah, Ralph, my friend, how little does the landsman know of the perils and dangers to be encountered by those who have to plough the watery deep."

"True, Ben ;" replied his companion ; "and insensible must that individual be who does not admire and respect the character of the brave and hardy mariner. Truly this is a sight sufficient to appal even the stoutest heart. The burning vessel seems to be at some distance from the shore, and unless an all-merciful Providence should watch over them, I fear that few of the poor souls will escape from the dreadful and untimely death which threatens them. Come, let us hasten, for I am all anxiety to learn the results of this frightful calamity."

Accordingly they increased their speed, and in a few minutes more they arrived at the cliffs, and there the scene which presented itself was of the most exciting and painful description.

Nearly all the inhabitants of the village and the surrounding neighbourhood were congregated on the spot, and were watching the progress of the flames, which made all around as light as noon-day, with looks of pity, awe, and dismay.

The broad sheet of waters had all the appearance of liquid fire, and boats were hurrying from all directions towards the unfortunate ship, which, however, was at such a distance from the shore, and the flames seemed to have obtained so powerful a hold, that the chances of assistance were rendered still the more difficult, if not utterly hopeless; but many were the fervent prayers that were offered up to heaven for the preservation of the wretched sufferers.

"Alas! alas!" ejaculated Mr. Maitland, in a melancholy voice; "I fear all hope is at an end; all hands on board that fated ship seemed doomed to eternity. Oh, Ben, and to such a horrible fate as this those whom we so fondly love, and whom our hearts yearn so anxiously to behold again, may at this moment be exposed."

"Avast, avast, my friend," replied Ben; "do not give way to such sad thoughts; the great Commander above will surely preserve the poor boys from such a death as this."

A half-stifled and mournful cry at that moment caused them to turn hastily round, and they beheld Maud of the Ruins standing in a fixed and impressive attitude near them, and with her eyes bent wildly and earnestly upon them.

"The fierce flames rise to heaven," she said, in solemn accents; "the fierce flames rise to heaven, and the poor seaman, as he rushes madly to and fro among the blazing timbers, shrieks aloud, but in vain, for help and mercy! Who shall rescue them from impending fate?"

"Mysterious woman," said Mr. Maitland; "why comest thou, the harbinger of evil, in this fearful hour, to dampen the ardour of those humane beings who would risk their lives to save those of their unfortunate fellow-creatures who are thus exposed to such frightful danger?"

"Ralph Maitland," answered the old woman, "Maud of the Ruins is ever present in the hour of peril and woe. Her eye penetrates through the dark mist of fate, and can foresee the issue of events. Even now it sees that which you can little imagine."

"What mean you, old woman?" demanded Ben, in an impatient voice; "this is the time to listen to idle yarns. If you have any advice to offer, if you are woman, and really not devil, give it, and done with it; if not belay your jawing tackle and sheer off to frighten timid old women and land-lubbers."

"You scorn my words, and mock at my predictions," returned Maud; "but you would not do so if you knew all. Joy as well as sorrow this night awaits you, and even now there is that brooding in the dark web of fate for which you are little prepared."

Mr. Maitland and old Ben were about to return some answer, when they were prevented from doing so by an event which startled all present, and filled them with horror.

A terrific sound was heard, which seemed to shake the very heavens and earth; dense columns of smoke, and clouds of sparks, mingled with burning timbers, shot up high into the air, and the ocean hissed, and foamed, and bubbled like a burning cauldron.

The unfortunate vessel had exploded, and the work of destruction and of horror was complete!

Fearful was the excitement which now prevailed, and every one was transfixed to the spot in consternation and awe. Maud of the Ruins changed not her attitude, but pointed with a mysterious and ominous expression of countenance towards the spot where the frightful calamity had just taken place.

"All is lost!" exclaimed Mr. Maitland, in a melancholy tone of voice; "may heaven receive the souls of those unfortunate beings who have just met with such an awful and untimely end!"

"Oh, it is a melancholy sight," said Ben, in his most compassionate accents, and stretching his eyes anxiously across the ocean; "but still they may not all have perished. And see! a boat is making rapidly towards the shore, having doubtless picked up some of the survivors."

Mr. Maitland's eyes eagerly followed the direction in which his companion had pointed, and, as he had said, he then beheld a boat, which seemed to contain three or four individuals, struggling to reach the shore; but this was the only symptom of rescue that presented itself.

"They come! they come!" exclaimed Maud; "those long looked for, are rescued from a frightful death, and will once more be restored to the arms of those they love!"

"Strange being, what mean you?" interrogated Mr. Maitland, hurriedly, but Maud heard him not ; she was gone, and so sudden and so secret was her disappearance, that no one had observed how she vanished.

The boat now rapidly approached the land, and made towards a little creek, where it could put in without any danger.

Anxious to behold those individuals who were thus so miraculously saved when death seemed inevitable, Ben and Mr. Maitland quickly descended the cliffs, and hurried along the coast towards the spot where they were about to land. Another minute and the boat touched the shore, and was found to contain besides those who had gone to their assistance, two seamen, in an apparently exhausted state, and whose half-burnt clothes presented sad ravages of the dreadful conflagration. They were assisted on shore, and a number of persons crowded round them, among others Ben and Mr. Maitland. The light from several blazing torches glared full upon their pale faces, and Ben and his companion uttered a mingled cry of astonishment and delight, and immediately rushed towards them, when they recognised the well known features of the long lost Ben Bolt and his friend Harry Helm !

At that moment a fierce oath was heard, and the dark shadows of two tall forms were seen hastily retreating from the spot. They were those of Sir Raymond Perceval and Luke Harden, the pirate !

CHAPTER VII.

THE MEETING OF THE LOVERS—THE SAILORS' WELCOME HOME.

" Ben ! Harry ! noble lads ! oh, heaven be praised for this !" exclaimed Mr. Maitland and the old seaman in a breath, and clasping the hands of our hero and his youthful friend, the big and manly tears started to their eyes, and they were unable to give expression to the mingled feelings of transport and surprise that agitated their breasts by the utterance of another word.

The sound of their voices struck upon the ears of the young mariners with an effect which was perfectly electrical, and seemed at once to arouse them from every feeling of exhaustion ; nay, even all recollection of the dreadful calamity from which they had so providentially and miraculously escaped appeared, for the moment, to be banished from their minds in the excitement of their feelings ; and looking up, and in an instant recognising the features of those dear friends whom they so sincerely revered, but whom they had never expected to behold again, they rushed to their arms ; the intensity of their emotions completely overpowered them, and they wept and sobbed like children.

The spectators of this interesting scene, many of whom had known the young men from their earliest days of boyhood, stood by and looked on deeply affected, and with feelings of the utmost respect.

Ben Bolt was the first to recover the use of speech, and grasping the hand of his protector, and that of the father of that dear girl whose beauteous image was treasured in his heart's innermost core, in a voice that was broken by the vehemence of his glowing and struggling emotions, he ejaculated :

" Father !—Mr. Maitland !—oh, after weathering so many storms, and braving all the perils of the battle and the breeze, is the poor mariner saved from the jaws of a frightful death, to find himself moored in the arms of those whom he would lay down his life to serve ? I—I—I am taken all aback—sailing as it were in a fog, and without rudder or compass. Am I awake ?—or are my upper works out of order ?"

" No, no, Ben, my dear boy—my young sea-lion, you are not dreaming ;" replied his adopted father, still grasping his hand with a fervour which nothing could equal ; " you are all tight and sound, safe in port at last,—and piloted by Providence to the arms of those who have so long and so anxiously watched for your return. Shiver my topsails ! I can scarcely believe the evidence of my senses ! Oh, that old Ben Bolt should have lived to see this happy hour ! God bless you, my dear boy !—God bless you !"

And the poor old man's further utterance was stifled by sobs, and the tears rolled down his furrowed cheeks.

" And my Alice ! my pretty Alice !" cried our hero, with eager emotion ; " oh, tell

THE MEETING OF ALICE AND BEN BOLT.

me all about her, for my heart is now ready to burst with anxiety and impatience.'

"Alice still lives and loves you, Ben." answered Mr. Maitland.

"Heaven bless you for those words!" exclaimed the young man, once more grasping him by the hand; "they have set my heart in full sail, and going at the rate of fifty knots an hour! My Alice, my own sweet Alice, still lives and loves her toil-worn sailor!—Hear that, Harry; lashed to the helm, and true as the needle to the pole! But could I ever doubt the dear girl? No, I must have been a lubberly scoundrel if I could have done so. Oh, with what fond anxiety, and devoted affection have my thoughts been ever fixed on her during the long and painful period of our separation. In every clime, in every danger, her beloved image has ever been present to my mind; and though death hath often stared me in the face, the sweet anchor of hope ever kept my vessel from foundering, and dared the fury of the angry breakers. And now I shall behold her again; I shall clasp her precious form once more to my throbbing heart, and read the faithful sentiments of her innocent soul in those bright eyes that have so often beamed with affection on her sailor-love! What a happy fellow I am to be sure. Here's a cargo of joy in store for me! I—I—oh, splice my timbers, if my scuppers ain't beginning to run over, and I shall blubber like an infant presently!"

No. 5.

"But my Rose;" said Harry; "my little merry-hearted, loving Rose! Have none of you a word to say about her?"

"Yes, Harry," answered Mr. Maitland, "all that I have said of her sister Alice; set your heart at rest, for heaven be thanked she is well, and Harry Helm is as dear to her as ever."

"Hurrah!" shouted Harry, his fine intelligent eyes sparkling with joy;—"Here's news for you! Rose is faithful to her Harry Helm, and I am as proud and happy as if I had been made Lord High Admiral at this moment."

"Bravo Harry! bravo Ben!" shouted old Bolt, in high glee; "pitch dull care to the devil, and pipe all hands for gladness!"

"Oh, my dear boys," observed Mr. Maitland, "from what an awful death have you been rescued. But you have suffered much, and—"

"Avast! avast!" interrupted our hero; "a fig about suffering;—'tis all over now. I feel as well and as hearty as if I had been sailing in the fairest of weather; but why do we stand palavering here? Spread every stitch of canvass, and crowd all sail for those we love!"

"But we must act with caution," said Mr. Maitland; "or this great and unexpected surprise may be too much for my poor girls. Had we not better defer the meeting until I have broken the joyful intelligence to them?"

"No, no," replied young Ben, impatiently, "I cannot hear a word about delay. Would you be drifting out to sea, with a gale threatening, when a friendly port is in sight? Let us weigh anchor directly. Dear Alice, my happiness will not be complete till I enfold you once more to my throbbing bosom."

Mr. Maitland offered no further opposition, and followed by the hearty congratulations of all who had witnessed the scene, they departed towards the cottage.

And what a noble specimen of Great Britain's hardy sons of the ocean, was young Ben Bolt. Nothing could be more perfect than the graceful and manly proportions of his form; or more expressive and intelligent than his handsome features. His eyes spoke the language of his soul, which was open and generous, and sooner could he have suffered death than have been guilty of a single act that his tongue would be ashamed to acknowledge. Well worthy was such a youth of the love of so fair and innocent a being as the captivating Alice Maitland.

Harry Helm, his friend, was also a brave and warm-hearted fellow, of handsome exterior, and esteemed and admired by all that knew him. Having lost his parents when a boy, whenever he came ashore he always resided with his friend and shipmate at the cottage of old Ben Bolt, and had the young seamen been brothers they could not have been more faithfully or devotedly attached to each other.

But we must leave them for awhile on their way to Woodbine Cottage, and return to Alice and her sister.

We left them in the company of their mother, and in a state of the greatest agitation and anxiety of mind; and that was by no means diminished, as, from the parlour casement, they still continued to watch the progress of the devouring flames; and most impatiently did they await the return of their father and old Ben.

The singular appearance and ambiguous words of the wierd woman continued to haunt their imagination; and various were the conjectures that arose upon their minds.

Mrs. Maitland, to whom they had related all the particulars, tried to dissipate all their doubts and uneasiness; but with Alice especially she succeeded but indifferently, and she could not but continue to express her forebodings of some approaching calamity.

"Would to heaven that my father would return," she said; "though, alas! I fear the news he will have to tell us will be of the most melancholy and painful description. How does my heart bleed for the poor creatures whose lives are at this moment placed in such imminent and frightful peril."

"Providence will watch over them, my dear child," replied her mother; "and ample assistance being so near at hand, a great portion of them, if not all, may probably be saved. God grant that they may, for it is terrible to perish by such a fate."

"Alas! it is," sighed our heroine; "and," she added, with a shudder; "how my heart trembles when I reflect that even at this moment poor Ben, and his faithful friend, Harry Helm, may be exposed to similar horrors."

"Why torture yourself with such fearful surmises?" said her mother; "would to heaven that you could banish those gloomy thoughts from your mind. I cannot help thinking that, notwithstanding the lapse of time since Ben and Harry quitted these shores, and the numerous dangers to which the gallant sailor's life is exposed, they will yet be restored to us, and that even much sooner than we can now possibly anticipate."

"And I still hope for the best, my dear mother," remarked Rose; "and would fain inspire Alice with the same feelings."

Our heroine was about to make some reply, when she was interrupted by a knock at the door, which made them all start, and inspired them with the hope that Mr. Maitland had returned; but on Rose opening it, they were much disappointed on seeing the loquacious barber Mr. Jingle (who appeared to be much excited and out of breath), enter the room.

"Oh dear, oh dear!" he exclaimed; "such an adventure!—such an incident! So full of romance and exciting interest; won't it form a capital subject for my next poem.

> "The ship was tossing on the sea,
> As comfortable as it could be;
> When, what the crew did not admire,
> They found it all at once on fire!
> Up shot the flames like winking then,
> And—"

"Pray, Mr. Jingle," interrupted Mrs. Maitland, impatiently; "defer your poetic effusion to some more suitable occasion, and if you have been to the scene of destruction, which I imagine from your observations that you have; let us know the particulars."

"Been to it," returned Jemmy; "I believe I have too, and a most awful scene it was; I shall never forget it, it was what I had been praying to see, and I would not have lost the sight for the world. If it don't make my fortune, my name's not James Jingle, Esquire, Poet Laureate what is to be.

> "Now to the clouds the flames they soar,
> Which to the crew must be a bore,
> And showers of sparks, and smoke and all,
> Which some a reg'lar flare-up call."

"For Heaven's sake, Mr. Jingle;" said the anxious Alice; "do be serious, and do not exhaust our patience in this manner."

"Serious!" repeated the barber; "I was never more serious in my life. Oh, Miss Alice, and you too, Miss Rose, there is such a surprise for you; I have run myself quite out of breath to be the first to come and tell you. But you interrupt the sublimity of my ideas:—

> "On board that burning ship so drear,
> Two noble sailor lads were there,
> Who well had earn'd their country's fame,
> Ben Bolt, and Harry Helm by name!"

"Gracious heaven!" shrieked Alice, wildly, and clutching at the arm of Jingle, while she looked with the most indescribable emotion in his face; "is this done to torture me?—is it only the offspring of your imagination, or have you indeed spoke the truth? Speak! speak, I conjure you, and keep me not in suspense."

"It is all a fact, I assure you;" replied Jemmy. "Poor Ben Bolt and Harry Helm were both on board that very unfortunate ship, and out of all the crew and passengers, they are the only two that are saved!"

Alice and her sister uttered a simultaneous cry of mingled astonishment and gratitude, and the former immediately fainted in the arms of her mother, while Rose was almost as much overpowered as herself.

"Poor things!" said Jemmy Jingle; "I thought how much it would surprise them. Here's another affecting incident for my poem. But they are conducting Ben and Harry this way, and I must go and meet them."

Thus saying, before Mrs. Maitland or Rose could recover from their surprise, Jemmy Jingle hastily quitted the cottage.

"Good God!' exclaimed Rose; " can what Mr. Jingle has said be true? It seems almost too wonderful to be believed."

" Oh, yes:" answered her mother, "most surely he would not be so cruel as to sport with our feelings thus. Courage, courage, my dear girl, and prepare yourself for that unexpected and joyous meeting which must shortly take place."

The words had scarcely escaped her lips, when the room door was thrown open; there was a loud cry of transport, and astonishment, and Alice Maitland and her sister were frantically clasped to the hearts of those beloved beings whose uncertain fate they had so long mourned; while the old people stood by deeply affected, and in mute gratitude to heaven.

"Alice! beloved Alice!" exclaimed our hero, in accents of transport, and covering the beauteous face of the insensible girl with his kisses; ' oh, revive, my poor lass, revive and speak to me! It is your own true sailor-love who now clasps you to his panting bosom, and could give his life away in retracing those matchless charms that have ever in absence been present to his fond imagination. And do I indeed behold you again? Oh, joy! joy!—All now is calm and sunshine, and the hardy mariner fears no more the shoals and the rocks, the storms of life!"

"Darling Rose," said Harry, as he also pressed the tender form of the trembling and blushing maiden to his heart, and kissed her rosy and unresisting lips again and again; " once more we meet, and joy and gratitude are ours. Pardon these tears, my sweet girl; the source they spring from is such as any man should feel proud to acknowledge."

Rose could only reply with her looks, which spoke more than any language, however powerful, could describe, and she returned the embrace of her lover with equal fervour.

At this moment our heroine breathed a gentle sigh, and opening her eyes, and fixing them tenderly on the enraptured Ben, ejaculated:—

"Gracious Heaven! then it was no delusive dream, conjured up by busy imagination to torture and distract me!—Ben, dear Ben; thou art saved, thou art restored to me, and I am happy!"

"Blessed words!" cried our hero; " what feelings of transport do they impart to my soul, and with what fond delight, my Alice, my own sweet Alice, do I listen to the music of thy voice. Oh, how often in the dreary hours of the mid-watch, has my vivid fancy pictured thy loved image; and I have prayed to heaven for this glad moment to arrive; though, exposed to the perils and dangers that I have been, frequently have I despaired of ever beholding it. But all is over now; every danger I trust is past, and Ben Bolt is the happiest lad in the British Navy."

The eyes of Alice told how heartily she responded to his feelings, and her bosom swelled with sensations such as she had seldom before experienced.

We cannot do adequate justice to the scene that followed, and we must therefore leave it to the imagination of the reader. The lovers had much to explain, many plans for the future to lay down, and vows of everlasting constancy to utter; and the hour of midnight had long since flown ere they could think of parting, and then they did so with regret and hesitation, promising to meet again at an early hour in the morning. But with what different feelings to those which had inhabited their breasts a few hours before, did Alice and her sister separate from their parents and retire to their chamber! So wonderful were all the circumstances that had occurred on that eventful day, that they could scarcely believe in their reality. Their hearts overflowed with gratitude, and fervently they returned their thanks to heaven for its boundless mercies.

CHAPTER VIII.

THE RAGE OF SIR RAYMOND PERCEVAL—THE SCENE IN THE PIRATE'S HAUNT—
DESIGNS AGAINST BEN BOLT.

From the lofty window of his chamber, where he had been seated absorbed in the most gloomy and guilty reflections, Sir Raymond Perceval had beheld the red glare of the burning ship, and the sight, though it excited no sympathy in his hardened breast, gave rise to various doubts and surmises.

He stood watching it for some time with folded arms, when taking up the lamp, he made his way towards the pirate's cave, in order to apprise Luke Harden of the circumstance.

Having left the cavern together, they made their way to the cliffs, from the loftiest summit of which they contemplated the awful scene with some degree of curiosity and wonder.

"The ship is doomed," observed Luke; "see how the fierce fire blazes and crackles. Poor devils, there is not many of them will live to tell the dreadful tale."

"True" answered Sir Raymond; "their fate is sealed; would that the boy whom I dread might be placed in a similar situation."

"Psha!" returned the other, impatiently, "why should you have him constantly in your thoughts? It is not likely that he will ever again return to annoy you."

"Be not too positive of that, Luke," said the baronet; "for I have my doubts. Even this night strange and unaccountable forebodings haunt my mind."

"Ridiculous!" ejaculated Harden; "it is sheer madness to talk thus. What can have put such a wild notion into your head? Young Ben Bolt no doubt has gone to the bottom of the deep months ago; and even if he has not, and should ever arrive in this country again, what have you to fear from him?"

"Should him and Maud of the Ruins encounter each other, she would doubtless divulge every thing to him, and then—'

"Bah!" interrupted the pirate; "you meet troubles half way. We must take prompt means to prevent that, and we shall find no difficulty in doing so"

At that moment the fearful explosion took place, which has been described in the preceding chapter, and they both stood for a minute or two in silent awe and wonder.

"There is the last of her, at any rate," remarked Luke; "and a pretty row she made in making her exit. But see, a boat is approaching the land, no doubt containing one or two that are saved. Let us go and learn the facts, we shall not be observed in the crowd."

Sir Raymond assented, and they took their way to the beach, concealing their forms and features as well as they could.

They had not been long there when the boat reached the shore, and Ben Bolt and Harry Helm were landed. It was at the moment that Sir Raymond and Luke discovered them, that the former gave utterance to the dreadful oath overheard by the spectators, and the pirate fearing that he would betray himself, took his arm, and hurried him away from the spot, and by a circuitous path towards the manor-house; where they soon arrived, and entering unobserved by any of the domestics, hastened to the secret haunt, where they might more safely confer.

The baronet was in the greatest state of excitement, and for some minutes after they had entered the secret haunt, he traversed the place backwards and forwards with a scowling brow and disordered steps, and Luke Harden, who was indeed as much surprised and disappointed as himself, did not attempt to break in upon his meditations. There was no one present but themselves.

"So you see, Luke Harden," he said at length, and with a sardonic smile upon his angry features; "with all your superior sagacity, my predictions and forebodings have turned out to be not exactly erroneous. The dreaded boy, the son of the ill-fated and much wronged Emeline, by some miraculous means has been preserved from the fate which you anticipated had long since befallen him. He is here to annoy me. What think you now of the doubts and fears that beset my mind?"

"Why," replied his companion, bluntly; "that they are weak and childish, Sir Raymond, and totally unworthy of you. What have you to dread from this young seaman, if you only act with due precaution, and do as I advise you? Nothing. One plunge of the knife, and your fears are quieted for ever."

"More bloodshed—more bloodshed!" said Sir Raymond, in a hoarse voice, and with a shudder; "I tremble at the thought, there has been too much of that already; methought as I gazed at his pale features in the glare of the torchlight, that I again beheld the ghastly countenance of his murdered mother, as she looked upon me in her dying moments, and conscience—"

"Hold" interrupted Luke, sternly; "enough of that nonsense, are you going mad? Why let the dark deeds of the past trouble you now? The bones of Emeline have long since mouldered with the dust, and let her memory therefore, also be blotted from your brain."

"It is impossible," answered the guilty baronet: "it is written there in characters that nothing can ever efface. Hark!" he added, starting, and looking round with fear and trembling, as if he expected to encounter the ghastly features of some frightful object.

"What now?" demanded the pirate, with a look of scorn.

"Did you not hear a groan?"

"Psha!—your mind is disordered."

"'Tis not. I was not deceived. I heard a cry, like the mournful expression of some poor wretch in his dying agony."

"Ridiculous!" returned Luke; "I heard nothing, and if you did, it could only have been the sighing of the wind.'

"Oh, no," observed Sir Raymond; "I could not have been so mistaken. Are you certain we are quite alone?"

"Quite," replied Harden; "the lads have been at the ship during the whole of the day, and I do not expect any of them to return till after midnight. But you must shake off those wild fears and fancies, and let us talk about business. Young Ben Bolt, as he is called, it is true has returned, and is with his friends again; and now our first object must be to prevent his meeting with old Maud, and afterwards to get him in our power."

"Aye," answered Sir Raymond, somewhat more composed; "you advise well, Luke Harden, but how is it to be accomplished?"

"Fear not but I will devise the means easily enough," returned his companion; "but if you show the white feather, of course I cannot be answerable for our success. I suppose you are not exactly disposed to abandon all thoughts of the fair Alice Maitland, simply because her lover is restored to her?"

"By all my hopes, never!" cried the libertine, and a fresh expression of desire and fierce determination lighted up his features as he spoke; "the lovely Alice holds firmer possession of my heart than ever, and I am resolved to leave no means untried to triumph over her obdurate spirit."

"Well spoken," said Harden, "keep in the same humour, and you may depend upon my most strenuous exertions in your cause."

"But Ben will doubtless be informed of what lately occurred between me and Alice," remarked Sir Raymond.

"And if he should, it matters but little," replied Luke; "an apology from you will easily quiet his suspicions; you can, with common prudence, regain the lost confidence of Alice and her friends, and then our designs will work well, and we may reckon our ultimate triumph as certain."

"You are most sanguine, Luke."

"Aye, it is only your own folly that can prevent the success of our plans. For my own part, I am determined that the lovely Rose Maitland shall not escape me. Why do you again start, and look so ghastly pale?"

"'Twas there again," answered the baronet, in a tremulous voice, and with quivering lips; "did you not hear it then?"

"What fresh vagary has seized your brain?" interrogated the pirate; I heard nothing. Such groundless fears are sickening."

"You may mock me," said Sir Raymond, with increased terror depicted in his countenance; "but I am positive. The voice of the dead sounded in my ears, I can remain here no longer."

"I am ashamed of you, Sir Raymond," said his companion; "I never thought that you could give way to such cowardly feelings as these."

"You may call them cowardly, if you please," he returned; "but I cannot subdue them. A strange gloom hangs upon my mind, and daunts my spirit, for which I can hardly account. I must begone from here, and in the solitude of my chamber seek to conquer my feelings."

"Bah!" cried Luke Harden, passionately, "can nothing arouse you from this morbid state of mind?"

"Not at present," replied Sir Raymond; "the feeling is too powerful for me to combat with. You will accompany me, Harden, along these subterranean avenues?"

"What then," demanded the pirate, with a look of scorn ; " does fear indeed thus powerfully assail you ?"

"The hour is lonely," returned the baronet. "Mock me not, for I am in no humour to bear with it at this moment."

"Then be it as you will," observed his companion, taking up the lamp, and preparing to lead the way ; " I am ready to attend you."

Sir Raymond cast one timid and hasty glance around the cavern, and then closely followed in the wake of Harden.

As they traversed the long and dreary passages, it was evident that his mind laboured under the influence of fear, for he frequently started, and glared wildly around him, as he fancied some dismal and unearthly sound saluted his ears, and he kept close to the heels of Luke Harden, for fear of losing sight of him even for an instant. At length, however, they reached the chamber, apparently much to the relief of Sir Raymond.

"I suppose you can dispense with my presence now," said Luke ; "so I wish you good night, and I hope when we meet again to find you in a much more agreeable humour."

With these words, the pirate departed, and the baronet was left to his own gloomy meditations.

CHAPTER IX.

BEN BOLT'S ADVENTURES—THE TAR AND THE LIBERTINE—FALSE COLOURS.

The slumbers of our heroine and her sister on that auspicious night which had restored their long absent lovers to their arms, were calm and serene, and bright were the visions that were presented to their busy imagination. They awoke on the following morning much refreshed, and with spirits more light and buoyant, and hopes more brilliant and sanguine than they had experienced for many a day before.

How marvellous and how joyful was the change, which only a few brief hours had wrought in their present circumstances and future prospects ; indeed so wonderful was it, that they were at times almost disposed to doubt its reality.

The first thing the lovely sisters did on leaving their couch was to kneel down and with clasped hands and upraised eyes, devoutly to pour forth the gratitude of their souls to that beneficent power, who had so far extended his mercies towards them, in the restoration of their lovers, and their preservation from a frightful death ; and most fervently did they pray for a continuance of that happiness which had so fair and promising a beginning.

The morning was lovely, and the golden orb of day shone resplendently on all around. It seemed to Alice and her sister a bright augury of that which was now in store for them. All those cares and anxieties, that had pressed so heavily on their hearts and crushed the youthful ardour of their spirits, were for the time banished, and they looked upon the past only as a troubled dream.

Most anxiously they awaited the arrival of those gallant youths, in whom their whole hopes of happiness were centred ; and on whom their fondest thoughts and wishes were fixed.

Hearing their parents were about, they hastened to meet them, and by them were greeted with all the sweetest demonstrations of parental affection. The alteration in their appearance, which such a short time had wrought, was to them a source of the purest delight and satisfaction, and they listened to their sanguine anticipations of the future with every feeling of encouragement ; and sincerely did they pray to heaven that expectations so fondly raised might not again be blighted by disappointment.

"Yes, my dear children," observed their father, whilst a tear of gratitude trembled in his eye ; "Providence has indeed been most kind and merciful to us, and we can never be sufficiently thankful for it. But a few hours since, and all was darkness and despair ; but now the clouds have passed away, and a bright horizon of hope and happiness opens to our mental vision. Oh, may it not again be interrupted ; and may the sorrows of the past be buried for ever in oblivion."

The eyes of Alice and Rose showed how heartily they responded to this prayer, and they returned the affectionate embraces of their parents with equal fervour.

"Oh, how wonderful must have been the events that kept them so long away from us," remarked our heroine; "and how great must have been the anguish of mind they endured. Poor Ben, little could you ever expect to behold those so dear to you again; and great indeed was the mercy that sustained you throughout so many severe trials."

"Ah! my dear sister," added Rose; "and to think that they should be exposed to all the horrors of so terrible a fate, when just within sight of their native home. My mind is lost in wonder and awe."

"But surely they tarry this morning," said Alice, looking anxiously towards the window; "I wish they would arrive, or really we must chide them for their delay."

"Nay, Alice," said her mother; "you really must not be so impatient; remember it is early yet, and considering the excitement and fatigue they have had to undergo, their tardiness this morning must be excusable."

"House ahoy! Ralph Maitland ahoy!" now saluted the ears of the anxious listeners, shouted in a stentorian voice, and the eyes of the sisters sparkled, and their hearts palpitated with delight and fond expectation.

"'Tis the voice of old Ben," observed Mr. Maitland; "they come; so there is an end to your anxiety, my dear girls."

Before Alice or Rose had time to make any reply, the cottage door was thrown open, and they found themselves again clasped in the arms of Ben and Harry.

"Here they are, the young dogs," said the veteran; "I have conveyed them safe into harbour, and I see that they have met with a worthy salute. My eyes, what kissing and embracing, if it does not make me feel quite young again to see 'em. Ralph, my old tar, give us your flipper; damme, your's—if we don't splice the mainbrace this day, may I be placed upon six-water grog for the rest of my cruise."

Ralph Maitland and his wife could not help smiling at the hearty humour of old Ben, and they returned his greeting with equal cordiality.

The lovers continued to give vent to their joyous feelings for some minutes, and the old people did not offer to interrupt them; but at length becoming a little more composed, they took their seats at the table, and the morning repast was accomplished in the most cheerful and agreeeable manner.

A night's repose, and the happiness of their minds, had effected a most favourable change in the appearance of the young seamen; and health, hope, and cheerfulness of spirits, animated their handsome and manly features, and imparted additional interest to the general expression of their countenances.

How affectionate were the glances that the lovers exchanged with each other; and which told so forcibly the feelings that inhabited their bosoms.

As our heroine gazed upon the noble features of the youth she loved, and caught his impassioned glances fixed full upon her, deep blushes suffused her cheeks, tears trembled in her eyes, (but they were those of joy and gratitude), and her heart palpitated against her side with the fondest emotion.

"Dear Alice," observed Ben; "how little did I expect that after so rough a voyage as me and my friend and shipmate Harry encountered, we should thus have been safe anchored in the haven of happiness at last. And yet the certainty of your constancy and love, was my sheet-anchor, and sustained me manfully throughout those dangers that otherwise might have caused me to founder. Bless those dear eyes that now beam so brightly and affectionately upon me; they were the sweet beacons of my memory that lighted my soul, when all else around was darkness and despair."

"Oh, Ben!" replied Alice; "how can I describe the emotions of my throbbing heart at this moment? They are far too powerful for utterance."

"And, oh how terrible must have been the sufferings you have endured, during the long time you have been away, and tossed about on the rude billows of the broad ocean," said Rose.

"Aye, my dear lass," returned Harry; "we have had a rough time of it; and had to experience such dangers as would have appalled and daunted many a stout heart. But my friend Ben will relate to you all the particulars, for he has got them better stored in the log-book of his memory than I have, I imagine."

"And what was the name of the unfortunate vessel, from which you were so providentially rescued?" asked Mr. Maitland.

SEIZURE OF THE WIERD WOMAN.

"The Boraus, trading-ship, homeward bound, from the coast of Borneo, with fifty-six, crew and passengers on board, the whole of whom, with the exception of ourselves, have perished;" replied our hero.

"Poor souls!' ejaculated old Ben, compassionately; "may they all find safe and pleasant moorings aloft, for it was an awful fate to meet with. But how came you aboard of her, Ben?'

"She mercifully picked us up, when we were cast upon an uninhabited island, where we had been three days and three nights, and must otherwise have perished;" returned Ben. "Much I fear that it was no accident which caused the burning of tha ill-fated ship, but that it was the work of some base incendiary."

"Heaven pardon him the frightful deed, for his guilty soul is now in eternity!" said Mr. Maitland.

Alice and her sister shuddered when they thought of the narrow escape their lovers had had, from so horrible a death.

"But the gallant Dauntless, in which you and Harry sailed from England, Ben," enquired the old seaman: "what became of her?"

No. 6.

"Contrary winds separated her from the rest of the fleet," answered Ben; she was afterwards much disabled in a heavy storm, and lost several of her hands, being unable to make any port. In this manner we were tossed about for several days, and were compelled to part with some of our heaviest guns. Then sickness broke out among the crew; a most malignant fever raged on board, and the poor fellows died like rotten sheep, among the rest, our brave commander, and the first and second lieutenants. In this wretched plight a formidable pirate-vessel bore down upon us, and crippled as we were, no wonder that we became an easy prey. A great number of our poor fellows were slaughtered by the fury of the pirates, and the rest, with the exception of myself and Harry, were left to perish in the sinking ship, which they had previously scuttled."

"And such was the fate of the poor Dauntless, as gallant a craft as ever stemmed the waters?" said old Ben.

"It was," returned our hero; "and we were only preserved to experience still greater sufferings. Forced to join the pirate crew, I need not describe to you the horrors we had to witness, though, thank heaven, we managed to take no active part in them."

"And how did you contrive to effect your escape from these wretches?" interrupted Mr. Maitland.

"After we had been some months on board of her, she was attacked by a British schooner, and totally destroyed. Having told our tale, of course we were set at liberty and treated with every kindness. And now we hoped soon again to behold the happy shores of old England, for the schooner was homeward bound. But our troubles were not yet over. We were exposed to all the fury of a dreadful storm, and after bravely endeavouring to weather it, our hapless vessel struck upon a rock, and almost immediately went to pieces. Myself and Harry clung desperately to a portion of the wreck, and by that means, after the most indescribable difficulties, we succeeded in gaining a small island, which we found to be totally barren and uninhabited. Here for three days and nights we were forced to remain, subsisting only on shell-fish and sea-weed, and and I need not attempt to describe our sufferings. At length a distant vessel met our gladdened sight, and when it approached nearer, with frantic eagerness we hoisted a signal of distress, which they fortunately observed, and sent a boat off to our rescue, and we shortly found ourselves on board the Boreas, where every attention which humanity could suggest was paid to our necessities. Favouring gales wafted us speedily on, and again the blissful thoughts of home and those beloved beings from whom we had so long been separated, gladdened our hearts, and fully repaid us for the many troubles we had undergone. We had just got within sight of our native shores, when the fearful cry of 'Fire! Fire!' was raised, and soon the unhappy ship was in flames from stem to stern. The rest you know."

Thus Ben Bolt concluded the brief narrative of the perils and dangers that he and Harry Helm had encountered, and to which his auditors had listened with the greatest attention and interest.

The eyes of Alice expressed much more than she could find language to give utterance to; and when she reflected upon all that her lover had undergone, his many narrow escapes from death, and that he was now once more restored to her, she could scarcely believe that she was not labouring under the delusive influence of some deceitful dream; whilst, at the same time, her soul rose in gratitude to the supreme for the infinite goodness and mercy he had extended towards them.

The feelings of Rose were in perfect unison with those of her sister; and, for some minutes after Ben had ceased speaking they remained silent, unable to give vent in words to the various emotions that animated their bosoms.

'Oh, Ben;' said our heroine, at length, and her fine eyes beamed with an expression of redoubled affection upon his handsome countenance as she spoke; "how wonderful are the ways of Providence, that have sustained you throughout so many trials and vicissitudes. We meet again, thank heaven; and shall the broad waters of the perilous ocean ever more separate us?"

"Why, as for that, my pretty Alice," he replied; "while there are any of the enemies of his country left to drub, the true British tar will never shrink from his duty, for fear, you know, is a stranger to his breast. The war still rages, and you do not think, I hope, that I and my friend Harry here, are two such lubbers as to remain skulking ashore. No—no, we should be unworthy of the love of you and Rose if we could."

" Alas! alas!" sighed Alice; "and must those bright hopes so fondly excited in my breast so soon be blighted? Oh, Ben, are we doomed again to part?"

" Why, you see, my dear Alice." returned the young mariner; "it can't be helped; but cheerly, cheerly; it will not be for long mayhap, and the same Providence that has hitherto protected me through every danger, will, I trust, not now desert me; but once more convey my vessel into port, to love and you."

" Bravo, Ben!" exclaimed his friend and protector. " Bravo, Ben; spoke like a man, and it does my heart glad to hear you. He must be a cowardly swab who does not entertain the same feelings. Come, Alice, lass, belay your fears; the time has not yet come for your lover to weigh anchor, and when he returns, what say you to starting in a matrimonial cruise together?"

" Right! right!" said our hero, "and I fancy that Alice will have no objection to accept me as her skipper?"

Our heroine blushed, but at the same time she could not help smiling at the observations of Ben and the old seaman.

" Ah! now it glads my heart to see you smile, dear Alice," observed her lover; " bless those pretty lips! What a scoundrel that man must be who could raise one guilty thought towards you."

Alice sighed, when she thought of Sir Raymond, and a dismal foreboding came over her.

" What means that sigh, Alice?" interrogated Ben, anxiously; " you are agitated."

" 'Tis nothing, Ben," she replied, in a faint and hesitating voice; " 'twas only a slight emotion, and—and—"

" Nay, nay, Alice," he interrupted; " I am certain there is something more than you think proper to divulge. Come, my lass, you must have no secrets from me."

" The fact is, Ben," remarked Mr. Maitland; " I guess well the thoughts of Alice, and consider it is only right that you also should be made acquainted with them. Sir Raymond Perceval—"

" Ah! what of him?" demanded the young seaman, hastily; " I like him not; if he is not some rascally pirate, sailing under false colours, I am much mistaken; but, if I imagined that he had dared to encourage one thought to the injury of my innocent Alice, it should not be his rank that should shield him from my resentment."

" Hold hard, Ben, my boy," said old Bolt. " 'Tis true the lubber did venture to utter some rather bold lingo to Alice; but I happened to bear down upon him just in time, and so, like a cowardly cur as he was, he lurked about and sneaked off in a moment, and I do not think he will venture the same game in a hurry "

" The daring ruffian!" cried our hero, passionately; "he insult 'my Alice! He presume to utter a word which could call the blush of shame into her cheek! May I never go aloft again if he shall not dearly pay for this."

" Forbear, dear Ben," said the damsel, a sensation of fear stealing over her; " the baronet was wrong, but I trust that he is convinced of his error, and will not repeat the offence. I would not that you and him should encounter each other."

" And think you, Alice, that I fear such a dastardly land-lubber as him?" cried her lover, his cheeks still glowing with the indignation of his excited feelings; " I can read his character, and I am much deceived if he is not as great a villain as was ever strung up to the yard-arm."

" Well, Ben," observed the veteran tar; " I think you have taken the right soundings there, my boy; but we have only to keep a sharp look out, and he will not be able to do any harm."

" True," remarked Mr. Maitland; "and, as he has now unmasked himself, and boldly appeared in his true character, we can be every way on our guard against him. It is necessary that I should demand an explanation and apoligy from him; for he must be given to understand he cannot commit such outrages with impunity."

" Aye," coincided Ben; "and I shall not rest satisfied till I have overhauled him, and woe to him should he attempt to defend his behaviour. But be firm, Alice, and do not fear this wealthy libertine; he will not attempt to insult you again fancy, now I am within hail to protect you, or may I never see salt-water again if I do not open such a broadside upon him that will pack him off to old Davy in the turning of a handspike."

"Indeed," observed our heroine, "I hope there will be no occasion to go to any such unpleasant extremes. Come, let us drop the subject, which is calculated only to give rise to painful feelings."

"Aye, aye, wisely spoken, lass," observed old Ben; "the return of your lover and Harry Helm should meet with a hearty welcome; so I propose that to-morrow we should pipe all hands on deck for mirth and festivity. What say you, friends?"

"Agreed, my old friend," replied Mr. Maitland; "I can only say that I cordially approve of your proposition."

"Hurrah!" ejaculated the veteran; "we will have a jovial day of it. Several of Ben and Harry's friends and shipmates are now in this harbour, and they must be pressed into the service. We will invite them all, and won't we have the grog and baccy aboard? The first one that flinches shall be branded as a mutineer directly."

Thus was the merry-hearted old man proceeding to give vent to his feelings, when he was interrupted by a knock at the door, which being opened, much to the surprise and confusion of all present, Sir Raymond Perceval entered the room.

The blushing Alice felt a sensation of dread steal over her, especially when she marked the looks of indignation which her lover fixed on the baronet; but the latter was all smiles and condescension, and bowed politely, apparently being fully prepared for the task he had assigned himself.

"Wheugh!" exclaimed our hero; "there's breakers ahead, I see!"

Alice looked at him imploringly, and he re-assured her with a smile.

To what may we attribute the *honour* of this unexpected visit, Sir Raymond?" enquired Mr. Maitland, in a sarcastic tone but which the former affected not to notice.

"I must apologise for this intrusion, Mr. Maitland," he replied; "but I could not resist the temptation I felt to congratulate our young friends here on their miraculous and p ovidential deliverance from a frightful death, and their restoration to the shores of old England."

"Hark ye, Sir Raymond Perceval," observed our hero, with mingled resentment and suspicion; "you are a rich man, while I am but a simple sailor, rough and plain spoken; but still I flatter myself as honest a heart beats beneath this humble jacket as ever swelled the breast of the proudest nobleman in the land; nor am I either afraid or ashamed to remind those who deem themselves my superiors, of their faults, whenever I see occasion for it. You will understand me, no doubt; however, to speak more distinctly, if you ask your own conscience, you must admit, I think, that you owe an apology of a very different descripton to that you have just alluded to; so, in order to belay all unnecessary trouble and palaver, the sooner you make it the better.'

The bold and haughty tone of the young mariner filled the guilty breast of Sir Raymond with rage and indignation, but stifling his feelings as well as he could, and beneath that cloak of hypocrisy he could so skilfully assume at pleasure, he said:—

"It would be useless for me, my gallant young friend, to pretend that I do not understand the drift of the observations you just made use of; and, when in all sincerity I am ready to acknowledge my error, and express my regret that, in a moment of foolish thoughtlessness I so committed myself; I hope my apology will be received by yourself and your friends in the spirit with which it is offered."

Mr. Maitland looked at the baronet with an expression of doubt and suspicion, as he replied:—

"Sir Raymond Perceval will be pleased to understand that, while animosity is not one of the passions inherent in my nature, and myself and my family are always ready and anxious to pay due respect and deference to those whom fortune has placed above us; we will never fail to resent an insult, come from whatever quarter it may. You have admitted your error, sir, and I trust that your regret is sincere."

Sir Raymond bit his lips, and his pride was mortified in the extreme; nevertheless he had a nefarious game to play, the success of which entirely depended on his using the utmost precaution; he therefore subdued his wrath, and still endeavoured to conceal the real thoughts and feelings that were passing in his mind form observation.

"Believe me, Mr. Maitland," he observed; "I fully appreciate all that you have said, and respect and honour you for your sentiments and forbearance. That I am sincere, I must leave my future conduct to demonstrate. But what says your daughter, the fair and gentle Alice ? Surely after this explanation, she will not entertain any angry feeling towards me ?"

Our heroine blushed, and casting down her eyes, she was unable to reply, while her bosom was agitated with mingled emotions of fear, doubt, and misgiving, which she could not conquer. The keen eye of Sir Raymond penetrated her thoughts, and he felt chagrined, abashed, and disappointed.

"Avast there, Sir Raymond," said Ben; "let's have all fair and above-board, if you please. My Alice possesses too kind and forgiving a spirit to bear animosity towards any one; and the man who would dare to insinuate anything of the kind towards her, no matter who, even if he were one of the Lords of the Admiralty, must answer the same to Ben Blot. However, there has been enough said upon this subject, and, as your honour has lowered your flag and cried for quarter, why, with the plain and honest feeling of a British seaman, I say I forgive you—everybody forgives you I suppose, and that's all about it."

"Bravo, my lad!" said old Ben; "there spoke the spirit of a British tar, every inch of him, and those are exactly my sentiments. After a storm comes a calm, and so now, if your honour is agreeable to bring yourself to an anchor, just to settle the business, we will splice the mainbrace in the cracking of a biscuit."

The baronet affected to smile at the bluff good humour of the old man, while he cursed them all in his heart, and secretly resolved to lose no opportunity to gratify his revenge, and to effect the accomplishment of his diabolical designs.

"I thank you for your kindness, my worthy old friend," he remarked; "but business prevents me accepting your invitation. I wish you all good day, and once more congratulate you on the events that have recently taken place. Remember that the doors of the Manor House are always open to receive you all with a hearty welcome."

Bowing politely to them, but scarcely daring to direct his gaze towards Alice, (for the eyes of our hero and Mr. Maitland were upon him,) he retired from the cottage as he spoke

"Indeed?" said Ben, when he was gone; "this invitation may be a very friendly one, but I have my doubts upon that subject, and I think we had better steer clear of that coast as much as possible. I like not this Sir Raymond Perceval, and am glad he is gone. Years ago I could never look upon him without an unpleasant feeling stealing over me, for which I could not exactly account. I am certain he is a villain inherent, and that, if his past actions could be overhauled, his character would not stand very well upon the ship's books. But what say you, my dear Alice?"

"Heaven forbid that I should judge him or any other person wrongfully," replied the damsel; "but much I fear that the baronet's conscience is not clear of crime, and that the strange observations of Maud of the Ruins are not without foundation. God grant that we may experience no further trouble from him, but I would that we resided not near him.

"Nay, my love," remarked Ben; "You must not encourage those fears altogether, though, after what has occurred, notwithstanding his present plausible manner, we have a right to look upon him with suspicion. Should he again venture to annoy you with his insolent addresses while I am near you he will have good cause to repent it, depend upon it."

"But you will ere long be again separated from me, dear Ben," she sighed, and tears of regret trembled in her eyes; "distant lands will divide us once more and then—"

She could not finish the sentence, for her vivid imagination pictured the future in the most fearful colours, and her emotions overpowered her.

"Now, Alice, lass," said Ben, and he kissed a tear from her cheek; "I shall chide you if you give way to these gloomy ideas. Will you not have your parents and friends to watch over your safety? And when I am away, you should console yourself with the reflection that I am doing my duty to my king and country, and fear not but your lover will meet with an ample reward. Come, come, away with all sad misgivings, and look forward with bright and sanguine feelings of hope to that happy time when I shall again return, with plenty of shots in the locker, a heart throbbing with love and constancy, and kind friends and cheerful hearts shall be making merry on our wedding day."

"Aye," said his friend and benefactor, "won't that be a joyful day? Lor'—lor'—

how I do wish it was to-morrow. But I feel confident that this old hull of mine will
not be placed under hatches before it arrives, and that all will turn out as Ben has
foretold."

The observations of her lover and old Ben, did re-assure Alice, and struggling with
her feelings she became more composed. An animated conversation then ensued, in
which they all took an active part, and the day having passed away in the most agreeable manner, they did not separate until they had made arrangements for the festivities of to-morrow, which they resolved should be celebrated with all the spirit that the
occasion demanded.

Alice and her sister retired at an early hour to their chamber, and bright hopes once
more dawning upon their minds through the restoration of their lovers, those cares,
those fears and anxieties, that had before crowded them were dissipated, and they slept
more calmly and serenely than they had done for some time before.

CHAPTER X.

THE GUILTY DETERMINATION OF SIR RAYMOND—SEIZURE OF THE WIERD WOMAN—
SCORN AND DEFIANCE—THE FEARFUL DOOM.

Hearing the voices of the party assembled at Woodbine Cottage in loud conversation, Sir Raymond Perceval thinking he might hear something which might be useful
to him in the furtherance of his guilty plans, and put him on his guard how to act;
paused for some time outside and listened, and by that means was enabled to gather all
the particulars that have been related, their opinions of his recent conduct, and
arrangements for the celebration of the return of our hero and Harry Helm on the
following day, an arrangement which afforded him much satisfaction, as he hoped it
might be productive of some favourable result to his own nefarious wishes.

" 'Tis well," he muttered to himself; " the opinions you form of my character, are
no more than I anticipated, but they shall not daunt me from the execution of my purpose. The proposed festivities of to-morrow I may be able to turn to some account ;
at any rate, it shall be no fault of mine if I do not. Fair but scornful Alice, in spite
of the return of your lover, the fate to which I have doomed you may be nearer at
hand than you or your friends can dream of. Now to conceal my real thoughts and
intentions under the mask of the hypocrite."

Having thus soliloquised, the baronet knocked at the cottage door, and being
admitted, with what followed, the reader has been already made acquainted.

On leaving the cottage, Sir Raymond walked slowly on towards the Manor House,
reflecting deeply upon all that had passed, and in a frame of mind which we need not
stop minutely to describe.

" Fools !" he said; " in spite of your sarcastic observations, and the suspicions
which you evidently entertain of me, methinks I have now succeeded in deceiving
ye; and I will not fail to take advantage of the opportunity I have thus obtained.
Alice is more surely mine than ever; and to morrow's sports and revels will terminate
far differently than what they imagine, or I am much mistaken. It would be folly of
me to hesitate, or neglect the chance which now presents itself. Let me but boldly
venture, and certain triumph must be mine."

He paused for a moment or two and reflected, and some ideas and remembrances of
a torturing nature seemed to flash across his brain, which somewhat damped the ardour
of his recent feelings.

" Why does the fearful past arise to my memory in such vivid characters," he said,
in a hoarse voice, and looking hastily around as though he was fearful of being overheard by some one; " would that I could bury it in oblivion. But no, it will not be;
it is written in characters of blood; those nothing whatever can efface. To gaze upon
the features of that noble-minded youth makes me shudder, and I must be cautious
when in his presence, or one single word, even a look, might betray me, and then I
should be inevitably ruined. Why did not the angry billows overwhelm his hated and
dreaded form or the sword of the enemy lay him low? His features haunt my ima-

gination like a ghastly phantom, and—but, psha !—this weakness is unworthy of me ; let me be firm, and banish all such cowardly thoughts from my mind. It is the woman, Maud, whom I have most cause to fear, for should she appear at the revels to-morrow, she would probably denounce me, and a terrible retribution would then be sure to overtake me. Are there no means of preventing that ?" he added, after another pause. " There are. Why should a feeble old hag like her be permitted to keep me in a constant state of dread? This night, this very night shall secure her person in my power, or Fortune will prove a jilt to me altogether. To Luke Harden, and let together arrange our plans without delay."

As Sir Raymond came to this determination he increased his speed, and in a short time afterwards arrived at the Manor House, and without any more delay sought the presence of the pirates to whom he disclosed all that had passed at the cottage, and unburthened his plans in as few words as possible.

" And do you not think," said Luke, after he had listened to him ; " that what you have just proposed is rather precipitate, and might be frustated ?"

" No," replied Sir Raymond, hastily ; " my impatience will admit of no more delay, and I am most sanguine in my expectations of success. We must hit upon some plan by which you and your associates may take the persons assembled by surprise, and, in the confusion that will naturally ensue, Alice may easily be seized and hurried to this secret retreat of which no one has the least suspicion."

" And yourself, Sir Raymond," demanded Harden.

' Of course I will be present at the sports," replied Sir Raymond, " to prevent all surmises of the intrigue originating with me ; and when you make the attack, I shall appear to take an active part in attempting to defeat you, and to rescue the girl. So you will be on your guard !"

" Aye, that shall be attended to," answered his companion ; " though I still think the scheme is a hasty one, and may be fraught with danger, so soon after what has occurred between yourself and Alice."

" Psha !" ejaculated the baronet, impatiently, " I never knew you so doubtful, and to hesitate so much before, Luke. My determination is fixed, and a bold venture is almost certain to command success."

" Well be it so. But what is it you propose respecting old Maud ?"

" She must not be permitted to be an obstacle to the accomplishment of our wishes. That must be prevented this very night."

" By her death, I presume ?" said the villain, Luke.

" No," returned Sir Raymond ; " I would not that her life should be sacrificed at present. I am anxious to know more about her. Could she be secured it would answer every purpose."

" There will be no difficulty in accomplishing that," observed the pirate. " We will arrange everything between this and night."

" Enough," said the baronet ; " be prepared to see me again in a few hours, by which time we may be able to make up our minds what is best to be done."

To this Luke Harden assented, and, after a few more observations, they separated, Sir Raymond betaking himself to his study, where he gave way to the busy train of thoughts that crowded upon his brain, and flattered himself with the idea that his villanous projects were now in a fair way of speedy accomplishment, and exulted in the thought that the beauteous Alice Maitland would soon be in his power.

" I will run every risk," he soliloquised ; " for what danger is there which I would not boldly brave to achieve so great a triumph? Lovely Alice, little do you even dream of the fate with which you are now threatened. Every moment of delay does but increase my impatience, and heighten still brighter visions of the future in my fertile imagination. Sweet Alice ! the village pride ! must be mine, and now I swear that no earthly power shall prevent her."

An unnatural expression of exultation and guilty determination overspread his features, as he gave utterance to these words, and he looked forward to the arrival of the morrow with the greatest anxiety.

* * * * * * * *

Night set in, sad, sombre, except when at lengthened intervals, the moon for a brief space, peeped from behind a heavy cloud, and then again retired, making the darkness if possible, appear the more intense. The solemn silence of the hour was only inter-rupted by the low murmuring of the wind, or the dashing of the waves against the rocks, and all nature seemed otherwise wrapped in sleep.

Again the moon for a minute showed her pale face, shedding a ghastly light upon the old castle ruins, and a tall dim figure issued forth, and, after pausing a moment or two at the entrance, slowly descended the narrow and dangerous path which led from the cliffs to the beach below.

It was the mysterious wierd woman. Any one who could have seen them must have observed that there was even a more wild and anxious look in the expression of her features than usual on that occasion; and that it was quite evident that her mind at that moment was pervaded by thoughts of the most torturing and conflicting kind.

She paused when she reached the sea-beach, folded her arms across her breast (for she was without her usual companion, her staff), and as she gazed through the heavy mist which hung upon the waste of waters, her eyes seemed to penetrate the darkness, and a deep sigh escaped her bosom, which spoke of some agonising feeling within, which only in the silence and secresy of solitude she would suffer to find vent.

At length the wretched and mysterious woman spoke, and solemn and impressive were the tones of her voice as she thus gave utterance to the feeling of her troubled breast :

"How dark—how lonely—and how ominous is the aspect of all around; and yet how truly in keeping with the wild tempest of passion that hold dominion in this wretched care-worn heart. 'Tis such a night as would aid the murderer in the perpe-tration of his dark and hideous crimes, when no eye might watch his actions but that of heaven. 'Twas on such a night as this when I lost all that was dear to me in life, and nothing was left me but misery, despair, and the hope of vengeance. Oh, Alfred! Alfred!—noblest of men, and best of sons, why did cruel fate thus rob me of thee? Here stands the aged wreck of what was once so fair, so gentle, and so pure! May lightnings blast the guilty wretch who has been the cause of all!—But patience, patience, Geraldine; you have hunted the villain to his lair, your eye constantly watch his actions, and when the fitting time shall have arrived, a terrible revenge shall be yours."

A noise as of several approaching footsteps at that moment interrupted Maud in the midst of her soliloquy, and starting hastily round, she beheld several armed and masked ruffians standing with threatening attitudes before her, while one stood by, whose form was enveloped in a large cloak, and his hat so drawn down over his brows as to completely conceal his features.

Perfectly convinced of the danger which menaced her, and aroused into action, in an instant she drew forth from her bosom a couple of pistols, and in a fierce and determined voice exclaimed :

"What dark and guilty purpose brings ye hither? What seek ye with old Maud of the Ruins? Back, back! cowardly ruffians, bloodhounds, back! or this arm, old and feeble as it is, shall deal the first who dares advance a step towards me, death!"

"Heed not her threats!" cried Sir Raymond, (for he it was who has been described as enveloped in the cloak) "heed not her threats, but seize her and away with her!"

"Ah!" exclaimed old Maud; "'tis you, villain!—murderer! I know you now, and will not tamely yield to the fate you have doomed me to. Begone! or at your peril seek to molest me, miscreant."

"Why do you all stand as though petrified and alarmed by the idle threats of this wretched old hag?" passionately demanded the baronet. "Perform my bidding, I say, if ye are not cowards all!"

The pirates now made a rush towards her, but the moment they did so, Maud dis-charged the contents of both pistols, and the foremost of them, with a loud cry of agony, made one slight bound into the air, and then fell to the earth, weltering in his blood, and a ghastly corpse

With a bitter oath, the enraged Luke was about to rush upon her, and bury his deadly weapon in her breast, but Sir Raymond arrested his arm, and, in a voice of command, cried :

"Hold! hold, Harden! shed not the wretched being's blood! I have a more terrible and lingering fate in store for her!"

"Monster!" returned Maud, in tones that made the adjacent rocks reached again

FESTIVITIES ON THE RETURN OF BEN BOLT.

"fiend in human form ; I scorn, I defy your threats ; you dare not put them into execution ; vengeauce is mine upon your guilty head !''

"Stifle her cries,'' said the baronet ; "and let us begone ; we do but waste time.''

In a moment the villains rushed upon the now defenceless woman, and, in spite of her violent struggles drew a cloak so closely over her head that she could scarcely breathe, and pinioning her arms, she was completely at their mercy.

"To the boat ! to the boat with her !'' directed Sir Raymond ; " and convey her, with all speed to the secret entrance in the rock, where your associates are waiting to receive her. I will go by another route, and meet you there anon.''

The pirates immediately obeyed these commands, and raising Maud in their arms, proceeded towards the boat which they had moored in a convenient place close by.

" I triumph, I triumph !'' cried the baronet, in a voice of exultation, as he watched them away, and then departed from the spot; "Maud of the Ruins, one of the principal objects of my dread, is now secure in my power, and my future designs no doubt will work well. This is but a prelude to my future success. Now shall I be able to

No. 7.

ascertain who this mysterious woman really is, and my fearful secret will be safe from discovery."

He hurried on his way as he thus gave an expression to his feelings, and soon arrived, without being observed by any one, at the place of his destination. Immediately he made his way to the cavern, and was somewhat disappointed when he found that the pirates, with their prisoners, had not yet arrived.

"The tardy knaves," he said, in an impatient tone, as he hurriedly paced the cavern; "what can detain them."

He had scarcely spoken the words, when the paddling of oars was heard outside, followed by a shrill whistle.

"Ah !" he cried, as he advanced towards the secret entrance, which two or three of the pirates ascended too; "'tis well, they are here. Assist them to hand in the prisoner.

Luke Harden now appeared at the mouth of the cavern, followed by two more of his companions, hoisting up their helpless burthen, who was soon handed safely into the place, and the pirates following, the aperture was closed, and Sir Raymond stood for a few moments and gazed with a look of malicious triumph upon his unfortunate victim.

"Fortune has favoured us," he said, "my mysterious enemy is safely lodged at last. Let her view the pleasures of her situation."

The arms of poor old Maud were now unbound; the cloak was removed from her head and shoulders and having fixed one look of mingled reproach, hatred, and defiance upon the guilty baronet, completely exhausted with what she had to undergo, sank on a seat, and covered her face with her hands.

Sir Raymond could not restrain a laugh of exultation, as he said, in accents that showed the malignant nature of his feelings :

"So I have already found the means to crush the spirit of her who so boldly dared to threaten and denounce me. 'Tis well; the power of the hag is not then so great as she was wont to boast of."

Aroused at his words, and quickly recovering her usual demeanour, Maud started to her feet, and boldly confronted him.

"Miscreant ! murderer !" she cried, " and thinkest thou that the spirit of Maud can ever quail before thy proud yet empty menances; or that thy triumph o'er her shall continue? No, thou mayest taunt and mock me as long as thou think'st proper, but still will I scorn and defy thee !"

"Indeed ?' returned Sir Raymond, "those are bold words, old woman, but they fall harmlessly on my ear. We shall see what time can effect; and methinks you will yet be glad to sue for mercy to him whose helpless prisoner you now are."

"Sue for mercy to thee !" she repeated, and her eyes for the moment seemed to flash fire; " fool ! sooner should thy murderous weapon pierce my heart, than I would succumb to thy power. Oh, man of blood think of the fiendish deeds of the past, perpetrated by thy remorseless hand, and tremble ; for the hour of retribution will come, and a terrible fate hurls thy black and guilty soul to perdition !"

" Why do you thus stand to listen to her wild taunts, her threats and denunciations, Sir Raymond?" said Luke; "why not at once exercise your power, and stop her bold tongue for ever."

"Aye," returned Maud, glaring fiercely upon him; "I know thee well, Luke Harden ; thou art the fit associate of him whose ready instrument thou hast ever been in deeds of blood. Fear not but thou wilt yet meet with thy due reward, villain. For what purpose am I brought hither?" she sternly demanded, turning to the baronet.

"Need you enquire ?" he returned. "Have you not proved by your conduct that you are my bitterest enemy, and that you are possessed of dangerous secrets ?'

"Aye !" replied Maud, with an expression of triumph; "and dost thou doubt my knowledge, Sir Raymond Perceval? Oh, it should make thy guilty soul quail, to recapitulate the fearful deeds of the past, and which now call aloud to Heaven for vengeance. Rememberest thou that man, thy friend, whose dearest confidence thou didst betray? Rememberest thou his unfortunate wife, the beauteous Emeline, whose blood—"

"Hold ! hold !" interrupted the baronet, in a hoarse voice, and trembling violently ; " dare not to repeat that dreadful tale, or shudder at the consequences."

"Oh, then," said Maud, sarcastically; "thou canst not deny the truth of my words, Sir Raymond, with all thy boasting? And thy cheek is blanched with terror; and thy quivering lips, show the workings of thy guilty conscience, notwithstanding all thine efforts to conceal them. The despised Maud of the Ruins has still food for exultation. Ha! ha! ha!"

"Taunting devil!" shouted Sir Raymond, passionately; "I know you not; why then thus pursue me with your fiendish malice? Who are you?"

"That wilt thou know anon, to thy cost," she answered; "but not all the tortures thou mayest think proper to inflict, shall at present force the secret from me."

"Fool that I am to heed what you say," observed the baronet, after a brief pause; "you are either mad, or some base imposter, who seeks to intimidate me."

"Imposter!" repeated Maud; "thou knowest that thou liest in thy guilty soul, Sir Raymond Perceval, or why dost thou fear me? Why tremble to gaze upon me, even though I am now in thy power?"

"And shall I submit to be thus braved, defied, and insulted?" demanded the baronet, fiercely; "what folly and weakness is this?"

"Folly and weakness," repeated Luke Harden; "aye, you may well say that, Sir Raymond, and I am surprised at you, when in a moment you could rid yourself of the annoyance."

"But I have yet other means to quiet her bold tongue, and to make her yield to my demands," said Sir Raymond.

"I scorn all that thou canst do," returned Maud; "do thy worst, I am prepared to meet it."

"I will hear no more," he cried; "away with her to the dungeon; and there let her ponder in silence and horror on her wretched fate."

"Aye, villains, away with me," said Maud of the Ruins, firmly; "there are no terrors to which you may consign me that shall daunt my soul; but rest assured, Sir Raymond Perceval, that my predictions will be fulfilled, and that the fearful vengeance of outraged heaven will shortly descend upon your head. Lead the way; I am prepared to meet my fate, whatever it may be!"

Sir Raymond motioned the pirates impatiently to execute his commands, and they obeyed, leading Maud from the cavern, as she fixed a look of deadly malice upon him.

CHAPTER XI.

THE DUNGEON—SIR RAYMOND'S EXULTATION—THE CELEBRATION OF THE RETURN OF BEN BOLT AND HARRY HELM—THE ATTACK, AND THE RESULT.

For two or three minutes after Maud had been forced away, Sir Raymond traversed the cavern with disordered steps, and reflected deeply on her observations. At length he was interrupted in his meditations by the return of Luke Harden and his companions.

"Have you secured the hag in the dungeon?" he enquired of Luke, eagerly.

"Aye," replied the latter; "and if the terrors of the place do not soon cool her courage, I am much mistaken."

"Methinks it will be no easy task to do that," observed the baronet; "how her bold taunts and bitter denunciations annoyed me."

"Aye," replied the pirate, "and I marvel not that they should do so; all that surprises me is that you should have borne them with the patience and forbearance you did, when one plunge of the knife would have rid you of one, who must after what has taken place, ever be so hateful to your sight."

"You are too rash, Luke," said his companion. "I tell you again that I would avoid the shedding of more blood at present, if possible."

"But there was a time, Sir Raymond Perceval, when you were not wont to be so particular," observed Harden.

"Remind me not of that now," returned the former, with a shudder; "for I am in no humour to bear with it. I must, if possible, learn who this woman really is, and by what strange and unaccountable means she has become acquainted with that fearful and important secret, which I thought was hidden from the knowledge of every one but ourselves."

" Well," said Luke, " I do not wonder at your anxiety ; but it strikes me that old Maud, in spite of all the tortures that may be inflicted on her, is likely to remain obstinate. Curses light upon her ! she has this night slain one of the bravest of my crew ; and but for you, her own life should immediately have paid the forfeit of her daring."

" Well, it was a bad job ; but you did not leave the corpse behind, did you ?"

" Certainly not, for that might have led to our detection."

The baronet paused and reflected for a few minutes, and then observed :

" Tis well, 'tis well ;—the old woman secured, the success of my designs against Alice Maitland to-morrow seems all but certain. You will hold yourself in readiness, Luke, when the shadows of evening have fallen upon the earth, to act with promptitude."

" Aye," he replied ; " you will have no cause to complain of me, Sir Raymond. But we must call stratagem to our aid ; for, when there are likely to be so many persons assembled it might be dangerous to make an open attack."

" True," coincided Sir Raymond ; " we must hit upon some plan by which their attention may be diverted. We will arrange that anon."

" Be it so."

" And now," remarked the baronet ; " I must be gone. I will meet you again at an early hour in the morning, Luke ; in the mean time look well to your prisoner."

" You need not enjoin me to do so, Sir Raymond," returned Harden ; " a more watchful gaoler than myself she could not have."

" I am satisfied," said Sir Raymond ; " I know I may safely depend upon you. If fortune still continue to smile upon me, before this time to-morrow night the fair Alice Maitland will also be in my power. Oh, how exquisite is that thought !"

" Yes," replied the pirate ; " and it will be strange to me if I do not also, before long, obtain possession of the person of her equally lovely sister. You know that is a part of our bargain, Sir Raymond."

" True," agreed the latter ; " Rose Maitland is indeed a prize worth seeking to secure, and you have my best wishes for your success, Harden. The Bloodhound will be ready for sailing on the shortest notice, should we see occasion, will she not ?"

She will," answered Luke ; " my preparations are all made, and I flatter myself that we may weigh anchor at any time without exciting the least suspicions in the breasts of the land-sharks."

" All then, at present, goes well," said Sir Raymond ; " even much better than we could have expected. My hopes are sanguine, and increased determination urges me on to the completion of my designs."

In this state of mind Sir Raymond left the cavern, and once more returned to his chamber to brood over his guilty projects. The adventure of the night and its result had excited the most lively interest in his breast, and he looked forward to the morrow with the utmost confidence.

" The principal obstacle is removed," he soliloquised ; " old Maud is secured ;—she is safely in my power, from which it is impossible for her to escape, and I have nothing now to fear from her fierce denunciations. And yet," he added, after a brief interval, during which some torturing thoughts flashed across his brain ;—' and yet, how her observations have appalled my guilty soul, and conscience, with its iron tongue, continues to haunt my troubled fancy. Curses light upon her ! why was she ever permitted to cross my path ? But away with these thoughts. Be the past blotted from my memory, and let me look forward to the future with certainty and hope. To-morrow—to-morrow shall see my fondest wishes realized, even at every risk. Luke Harden and his daring associates in crime I know I can depend upon, then what should daunt me in the prosecution of my designs ? Let me but be firm, and I have no reason to entertain any fears as to the result."

Thus he continued to reflect for some time longer, until the lateness of the hour warned him to rest. Rest !—what rest is there for the mind blackened by crime ?

The dungeon to which poor old Maud was consigned, was indeed a fearful place ; and many were the unfortunate individuals, no doubt, who in years past had there met with a dreadful and lingering death. It was situated on the left of the subterranean passage which led to the cavern, and was secured by an iron door.

The bare contemplation of this place was enough to strike the soul of the beholder with terror, and it seemed totally impossible to exist in it for any length of time. It was a low vaulted cell of the smallest dimentions, and the only portion of light or air it received was from an aperture in one of the walls. The whole aspect of the place was black, dreary, and loathsome; and the air which the wretched occupant had to breathe was painfully oppressive and poisonous. The walls were reeking with unwholesome dew, and the damp earth was covered with filth, and the mouldering bones of those who had formerly perished there. A miserable heap of straw in one corner was the only substitute for a bed, and an old stool was everything in the shape of furniture it contained.

Such then was the frightful place where the unfortunate Maud was incarcerated. She uterred not a murmur of complaint when the villain Luke and his companions thrust her into it; and when they were gone, and she was left alone, she cast a feverish glance around the dungeon, and, in spite of the firmness of her spirit, and the gloom to which she had been so long inured, she could not help shuddering when she contemplated the horrors around her. She soon, however, recovered herself, and folding her arms across her chest, in a voice that showed the real state of the feelings that at that moment occupied her mind, she said:

"Blood-stained miscreant, and thinkest thou thus to daunt the spirit of Maud?—Fool! thou little knowest the character of her thou hast to deal with, or thou wouldst be convinced of the impotence of thy designs. Years of misfortune have rendered me reckless of suffering, and gloom and horror are in unison with my feelings. I will still scorn and defy thee. Still will I brave the worst, and live to see thee terribly punished for the monstrous crimes thou hast committed. Oh, how it glads me to know that I have already appalled thy guilty soul, and that, notwithstanding thou now holdest me in thy power, thou canst not look upon me without fear and trembling. And thou shalt have reason to dread me more yet, and thy present triumph shall be but of short duration."

Fresh courage nerved the wretched woman's breast as she thus spoke, and seating herself on the stool, she no longer noticed the dreadful situation in which she was placed, but abandoned herself to thoughts of a far different description.

*   *   *   *   *   *   *   *   *

The joyful morrow came at last, and nothing could be more propitious than the manner in which it was ushered in. The weather was all in favour with the glad occasion, and was as bright and cheerful as the happy hearts of all who were to take part in the pleasures of the day.

Old Ben, our hero, and Harry Helm had made the best use of their time, and numerous were the friends and acquaintances that were invited, and who thronged to welcome the return of those whom they so highly respected.

It was a perfect holiday in the village of Mayland, and might fairly vie with the scene of gaiety described in our first chapter. There was to be feasting and dancing on the lawn, and every cottage bore some simple decoration in keeping with the occasion. Jemmy Jingle and Sally Simper were arrayed in their best, and the former had set up the greater part of the preceding night to write a poetical effusion in celebration of the event, and by which he expected to win fresh laurels, and to astonish every one present. Matty Muggins was in his glory; his jolly round visage glistened with smiles; "The Jolly Topers," was rather tastefully decorated with flowers and evergreens, and from the top of the quaint old tavern waved the union jack. Then there was a little band of musicians, the best that could be found for miles around, and this promised to make the festivities go off with redoubled *eclat*.

The old Manor House, too, had a very gay appearance, with the colours of old England from every turret "waving in the wind."

At an early hour the guests began to assemble, and honest pleasure was depictured on every countenance. Among them were several youthful sailors, with their pretty lasses, and all seemed determined that nothing should be wanting on their parts to shed happiness and pleasure around.

As Sir Raymond from one of the windows of his mansion viewed the preparations making for the festival, and thought of the dark designs he had in contemplation, and of the complete success of which he felt quite confident, an expression of satisfaction settled upon his features, and exultation predominated in his breast. Himself and Luke Harden had held an early conference that morning, and finally arranged all their diabolical plans, which the baronet fondly flattered himself could be executed without the slightest suspicion falling upon him, and long before the hour of midnight he hoped to claim the beauteous Alice Maitland as his own.

Refreshed by tranquil sleep, Alice and her sister arose at an early hour on the morning of that eventful day; and having arrayed themselves in neat and appropriate attire for the occasion, descended from their chamber to the parlour to meet their parents, who embraced them with hearts o'erflowing with the fondest affection and delight.

And never had the fair sisters appeared more lovely than they did on this joyous morn. Health and hope lent their sweetest charms to their cheeks, and their bright eyes sparkled with even more than usual animation.

In a short time afterwards they were joined by old Ben and their lovers, and the greeting which then took place we must leave to the imagination of the reader.

Old Ben had set himself off to the greatest advantage, was " full rigged," as he characteristically called it, and wore his best pig-tail, which he only did on the most extraordinary occasions. It was quite evident that he had come determined to give the blue devils no quarter; to hoist the flag of mirth at the main, and to be friendly and happy with everything and everybody.

" Aye?" he cried. " this is as it should be, every ship in the fleet taut and trim; and all hearts on board as sound as a biscuit. Oh, splice my timbers, wont this be a happy day? I feel as young again as a boy on his first voyage. Alice; Rose—my dear girls, how pretty you do look to be sure. God bless you! God bless you! If it warn't that I'm afeared Ben and Harry might be jealous, I—I—oh, shiver me, it's no use;—my old heart's bounding right to my lips, so I might as well kiss you both first, and ax permission arterwards."

And thus saying, the kind-hearted old man suited the action to the word, and kissed the smiling lips of his fair and youthful friends respectfully, much to the amusement of their lovers, and Mr. and Mrs. Maitland.

" There," said the veteran, after the performance of this feat of gallantry; " I've done it, and now I feel as happy as if I had just received a whole cargo of prize-money."

" Bravo! my gallant old commodore !" said our hero, grasping the hand of hir aged friend and benefactor; " it glads me to see your noble old hulk in such good sailing trim. My dear Alice, when I gaze at your pretty figure-head, and see the sweet smiles of affection, happiness, and content beaming in those beautiful bright twinklers of yours, I feel myself one of the proudest and luckiest fellows in the British Navy. Tell me, my lass, is not your heart light and cheerful on this joyous occasion?"

" Oh, Ben," replied the blushing maiden, and the whole sentiments of her soul spoke in her eyes; " need you ask the question? It is to celebrate your restoration to those who love you, and who I know are so dear to you, and can I be otherwise than happy? Heaven grant that nothing may occur to mar it."

" Mar it, Alice ?" repeated Harry Helm; " oh, fear not, all is bright and fair, above and below, and all will go as merry as hearts can wish it. There will be no squalls to-day, depend on it, whatever point of the compass the wind may blow from. What say you, my pretty Rose? You see no clouds gathering aloft, do you, my dear girl?"

" No, Henry," replied Rose; " all is calm and sunshine, and the sweet hope animates my breast that nothing will seem to interrupt it."

" Well said, Rose, my lass," ejaculated old Ben; " spoken like a little Queen, as you are. But see, the lads and lasses are all gathering; so let us weigh anchor, and bear-a-head to meet 'em."

" Aye," observed Mr. Maitland; " we must not suffer our friends to think that we are tardy in welcoming them; so, come, my dear children—come, my friends, let us away at once."

To this they all, of course, readily assented, and the happy party issued from the cottage.

For the better accommodation of all, and to render the scene more joyous and animated, the festivities of the day were arranged to take place in a verdant meadow adjacent to the village; and tables for refreshments were laid out with much care and taste in front of the comfortable hostelrie of Matty Muggins, who, as has been stated before, was in high glee on the occasion; for it must be acknowledged that the worthy host calculated upon reaping the profits of a whole year at least, on that day.

And there was our eccentric friend, Mr. Jingle, mounted on a bench, and with peculiar emphasis and extraordinary gestures reading the lines he had taken so much trouble to compose, amidst the shouts of laughter and applause from the persons assembled.

"There!" he exclaimed, when he had concluded, almost out of breath, and addressing himself to Sally; "what do you think of that, Sally? Haven't I astounded 'em? Who'd imagine that the little village of Mayland could ever contain such a genius? Don't you admire me, Sally? Do you not worship me? Ain't you proud of me?"

"La! Jemmy," simpered Sally; "how can you ask me such a foolish question? You know I admire you above every other man in the universe."

"And so you ought, Sally," remarked her lover with a pompous and egotistical air; "so you ought, for genius, immortal genius, is stamped upon my brow. Oh, Sally, I should love you a thousand times more than I do, if you was only like me, a votary of the Muse!"

"The *Mews!*" repeated Sally, with much simplicity; "what's that, Jemmy? Oh, I recollect now, when you was in London, you did live in a mews and used to look after the horses."

"Shades of Milton, Pope, and Dryden," cried the indignant barber; "hear this! Here's ignorance! I'm ashamed of you, Sally; now I'll be bound to say that you do not even know what a couplet is?"

"*Couple it!*" replied Sally, archly; "oh, yes, I do;—that's what you and I shall do, Jemmy, when we get married, and make *one.*"

"Ha' ha! ha!" laughed Jemmy, good humouredly; "that's not so bad."

At this moment the party from Woodbine Cottage approached the spot, and loud shouts of joy and welcome rent the air, and every one gathered eagerly round to give the young seamen and their lovers and friends a cordial greeting, which was returned by them with the same warmth and sincerity.

A morning repast was set upon the tables, to partake of which all were invited, and which had scarcely concluded, when Sir Raymond Perceval made his appearance.

At the sight of him, an uneasy feeling came over our heroine, and the ardour of the joy she had previously felt was for a moment checked. Ben observed her emotion, and whispered in her ear:

"Be not alarmed, my love; it would be wrong to judge too harshly of Sir Raymond, after the apology he made yesterday; and I cannot for the life of me, bear malice towards any one. No doubt he comes in every friendly spirit, and not to interrupt our happiness."

Alice felt re-assured by the observations of her lover, but still she averted her eyes from the baronet, who advancing towards the happy guests, with a condescending air, said:

"Do not let my presence disturb or embarrass you, my friends; I came, a self-invited guest, with the hope that I may be permitted to take part in your festivities. Mr. Bolt, and you, my gallant young friend, Mr. Helm, it affords me much pleasure to have to congratulate you on this happy occasion."

"Your honour is very kind," said our hero, scraping a bow in true nautical style; "and I can only say that any one is welcome here who is a fair and honest craft, and would scorn to sail under false colours."

Sir Raymond felt rather abashed, for he saw plain enough that the young seaman viewed him with anything but confidence. However, he concealed his real thoughts, and with much apparent candour replied:

"True; he must indeed be a scoundrel and a hypocrite, who could contemplate any harm on the occasion of such a friendly meeting as this. But let me not, I beg, be any interruption to your sports, which it will afford me the highest pleasure and gratification to witness."

He then retired to a seat which was placed for his accommodation, and the guests encouraged by the urbanity of his manner, proceeded to enjoy themselves with the same freedom and hilarity as if he had not been present.

But dark and guilty were the thoughts that occupied the breast of the baronet as he viewed the joyous scene before him, and noticed the affectionate glances that were ex changed between Alice and her lover.

"Make the most of the present moments, hated rival," he muttered to himself; "for they are not fated to last long, depend upon it. The hour of my triumph is at hand, and your joy shall be turned to sorrow. Oh, how impatient am I for the time to arrive. But all is so admirably arranged that it is next to an impossibility for it to fail."

Luke Harden, in rustic disguise, now joined the happy throng, in order to watch the proceedings, and he and Sir Raymond exchanged significant glances with each other.

The mirth of the guests was rising to its full pitch; the health of Ben and Harry Helm, and our heroine and her sister had been pledged with the utmost enthusiasm and hilarity, and the joke and the song went merrily round; in all of which no one took a more active part than old Ben, who, it was quite evident, had never felt more happy than on this occasion.

"And now my lads and lasses," said the veteran; "having laid in a cargo of grog and provisions for the voyage, I think you cannot do better just by way of changing the scene than to enliven it with a dance."

"Aye, aye." shouted several voices; "a dance! a dance!"

And the rustic musicians did their best, and every one who took part in the sports did their best; some of the prettiest feet and ancles that ever nature in its happiest moods moulded, might be seen tripping it gaily on the light fantastic toe; and such a scene of joyous innocent revelry presented itself to the delighted view of the spectator, as had seldom before been witnessed in the at all times lively village of Mayland, and its neighbourhood.

While these festivities were going forward, and each one was too busily and too happily engaged to watch his actions, Sir Raymond Perceval took the opportunity of drawing Luke Harden aside, and speaking to him.

"So, Luke," he remarked; "all appears to go on as well as we could wish. These happy revellers little suspect the sad change which is in store for them, and which will turn their boisterous mirth to woe."

"True," answered the pirate; "I have prepared everything for action as soon as the shades of evening shall set in. Two or three of my crew disguised, are in the tavern, and at the proposed signal will execute my instructions. With the rest of my brave fellows I will be at hand, and in the confusion which will be sure to follow, we will rush from our concealment, and the abduction of Alice may be accomplished without much difficulty."

"Right, right, my worthy friend," said the baronet; "I depend upon you, and feel confident of success."

"But you must beware how you act your part, Sir Raymond," urged Luke; "you must remain here till the last, and then appear to take part and sympathise with the friends and lover of the girl."

"Aye," returned Sir Raymond; "I have already arranged that in my own mind. I will take good care to give them no room to suspect that I am in any way connected with the outrage. I am all impatience for the time to arrive, for the longer I gaze upon the transcendant charms of the innocent Alice, the more anxious am I to possess her. How do I envy my hated rival the looks of affection she bestows upon him."

"Psha!" replied Harden; "'tis folly to let such thoughts annoy you. But we had better separate, for we know not whose eyes may at the present moment be scrutinising our actions."

"True," coincided the baronet; "the utmost precaution is necessary. Leave me."

Luke obeyed, and leaving Sir Raymond to his own reflections, mingled with the guests.

The dance being now over, the baronet advanced towards them, and in the most affable tones, complimented them all highly upon the skill with which they had executed it.

"Aye, your honour," replied old Ben; "on such a joyful occasion as this, and with such light hearts as those here assembled, it would be strange indeed, if they could not find toes equally as light to match 'em. Yer see, yer honour, there's nothing ailing in their upper-works, so each one can sail along as merry as a grig. Even my old timbers are not so shattered, but they will be able to take part with the best of 'em,

THE INTERVIEW BETWEEN JEMMY JINGLE AND SALLY SIMPER.

as soon as I have got a little more of the grog on board, and there's nothing like it to set the timbers shaking."

"It delights me to see you all so happy, my friends," observed Sir Raymond. with an expression of countenance that might have deceived even the most penetrating eye, "and I assure you that I fully paticipate in your feelings."

Alice heard him with mingled feelings of doubt and dread, and would have felt much more satisfied had he not been present; but still her heart was too elated at the happiness around her, and in thinking of the occasion which had given rise to it, to suffer anything to trouble her for any time together, and she joined in the pleasures of the day with greater vivacity than she had done for many months before.

The revels were kept up with unabated spirit throughout the day, and no one seemed to enjoy them more than Sir Raymond Perceval; but as the hours, to him, wore tediously away, he awaited with the greater impatience for the time to arrive when he would see the result of his diabolical designs, and his guilty mind wavered between doubt and confidence.

At length evening set in, mild and tranquil, and the bright moon shedding her silvery beams over all around, gave additional effect to the scene. Several of the

No. 8.

guests, in merry groups, had dispersed themselves in different parts, and were gambolling away in all their heart's delight, while the more aged were seated at the tables, enjoying themselves, and looking on with admiration and pleasure.

Alice and her sister, with their lovers, somewhat fatigued with their unusual exertions, were seated at a separate table, deeply engaged in the most affectionate conversation, and their minds completely abstracted from everything else, when suddenly all were startled by a simultaneous cry of " Fire! fire!" and huge flames rushed forth from one of the upper windows of the old tavern; spreading instantaneously, and threatening the rapid destruction of the building.

It would be impossible to describe the scene of consternation that ensued; the revels ceased, cries of alarm filled the air, the females rushed about wildly, the men all made towards the burning house, to render what assistance they could in extinguishing the flames, and in the general panic and confusion that prevailed Alice and her sister found themselves alone!

Struck with awe and terror, they stood transfixed to the spot, and gazed aghast on the fearful scene. But they were not long suffered to remain so; a shrill whistle saluted their ears, which was quickly answered by another from a different part, and the next moment they found themselves surrounded by armed men, wearing masks, and before they had scarcely time to call for help, they were rudely seized, and hurried towards the wildest part of the coast. Still their piercing shrieks for help rent the air, and at that moment our hero, Harry Helm, Sir Raymond, followed by several others, rushed hastily to the spot and looked anxiously around them.

"What mean those cries of distress? From whom do they proceed?" exclaimed Ben, in breathless haste; "Alice!—Rose!—where are they? Oh, mad that we must be to desert them!"

"My children! my dear children!" cried Mr. Maitland, in a voice of agony; "oh, heavens!"

"Some foul treachery has been at work," observed the guilty Sir Raymond, with much apparent concern.

Loud screams were again heard, and with frantic eagerness all eyes were directed towards the place from whence they seemed to proceed, the reflection from the fire assisting their view.

"Ah! see!" exclaimed Harry, "the shadows of men are moving rapidly yonder in the distance. Ben, my friends—quick, let us pursue the villains, and we may not yet be too late to rescue the poor girls from their power!"

Ben, Harry, and most of the seamen, together with Sir Raymond, hurriedly started off in the pursuit, while others remained behind, to assist in subduing the flames. For a moment they lost sight of the ruffians, but the shrieks of the hapless girls directed them, and they again beheld them, and notwithstanding the advantrge which the pirates had had, they evidently gained fast upon them.

"Although Ben and his friends considerably outnumber them," muttered Sir Raymond to himself; "I fear not; Luke and his colleagues are so well armed that they must triumph."

Their pursuers had now gained so rapidly upon them that, the pirates seeing it was useless to attempt to avoid them, came to a stand, and prepared to defend themselves resolutely.

Alice, who was supported on the arm of Luke, and Rose on that of another of the ruffians, had now fainted, and the sight of this aroused all the courage and indignation of our hero and Harry.

"Damned villains!" exclaimed Ben, "thus to bear down with your heavy malice upon the weak and defenceless, when the fleet was out of the way. Release your hold of that innocent girl, you infernal grumpus, or I will scuttle your ugly hulk in less time than I could turn my quid!"

"Fool!" cried Harden, fiercely; "you do but rush upon certain death! There's a pill for you, to begin with."

He discharged the contents of a pistol at our hero as he spoke, but it missed him, and was spent harmlessly on the air.

"On to them, my friends," cried Ben, "we have justice on our side, and we will soon draw the teeth of the rascally sharks!"

In a moment, the gallant young mariner rushed upon one of the pirates, and so suddenly that he took him by surprise, and wrested his weapon from him without much difficulty. Harry Helm, and two or three others of the sailors followed his example, and the combat now commenced with the same obstinate determination on both sides. Several of the pirates were quickly disabled, but the others still fought with redoubled resolution, so that the issue for some time appeared to be extremely doubtful.

Our hero attacked Luke Harden with the most indomitable courage, and tried to tear the senseless Alice from his hold. Harry Helm also sought to rescue his beloved Rose, and fought with the most consummate bravery with the ruffian who held her ; but for some time success did not attend the efforts of the two friends.

Sir Raymond Perceval, who had pretended to take part in the rescue, seeing the danger of Luke, and that he was every minute becoming weaker, watched his opportunity when he thought no one could observe him, and aimed a blow with a poniard at Ben, but at the instant Luke turned suddenly round, and the deadly weapon entered the thick part of his arm.

" D—n !" exclaimed the ruffian, as he released his hold of our heroine, whom Ben secured ; and at the same moment Harry Helm succeeded in rescuing Rose and felling his assailant to the earth.

" The coast-guard ! the coast-guard !" cried two or three of the ruffians. This caused a general panic, and at once discontinuing the combat, the pirates fled in dismay, and were soon lost to the sight.

" Thank heaven ! oh, thank all-merciful heaven, our dear children are saved !" cried Mr. and Mrs. Maitland, fervently.

" The poor girls," ejaculated our hero, in a voice of the deepest emotion ; " that they should be exposed to such a monstrous outrage. But, thank God ! we have rescued them, and defeated these miscreants in their villanous designs. My dear Alice, oh what a shock will this event be to thy feelings."

But what was the tumult of fierce passions which raged within the breast of Sir Raymond Perceval at that moment ? The reader may easily imagine them, when he thus saw all the sanguine hopes he had formed at once annihilated. He, however, stifled his feelings as well as he could, and, assuming a tone of the deepest commiseration, he said :

" Who can possibly be the wretch who has concocted this villanous design against these innocent maidens ? But they have been defeated, and that affords me the most infinite satisfaction."

" I cannot imagine who the scoundrel can be who has thus dared to perpetrate so diabolical an act," answered Ben ; " but it strikes me that he will soon be discovered, and be he who he may, peer or beggar, he shall pay most dearly for his atrocity. My poor Alice look up and speak to me ; 'tis your faithful Ben who now holds you to his heart, and you are safe."

The baronet quailed beneath what his guilty conscience made him believe the rather pointed remarks of our hero, and he knew not what answer to make. But at length he said :

" I need not tell you, I presume, Mr. Bolt, how fully I appreciate your feelings, and I shall feel it my duty to assist you all in my power in discovering the villain and bringing him to justice. The fire at the inn seems to be now extinguished, and I hope that no serious damage is done. My presence at such a time as this must be an intrusion to you, my friends, and regretting that there should have been so sad a termination to your festivities I wish you good night."

Thus saying, and bowing to them all, the baronet quitted the spot.

At this moment Alice and her sister recovered, and opening their eyes and beholding themselves in the arms of their lovers and surrounded by their friends, they uttered a mingled exclamation of astonishment and gratitude.

" Dear Ben," ejaculated our heroine, in a faint voice, and looking almost incredulously round, " you and our beloved friends here ! Oh, what strange delusion, then, was it that for a time held possession of my senses?"

" It was no delusion, my poor lass," replied her lover ; " but the work of some secret villain, whom if I discover shall have true cause to repent of it, for, if I once get my grappling irons on him, Lord help his unhappy carcase. The rascally pirates did take advantage of the confusion which took place at the fire, and bear down upon you and the gentle Rose, sure enough ; a rare prize they thought to capture, and if your signals of distress had not reached our ears, and if we had not given chase to them so soon as we did, it is not at all unlikely that they would have succeeded. However, thanks to Providence, you are now safe."

"Oh, now I shudder to think of the fate which threatened me and my sister," said Alice, " and from which we have so narrowly escaped. Alas! who can that secret enemy be who thus seeks to destroy my peace?"

" Enemy!" repeated old Ben; " damme, he must be a rascally swab, indeed, who could think of injuring Alice or Rose Maitland. But courage, my good girls, he will not venture to come to the attack again; or, if he does, he will meet with such a warm reception as he little expects, I'll warrant."

"Sir Raymond Perceval," said Rose; " surely he could never—"

"No, no, Rose," interrupted Harry Helm; " it would be wrong, I think, to suspect him, after his friendly conduct to-day. Besides, he followed us in pursuit of the ruffians, and took an active part in defeating them."

"True," observed Mr. Maitland; " suspicion cannot possibly attach to him; ut by whom the villains who committed this outrage were employed I cannot conjectue. I am completely lost in mystery. But come, it is useless to tarry here; let us return home and endeavour to compose ourselves after this disagreeable adventure."

To this they all assented, and Ben and Harry, taking the arms of our heroine and her sister, they departed from the scene of the late conflict.

In the mean time the fire at the Jolly Topers was extinguished, having done far less damage than might have been anticipated, and when the party arrived there on their way home, they found a number of their friends waiting to receive them, and to congratulate them on the defeat of the ruffians who had put so alarming an end to their festivities.

On their return home the friends sat discussing the mysterious and alarming adventure of the evening for some time, and when Ben and his friend separated from their lovers, it was with the understanding that they would keep watch during the night, in case the ruffians should venture an attack on the cottage; and they had also the assurance of immediate assistance from several of their neighbours, who would arm themselves for the purpose. Independent of this, old Ben and our hero, having seen the officer of the coast guard, and made him acquainted with the whole particulars of the outrages, he promised that there should be a sharp look-out. Thus every precaution was taken to meet any danger which might threaten, that time and circumstances would permit. How the fellows could have escaped the coast-guard, who were so close upon them, was a mystery. They had vanished so suddenly among the rocks that it had seemed like the work of magic; and it was evident, if they were smugglers, as it was supposed they were, they had some secret place of concealment, which had hitherto remained undiscovered.

When our heroine and Rose separated from their parents and retired for the night, they sat for some time conversing upon the alarming subject. But they racked their brains to no purpose, for they found it in vain to endeavour to form the slightest conjecture as to who their secret enemy could be.

CHAPTER XII.

SIR RAYMOND PERCEVAL'S RAGE AND DISAPPOINTMENT—FRESH SCHEMES TO DISTURB THE PEACE OF ALICE MAITLAND.

The most ungovernable rage and disappointment held fierce dominion in the breast of Sir Raymond Perceval as he bent his steps to the Manor House. Fearful maledictions escaped his lips, and he felt in a fit humour to perpetrate any deed, however desperate and monstrous, to satiate his deadly feelings of revenge.

" To be thus defeated," he exclaimed, " when my plans were so well arranged and success seemed all but certain! Oh, curses light upon that wayward fate which has brought about this disappointment! Surely the rascals might have easily conquered the weak forces opposed to them had they been determined. Oh, how fondly had I cherished the hope that the beauteous Alice would this night have been in my power!

I would willingly have sacrificed half my fortune for the triumph of my plot. But no; at the very moment when I thought that the envied prize was within my grasp, accursed Fate snatched it from me, as if in mockery of my presumptuous wishes. And shall all my hopes be thus annihilated? Shall I suffer the girl to escape me altogether, and the young sailor to whom her affections are devoted to bear her off in triumph? No; by all the infernal host I swear, this shall not be. Let this disappointment bu make me the more firm and resolute, and I may yet surmount every difficulty.",

Deeply occupied by these guilty thoughts the baronet walked on, and having arrived at his mansion he lost no time in departing to the secret rendezvous of the pirates, whom he found had arrived there some time before him, and were in a state of great excitement and confusion, discussing the disasters of the night, and quarrelling among themselves.

Luke Harden was sitting in a corner, apart from the rest, his arm bandaged, and his compressed lips and contracted brows showed that he was in no very amiable temper. He arose on the entrance of Sir Raymond, and, advancing towards him, met his stern look with one of equal anger, but said nothing.

"So," said the baronet, in accents of rage, "a pretty job you have made of this, after all your boasting. You have suffered the girl to escape at the very moment when she seemed securely in our power."

"And who is to blame for it?" demanded the pirate, sternly. "Do you reproach me? Methinks I have more cause to complain, seeing the ugly wound I have received at your hands."

"Aye," remarked Sir Raymond; "that was, I admit, an unfortunate job, and I regret it. Need I tell you that the blow was intended for my detested rival?"

"Would that it had reached his heart," said the pirate, savagely; "it was that damned mistake on your part, Sir Raymond, which caused me to resign the girl; and it would have been madness for us to have prolonged the combat, on the appearance of the coast-guard. I think great credit is due to us for the way in which we contrived to elude them, and escape detection. Yet you now fix the whole onus of the failure on my shoulders."

"No, no," returned the baronet, seeing that the ruffian, Luke was in no humour to bear rebuke. and fearful of offending him; "you misunderstand me, Luke; bear with me. Can you wonder that I feel vexed and disappointed at our defeat at the very moment when I thought that the girl was securely mine? Curses light on the disaster which has thus marred my hopes. What is now to be done?"

"Done!" repeated Harden, sulkily; "nothing at present; we must wait awhile till the excitement consequent on this affair shall have somewhat abated. We could not, with any degree of safety, make any immediate attempt to put our designs into execution, for our enemies will now be on the alert."

"'Tis too true," coincided Sir Raymond, with an oath. "And yet my impatience can ill brook the delay."

"There is no alternative, and you must submit to it. Ben Bolt, it seem intends to go to sea again; he and his friend Helm, I heard to day, have already joined the Spitfire, which is expected to sail in a few days; when we have thus got rid of them, we may calculate upon the success of our plans."

"Ah!" exclaimed Sir Raymond; "then my hopes are not entirely crushed. But no, even at the cost of half my fortune, I am determined that Alice Maitland shall be mine. Present defeat does but make me the more anxious. I may still depend upon your aid, Harden?"

"Of course you may," answered Luke; "I have cause to feel as much anxiety upon the subject as yourself, for the fair Rose has excited passions in my breast as powerful as your own, and I am resolved that I will not rest until I possess her. So, you see, Sir Raymond, our interests are mutual, and if we only act in unison, and watch our opportunity, our triumph is certain."

"Your words revive me, Luke. And yet the failure of this night cannot but annoy me greatly. Oh, the transport I had anticipated would now have been mine. Alice never appeared more lovely than she did to-day, and as my eyes gloated on her superlative charms, my heated passion rose to such a pitch that it is a wonder I did not betray the nature of my feelings."

"'Twas well, however, that you were upon your guard. I watched your conduct narrowly, and consider that you acted your part well."

"Yes," observed the baronet; "I think my plausible manner completely quieted all their suspicions against me. The combat was a determined one, and I cannot but give you and your men every credit for the bravery you displayed."

"Aye," returned Luke, "the lads of the Bloodhound are no cowards, as they have proved in many a fierce engagement on the deep. Your rival and his friend fought like lions; two braver fellows are not to be found in the British Navy, I'll be bound."

"True, the boy does honour to the noble blood that flows in his veins," said Sir Raymond, and a pang of remorse shot through his breast. "Oh, how generous, how open-hearted was his father! Villain that I must have been to act the base, the treacherous, and monstrous part I did towards him. I—"

"Psha!" interrupted Luke, "what's the use of reproaching yourself with that now after the lapse of so many years."

"Ah, Luke! it is impossible for me to quiet the voice of conscience. Lord Alfred was my best, my warmest, most disinterested friend, and—"

"And you betrayed him," rejoined Luke, "that's all.

"I did," replied the baronet, "most brutally deceived and wronged him; heartless, ungrateful miscreant that I was!"

"Well, well—think no more of that. 'Tis strange, however, that you never heard what became of him afterwards."

"It is," said the baronet, "but something seems to tell me, notwithstanding so many years have gone by, that he still lives."

"That is not very likely," answered Luke, " or he would have sought you out ere this, and demanded satisfaction for his wrongs."

"Resolved to act the part of a villain from the first," returned Sir Raymond, "I introduced myself to him under a fictitious name, and he would therefore have no suspicion of me by my present title. Time, too, must have altered my features, that, even if we should ever meet again, I do not think it would be possible for him to recognise them."

"Then," said Luke, "at any rate, you may set your mind at rest on that score. Old Maud, however, is evidently acquainted with all the facts."

"True," answered the baronet; "and by what strange means they have come to her knowledge—who she is, and why she pursues me with such vindictive feelings, I cannot conceive."

"And it does not appear very probable that you will be able to force the secret from her," remarked Harden; "the old hag will remain obstinate to the last, depend upon it, and for my own part, I think it would be the wisest and the safest plan to silence her at once. You know the dead tell no tales."

"No," said the baronet; " is she not safe from doing me any harm where she is? and why should I therefore recklessly embrue my hands in her blood?"

"Well," returned his companion, " be it as you will; but mind that she does not escape."

"Escape! How is it possible for her to do so, secure as she is?"

"It shall be no fault of mine if she does. Enough, however, on that subject for the present. We have met with one defeat to-night; but fear not, Sir Raymond; let but these young seamen slip their cable and once more quit these shores, then can we pounce upon our prey, and what will there be to frustrate our designs?"

"Nothing!" replied the baronet, confidently; " my hopes are reanimated. In a few days you say that the Spitfire is expected to sail."

"Yes," returned Luke; " she goes to join the English squadron in the Baltic, and—"

"Ben Bolt shall never behold his beloved Alice again," added Sir Raymond, vehemently, and with a look of guilty determination. "Deprived of the protection of her lover, what can save her from falling into my power? Oh, how impatiently do I await the time when the object of my heart's fondest desire shall be within my grasp. Alice Maitland, for the present you have escaped me; but your doom is sealed, and my triumph is close at hand."

An expression of exultation passed over his features as he gave utterance to these words, and conquering his rage and disappointment at the failure of that night, he looked forward to the future with the most sanguine hopes of complete success; and after some further conversation of no importance, he retired from the place and sought his own chamber.

But the mind of the guilty baronet was too busily occupied to suffer him to think of retiring to rest, and he remained absorbed in thought, and deeply reflecting upon all that had occurred on that eventful day and night, till the light of morning broke in at his chamber window.

Notwithstanding the defeat which Luke and the other pirates had met with, ne could not but acknowledge the courage and determination with which they had fought, and he placed every confidence in them. The information which Luke had given him of Ben and Harry having joined the Spitfire, also afforded him every satisfaction, and he impatiently awaited the arrival of the time for the vessel to sail; for then he flattered himself that there would be no further obstacle to the realisation of his guilty wishes, which he resolved should be accomplished even at all hazards.

" Yes," he soliloquised, as he traversed his chamber in a state of considerable excitement, " in spite of what has happened all promises well, and Alice—the beauteous, but scornful Alice—must fall a victim to my designs. That boy, so hateful to my sight, will be got rid of, and then my mind will be more at rest. May I never behold him; for I cannot gaze upon his features without the most powerful feelings of terror and remorse. Oh, that I could blot for ever from the tablet of my memory the fearful deeds of the past. But no, in spite of all my efforts they will arise upon my conscience, and make me look forward to the future with doubt and trembling. Will such guilt as mine be suffered to remain unpunished? Will the restless spirit of the murdered for ever call in vain for justice? No, no; sooner or later a terrible retribution will most assuredly overtake me."

He paused, and fear shook his guilty soul. " But," he said at length; " why should I thus torture myself, when all at present is so secure? Away with cowardly thoughts, and let me again become a man. I cannot retrace my steps, and therefore 'tis useless to give way to these gloomy reflections, and bitter self-reproaches."

He became more firm as he thus spoke, and, with the hope of snatching an hour or two's sleep, he threw himself on the bed.

We will now return to poor old Maud, who in the deep solitude of the frightful dungeon in which she was confined brooded gloomily on the sorrows of the past, and endeavoured to form some conjecture of what was in future in store for her.

" So," she muttered to herself, as she sat crouched in one corner of the dungeon, and her eyes fixed upon vacancy, " the savage murderer of the unfortunate Emeline holds me in his power, and thinks by exposing me to terrors such as those by which I am at present surrounded to intimidate me, and to draw from my breast the secret which has there so long been hidden. Miscreant! fool! he little knows the character of her he has to deal with, or he would cease to encourage any such futile ideas. He may rack me—torture me—tear these old limbs asunder, but still shall he find me remain inflexible! Wild Maud, the wretched outcast, is a stranger to fear, and years of suffering have taught her to treat it with indifference. And shall these black and gloomy vaults long confine me? Shall I remain caged like some wild beast? No! Maud of the Ruins shall soon again be free to wander the dreary waste and climb the craggy steep. Aye! and her hour of triumph will come; she will live to redress the wrongs of the injured, and to invoke the most terrible and overwhelming vengeance of heaven upon the head of the guilty. Sir Raymond Perceval, the time will come when, in abject fear and horror, thou shalt cry aloud for that mercy which thou refused to others and which shall be denied to thee. Oh, with what feelings of gratification and delight will I then gloat upon thy anguish, and mock at and triumph in thy despair. It is for this that I have continued to live, and those wishes he shall not fail to see accomplished!"

The wretched woman exulted at the thought, and a malicious grin disturbed her haggard and shrivelled features. But it was wonderful how any human being could possibly bear up with fortitude against the accumulated horrors of that awful place. It was impossible there to tell the day from night, but one of the pirates had left her a small lamp, whose sickly, feeble rays only served to render the terrors of the place more visible. Even the horrors of the charnel-house could not have been more revolting. For some hours after Maud had been incarcerated there no one came near her, and she walked backwards and forwards, muttering wild and incoherent words to herself, and in a state of mind which we need not attempt to describe. But at length one of the pirates entered the cell, bringing with him a pitcher of water and a black loaf, which he placed on the earth before the unfortunate prisoner, and then retired from the cell without saying a word, while the thoughts of Maud were too busily occupied to allow her to take scarcely any notice of him.

And thus the hours passed drearily away until the morning after the daring outrage which has been described, when as old Maud was seated in her usual attitude, immersed in painful reflection, she was suddenly aroused by hearing the door being unlocked, and the next moment Sir Raymond Perceval entered the dungeon.

Maud started to her feet when she beheld him, and fixed upon him a look in which deadly malice, revenge, and defiance were combined. The baronet, however, met her gaze with indifference, being fully prepared for the reception he knew he should be sure to meet with. Having closed the door after him, he stood for a moment or two with folded arms, and gazed upon the old woman with mingled looks of triumph and fear.

"Now, miscreant," ejaculated the unfortunate prisoner, in a stern voice; "what wouldst thou with old Maud. Is not thy vengeance sufficiently gratified now that thou hast her confined in this living tomb; or seekest thou to torture her with thy bitter taunts and feelings of exultation? Proceed; she is fully prepared for all that your narrow mind and implacable malice can give utterance to."

"Obstinate woman," replied Sir Raymond, "have you not brought your present miserable situation upon yourself? You have boldly dared to avow yourself my most inveterate enemy, and proved that you are dangerous to my peace, and can you wonder that I should thus prevent you from doing that mischief which you have threatened?"

"I can wonder at nothing which the villain Sir Raymond Perceval may choose to do," replied Maud; "thou dost well to acknowledge that 'tis fear, coward fear, suggested by thy guilty conscience, which prompts thine actions. And thou hast ample cause to fear, if thou didst know all. Nay, seek not to deny thy feelings; they are evident in thy blanched cheek, thy quivering lips, and restless gaze. And thinkest thou by securing me in this loathsome cell to avert the avenging wrath of heaven for the hideous crimes thou hast committed, villain? Tremble, I say; for the fearful doom, the doom of the libertine and the murderer, rest assured, sooner or later awaits thee. Darest thou venture within these dreary precincts? Fearest thou not that the ghastly shade of thy hapless victim, the innocent and unfortunate Emeline, shall rise before thy appalled sight to blast thee with its presence, and—"

"Cease! cease!" interrupted the terrified baronet, and almost fearing to look around him, lest the words of old Maud should be realised; "I will not listen to your wild and taunting observations. Beware, I say, or you may try my patience too far."

"Ha! ha! ha!" laughed the old woman, scornfully; "it amuses me to hear thee threaten, Sir Raymond Perceval; but I heed it no more than I do the idle wind; Maud of the Ruins, although thy prisoner, and apparently at thy mercy, defies thee, and dares thee to do thy worst. Thou canst not harm her, for she is guarded by a power which thou wouldst tremble to invoke."

"D—n!" cried the baronet, passionately, "and shall I stand here to be thus braved and insulted? Woman, again I demand, who are you, who thus seems to be able to penetrate the deepest recesses of my heart? Who are you, I repeat, and why do you express such implacable feelings of hatred against me?"

"And think'st thou," replied Maud, "that I am to be bullied into answering thy questions? No; it glads me to be able to keep thee in fear, and doubt, and suspense. Thou wilt know me soon enough; and woe to thee when that dreadful day shall come when I shall reveal myself to thee."

A fearful oath again escaped the lips of Sir Raymond, and he paced the cell for a minute or two with hasty and disordered steps.

"Woman," he said at length; "what think you this conduct will avail you? You talk madly. You are now in my power, and think you that I will ever allow you the opportunity to put your threats into execution? If you would expect any mercy from me, you will be more compliant with my wishes."

"Mercy from thee!" repeated Maud, contemptuously, "I ask it not, neither do I expect it; but in spite of all thy fancied security, mark my words, I will yet evade thy boasted power, and continue to be to thee a terror and a curse. Maud of the Ruins has not yet completed the mission she is destined to fulfill; and it is not in thy power to prevent her doing so. Aye, I read thy dark thoughts; the form of the fair

THE SEIZURE ALICE AND ROSE.

Alice Maitland occupies them, and already hast thou sought to accomplish thy diabolical ends ; but beware, there is one who will yet live to protect her, and to avenge her wrongs."

" I must be mad to endure this," observed Sir Raymond, with increased rage ; " however, I will leave you to reflect upon the folly and obstinacy of your conduct. No doubt a few days seclusion in this agreeable place will curb your spirit, and make you the more ready to succumb to my will."

" Indeed !" retorted the old woman, sarcastically ; ' continue to flatter thyself with the idea, villain, if thou wilt, but be not too confident lest thou shouldst be disappointed. 'Tis not the terrors of this wretched place, or all the sufferings thou mayest inflict on me that can shake my resolution or intimidate me to obedience. The time has not yet arrived, but it will anon, when the dark clouds now gathering in the horizon above thine head, shall burst and overwhelm thee. Scorn not my words, for sure as the purple current of life now circulates in thy veins, they will be fulfilled, and the awful fate thy crimes so justly merit, will most assuredly overtake thee."

The tone in which the mysterious woman uttered these words was most impressive,

No. 9.

and their ominous import sunk deep into the heart of the guilty baronet, who, in spite of his efforts to the contrary, could not help viewing her with dread, and for some moments, such was the power of his feelings, that he could not answer her; he, however, at last sufficiently recovered himself to observe:

"Woman, you seek to alarm me by your wild predictions, the emanations only of a disordered intellect; but you have much mistaken my character if you think that they can have any other effect on me than to excite my utmost contempt."

"Thou wouldst fain make me believe so," returned Maud; "but thou canst not deceive me, Sir Raymond Perceval; I know thee too well. Thy black conscience acknowledges the truth of my words, and fear and misgiving make thee tremble. But begone, and leave me to the gloom of my dungeon, and in secret exult if thou canst. Thou seest thou canst not shake the resolution of Maud, and it is only a waste of time to endeavour to do so."

"Rash woman!" exclaimed Sir Raymond, with indignation; "you little imagine what it is you brave. Beware; for much as you may affect to scorn me, you will find that I am not to be tampered with, and that I have both the will and the power to accomplish my wishes at any time I please. When next we meet, I shall expect to find you in a less obdurate mood."

Maud fixed upon him a contemptuous look, but did not condescend to make him any reply, and the baronet then retired from the dungeon, taking good care to secure the door after him.

This interview, as may be expected, was anything but satisfactory to him; on the contrary, it only served to increase the doubts and anxieties of his mind; and he saw plainly that old Maud was a being whom it would not be easy for him to mould to his will. Every time he had seen her had only served to involve him in still greater perplexity as to who she really was, and the pointed observations she had never failed to make use of served to convince him that she was one whom he had every cause to dread.

"And yet you will submit to be thus annoyed; to be thus taunted, threatened, and defied, when it is in your power at once to prevent it, and to get rid of all those apprehensions which at this time, I know, disturb your breast," remarked Luke Harden, when the baronet had related to him the particulars of the interview; "bah! Sir Raymond, I am surprised and ashamed of you."

"You would have me then at once embrue my hands in the blood of this mysterious woman?" said Sir Raymond, with a shudder.

"Aye," replied the pirate; "why should you hesitate to do so?"

"There has been too much bloodshed already, I say again," returned Sir Raymond; "besides, I would ascertain who she is, and—"

"Psha!" interrupted Luke, hastily; "you talk ridiculously, Sir Raymond; why should you be so anxious to discover who she is? It is enough for you to know that she is well acquainted with all your secrets, and to prevent her from having the opportunity of divulging them to any one else."

"You would have me be too precipitate, Luke; I cannot listen to your suggestions."

"Of course you are at liberty to act as you think proper, Sir Raymond; but it strikes me that you will have cause to regret, at some future period, that you did not follow my advice. Let the old hag croak to herself, you need not again expose yourself to her reproaches; leave her where she is to perish of starvation. The gloomy dungeon will be a fitting tomb for her bones to moulder in."

The baronet started at this monstrous proposal, and even he could not help viewing the blood-thirsty miscreant Harden with a look of disgust and horror.

"Luke Harden," he said, at last; "I can listen no more to such frightful suggestions as that which you have just now uttered. Even guilty as I have been, my soul recoils with horror at the thought of such a dreadful crime as that."

"Well," observed the pirate, coolly; "you can adopt your own course, certainly; I do not wish to persuade you either one way or the other, though I see nothing so precious in the life of this old harridan, that you should be so anxious to preserve it."

"Enough on that subject for the present," said Sir Raymond, impatiently; "we will discuss it at some future time. At any rate, old Maud has not now the means to put her threats into execution, and while I have her securely in my power, why should I recklessly seek her life?"

" And should our designs against the fair sisters succeed," said Luke; " I suppose it is your intention to bear them away on board my craft; and how will you then dispose of the old woman ?"

" Convey her on board also," answered the baronet.

" What, to be there a constant source of annoyance to us," said Harden, in a dissatisfied tone; " however, I suppose you must have your own way, and it is useless for me to argue the point with you. But there is one important thing I have been thinking of. Sir Raymond."

" And what is that ?" interrogated the latter..

" Of course you do not wish it to be suspected that the girl is in your power?"

" Certainly not; for in that case it would be impossible for me to show my face in this part of the country again."

" In what way, then, will you account for your abrupt departure from the Manor House at the same time as the disappearance of Alice and her sister ?"

" Ah! that must be managed," replied Sir Raymond. reflecting; " I have it," he added, after a pause; " a day or two before the sailing of the Spitfire, I will pretend to leave the Manor House for London, on particular business, and I can easily remain secreted here."

" A good plan," remarked Harden, approvingly; " no doubt it will serve to remove all suspicion from you."

" It must," said the baronet; " would that the time had arrived. Let me but witness the departure of the Spitfire, with Ben and Harry on board of her, and I shall consider that all obstacles are surmounted, and that success is certain."

" True," agreed his companion; " the girls once seized, must be conveyed on board the Bloodhound at the earliest opportunity, and then away from England with as little delay as possible."

" Aye," remarked Sir Raymond, and his eyes flashed with an expression of exultation at the thought; " and once on the broad waters of the ocean, with the wind in our favour, we shall have no cause to fear pursuit."

" Pursuit !" repeated the pirate; " no, that vessel must skim the water like a sea-bird that can overtake the Bloodhound, for she's a clipper, as has been proved in many a sharp chase. Rest your mind satisfied, Sir Raymond, the next attempt we make shall not turn out a failure, unless Fortune should have abandoned us altogether."

" Right, Luke," replied the baronet; " at any rate, I do not think there will be anything wanting on our parts if it does. I am most sanguine on the subject."

" Yes." returned the pirate; ' all now promises well, if we only act with due precaution."

' And there is not much fear of our neglecting to do that, when we have such a precious prize at stake. But I will to the village, in order to ascertain the surmises that are abroad respecting the outrage. It will be as well for me to appear to take the deepest interest in the event."

" True," coincided Harden; " it will still further quiet all suspicions."

Sir Raymond then departed.

CHAPTER XIII.

JEMMY JINGLE FORMS A BOLD RESOLUTION—THE SAILORS' DEPARTURE—SAILING OF THE SPITFIRE.

A week had now elapsed since Sir Raymond had made the daring attempt to accomplish his diabolical designs, and the excitement and alarm of the beauteous sisters had very little abated, nor had they since ventured to leave the cottage only in the daytime, and not then unless they were accompanied by their lovers.

The circumstance had created the greatest disgust in the minds of all who heard of it, and they would have been happy could the ruffians have been detected and brought to justice. But conjecture was exhausted in vain to imagine who they were, or who was the principal villain by whom they had doubtless been employed. In spite of the affability of Sir Raymond on the day of the rustic fete; the apparent aid he had rendered in defeating the fellow, and the disgust and abhorrence he had expressed at the outrage, at times Alice could not help entertaining strong suspicions against him, and it was therefore with no small feelings of satisfaction that she learnt from Sally Simper the intention of the baronet to leave the Manor House in a day or two, and that the time of his absence was uncertain.

The mysterious disappearance of Maud of the Ruins was a circumstance which likewise created no little surprise in the neighbourhood, and various were the surmises that were formed as to what had become of that singular being.

But Alice and her sister had now something more to agitate and distress their minds; their lovers had joined the Spitfire, then lying in the harbour, and which was expected to sail in a week at farthest, and it was in vain that their friends tried to arouse them from the deep melancholy which that thought excited in their breasts, whilst the most dismal forebodings constantly haunted their imaginations, and made them anticipate the hour of separation with the most unconquerable feelings of dread.

Jemmy Jingle and Sally Simper were seated in one of the kitchens of the Manor House, the former busily engaged in committing some doggrel lines to paper, and the latter watching with evident anxiety and impatience.

" What are you thinking about, my dear Jemmy?" interrogated Sally. " I declare there is no getting a word out of you. What's the use of folks who have got to make love to be sitting here mumchance in this manner?"

" Don't interrupt me, Sally," he replied, " don't you see that my fertile muse is in labour? I have got such a splendid idea!"

" Oh, bother your ideas," returned Sally, pettishly; " why will you rack your poor brain over such nonsense?"

" Nonsense!' responded Jemmy. " Sally I am ashamed of you. If you had any taste for the sublime and beautiful you would not talk so."

" Well now, my dear little Jemmy," said his companion, coaxingly, " can't you just put the sublime and beautiful off to another day, and let us talk about love, and such-like. You know, Jemmy, that you promised me you would name the happy day."

" Ah!" he returned; " but that's a matter for very serious consideration. It can't be yet, because I'm going to leave you."

" Leave me?"

" Yes; I've made up my mind. Ben Bolt has arranged everything for me with the captain of the Spitfire; and in a day or two I shall be tossed about on the billerous hoshen."

" Now, Jemmy, my dear Jemmy," ejaculated Sally Simper, " do not be rash. It is not yet too late to change your mind, and I shall break my heart if you leave me in this manner. What can you *see* in the *sea* that you should be tempted to leave your poor little Sally Simper?"

" What can I see?" answered Jemmy; " honour, glory—fame, immortality! The earth is not wide enough for a man of my expansive mind. My poetical genius yearns to pourtray the wonders of the boundless deep; that sublime task is for me to accomplish, and so Sally, I tell you once for all, it is no use trying to persuade me from it."

> " Oh, isn't it a scrumptious notion,
> To plough the *billerous* briny hoshen;
> And all its dangers to defy,
> When *billerous billers* rose sky-high?"

" Oh, dear!" sighed the disconsolate Sally; " then you will go?"

" Go!" repeated Jingle; " to be sure I will; it's all settled; my name is entered in the ship's books—my *chest* is on board, and in a day or two my *trunk* will be on board also. But cheer up, Sally, you will see me again, never fear; and

> " In whatever clime I be,
> I will ever think of thee;
> The voyage o'er, as her I *wallee*,
> I'll *sally* home to meet my *Sally!*"

" Now, dear Jemmy, do be persuaded by me," said his companion, with one of her most insinuating looks; but you cannot mean what you say; indeed you don't."

" But I do though," he replied; " my poetic soul hungers; it must be fed. I go in search of the sublime and beautiful !"

" A fig for the sublime !" ejaculated Sally; " what do you want with that ? As for the beautiful, can you look at me and say that you have not found it ?"

" Come now," said Jemmy, softening, " that is not so much amiss; it's the best thing I've heard you say for many a day. But I'll tell you, Sally--I think I can find the way to arrange this business to our mutual satisfaction. Would you have any objection to go to sea? "

" Not if I was near my dear Jemmy !"

" Sweet empress of my soul !" exclaimed Jingle, embracing her; " nobly spoken, and so that settles the business."

" La ! Jemmy, what do you mean ?"

" Why, you see, my dear, if you were my wife, and willing to make yourself useful on board, I have no doubt the captain would allow you to sail along with me."

" Ah !" replied Sally, disconsolately: " but you see I am not your wife, Jemmy, and that makes all the difference."

" True; but there is a very easy way of altering that."

" How ?"

" Why, you see, my dear Sally, I have always been a very prudent, saving fellow, and so I happen to have a nice handy little hoard of bright golden guineas by me at the present time, sufficient to start any happy couple in life. Now, as I always had a notion to do the thing in style, and suitable to the position of a man of my eminence, if you have no objection, to-morrow we will be married by licence, and there will be an end of the business. What say you, Sally, to my proposal ?"

" Oh, yes, anything, my darling Jemmy," she answered, " when you are by my side."

" Bravo !" shouted the eccentric barber; " what a happy couple we shall be to be sure. And should we meet the enemy, only see how I'll *extinguish* myself! What a splendid poem I will write too, on the *broad sheet* of waters! Depend upon it, Sally, when we return home, I shall be made poet laureate at least."

" No doubt of it," observed Sally; " and I shall be presented at court no doubt; and I shouldn't at all wonder if I am appointed maid of honour to the queen, or some such office. eh, Jemmy ?"

" To be sure you will, my precious !" he returned, kissing her. " Oh, what a brilliant prospect is now opened to us. But I say, Sally, will not Sir Raymond be much enraged at your leaving his service so suddenly ?"

" And what do I care for that ?" replied Sally. " I have long been tired of the situation, and I have looked upon the baronet with fear and mistrust, not to say dislike, ever since the insult he offered to Alice Maitland."

" True," said Jingle; " Sir Raymond is a very mysterious sort of person, and I do not half like him myself. I cannot help thinking (though I may be wrong) that he had something to do with the late outrage."

" Well," remarked Sally, " I should not like to judge him wrong, but I must say that I am very much of the same opinion, and I am not at all sorry that he is about to leave the neighbourhood, for a time at least. There is much more about his character than I can make out. See how sullen and reserved he is at times, locking himself in his study for hours together, as if he had something heavy on his conscience. Do you not also remember the observations of old Maud to him on the day of the festival ?"

" To be sure I do," answered Jingle; " and how he trembled at the sight of her. If that did not betray the reproaches of a guilty conscience I am no judge of human nature.'

" And there is another circumstance I have to tell you, which has often excited my suspicion."

" And what is that ?" inquired Jemmy.

" Why," replied Sally; " on more than one or two occasions I have known him to be closeted for hours together with a savage-looking man; and how he gained access to him no one could ever tell, but quite certain it is that none of the servants ever admitted him."

"That is very strange indeed," remarked Jingle. "Do you think it is true that there are subterranean passages and secret haunts under this old Manor House?"

"I do not doubt it," returned Sally; "but, la! I would not venture to penetrate them for the world."

"Well, Sally, if the baronet has been guilty of any crime, I only hope it may be discovered and he borught to punishment."

"And so do I, with all my heart. But do not let us talk any more upon the subject. What a sad time it will be for Alice and her sister on the day they have to part with their lovers."

"Ah! poor girls," said Jemmy; "so it will, but they will be restored to them, I hope, safe and sound, and then, if they only follow our example, you know, Sally, and get married, their happiness will be complete."

"Well, I hope no harm will befall them during the time that Ben and Harry are away. But you will not fail to keep your promise to me, my dear Jemmy, will you?"

"Keep my promise!" repeated her lover; "to be sure I will; do you think that James Jingle, Esquire, poet laureate, what is to be, could ever prove himself to be the heartless deceiver of female innocence? Perish the thought! To-morrow morning, as I said before, my dear Sally, we will be united in the holy bands of matrimony, and who will then be half so happy as Mr. and Mrs. Jingle?"

"Oh, dear!" said the damsel; "how delighted I am at the thought!"

"And so you ought to be," returned her lover; "look at the honour I shall confer on you. And won't all the other lasses in the village envy you your lot? But you will not turn faint-hearted when the ship is about to sail?"

"Oh, no," answered Sally; "I'm a true heart of oak, never fear, and I feel all the courage of the British lion within me."

"I will support and comfort you in the hour of danger. But I must leave you, my dear Sally, to go and prepare for the joyful occasion, and to make arrangements with the captain of the Spitfire for your accommodation on board. One chaste embrace, my dear Sally, and then farewell till we meet again."

Jemmy Jingle embraced the blooming and delighted Sally accordingly, and then took his departure.

The next morning Jemmy, true to his word, made Sally Mrs. Jingle, they being married by licence; and the occasion was celebrated in the village of Mayland with due spirit.

At length the day preceding that on which the Spitfire was to sail arrived, and a sad one it was in Woodbine Cottage, and the village altogether. Ben and Harry were to be on board in the evening, and the hours that must intervene previous to the separation must therefore be short.

The heart of Alice was full to bursting, and that of her sister was equally tortured. It was in vain that their lovers, their parents, and old Ben exerted themselves to the utmost to abate their anguish and inspire them with hope. Dark presentiments of evil crowded upon the imagination of the lovely sisters with overwhelming force, and baffled and defeated all their endeavours to compose them, and as the time rapidly wore away and the fatal hour approached, their anguish became the more intense.

And in spite of all their efforts to appear elate, and to animate the bosoms of their lovers with hope and confidence, our hero and his friend Harry could not help feeling low and dispirited, and the recent outrage, and the mystery in which it was involved, filled their minds with doubts and misgivings as to the future, and what might happen to Alice and her sister when they were separated from them by the perilous ocean, and had no means of flying to their protection, should any danger threaten them.

From this state of feeling, however, they endeavoured to arouse themselves, and at last succeeded much better than might have been expected.

"Come, come, my dear Alice," said Ben, and he imprinted a fond kiss upon her pale cheek as he spoke, and looked in her tearful eyes with an expression that told full well the feelings which at that moment were passing in his manly breast; "you must not take on so, lass, nor give way to fears of squalls and dangers which may never take place. Remember it is his duty to his king and country that calls your sailor-love away, and I know you would not have him shrink from that which honour demands. Think of the happiness which is in store for us when we shall meet again, and bear this parting with the fortitude of a woman!"

"Aye, that she will, I'll be bound for it," observed old Ben; "for Alice is formed to be a sailor's wife, and will not suffer such a thing as fear to take her in tow, when she knows that his heart will remain as true to her as the needle to the pole. Cheerly, cheerly, my pretty one, for it makes my old heart as sad as a tar without flip to see your pumps at work in this manner."

"Alas! my dear friends," sighed Alice, "can you wonder at my sorrow, when I reflect upon the brief period that I and Ben have been permitted to be together, after so long a separation, and the many fearful chances that may arise to prevent our ever meeting again? Should he fall by the hand of the remorseless foe, what would then be left to render life endurable to Alice?"

' And you, Harry," sobbed Rose; "to what horrors will you not be exposed? My heart misgives me; I fear that our parting will be for ever!"

"Nay, my dear Rose," replied her lover, "overboard with all such melancholy thoughts as these, I implore you; and try to hope for the best. The same Providence which has hitherto protected us, will, depend upon it, continue to shield myself and Ben from all those dangers you apprehend."

"But," said our heroine, and a sickly feeling of uncontrollable dread came over her as the thought flashed upon her brain, "it is but too evident that we have some secret enemies who seek to disturb our peace, and may they not take advantage of your absence to put their nefarious designs into execution?"

"Avast! avast! my poor girl," returned Ben, "should the lubbers harbour any such villanous thought, fear not but that Power above which ever keeps watch for the safety of innocence and virtue, will not desert you, but will defeat all their diabolical plans. Besides, you have those at hand who will ever be on the alert, and who will guard your security and happiness even more carefully than they would their own lives."

"To be sure they will," said old Ben; "there is not a man in the neighbourhood who would not stand up in their defence to the last. Should those rascally pirates again dare to bear down upon us, it strikes me hat they will meet with such a reception as they little anticipate. So let us belay this dismal palaver, and try to pass the few hours that we have to spare before Ben and Harry go on board in mirth and happiness."

Alice and her sister, in order to satisfy their lovers, and not to add to the anguish they well knew they must experience, though they tried so hard to conceal it, did struggle with their feelings, and sought to appear calm and resigned; but this was a most difficult task to accomplish, and they succeeded but indifferently; and gloomily and tediously the hours wore away.

The dreaded moment at last arrived. It was the time for Ben and Harry to go on board. Alas! the circumstances would admit of no delay, and the intense agony of all present may be readily conceived. With bursting hearts the beauteous sisters clung to their lovers; and with voices choked by sobs, and looks of frenzy and despair, in vain sought to detain them; whilst poor old Ben, and Mr. and Mrs. Maitland, in vain tried any longer to conceal the emotions that laboured in their breasts; and as they shook the hands of the brave and noble hearted young seamen, and bade them farewell, perhaps for ever, the big tears chased each other down their aged cheeks, and they felt completely overwhelmed with sorrow.

But why should we dwell upon the melancholy and affecting scene? The last moment arrived; the signal gun from the ship had three times sounded in their ears, the summons must be obeyed. In frantic haste our hero and his companion tore themselves away, followed by old Ben, and poor Alice and her sister fainted in the arms of their parents.

We will not attempt to describe their sufferings during that night. Sleep was a stranger to their eyelids, and it was all to no purpose that their parents (who remained with them till long past the hour of midnight) sought to console them.

As has been before stated, the vessel was to sail at an early hour on the following morning, and notwithstanding all the arguments and persuasions of their parents, Alice and Rose were resolved to be present at its departure; and for that purpose they were ready to leave the cottage by the first dawn of day.

Of course they were accompanied by Mr. and Mrs. Maitland, and at the door of the cottage they found old Ben ready to join them, and who tried his best to raise their spirits, and to banish all dismal forebodings and apprehensions from their minds.

On arriving in the harbour they found many individuals assembled on the same melancholy and affectionate errand as themselves, and with eager haste the eyes of the poor girls wandered to the noble and stately ship, which contained those whom they so fondly loved, and which was evidently preparing to weigh anchor.

How violently throbbed the heart of Alice Maitland as she gazed at the gallant craft, and she trembled so much that, had it not been for the support of her parents, she must have sunk upon the earth. Having entered a boat they put off towards the ship, which they approached as near as was convenient or practicable ; and the eyes of our heroine and her sister eagerly and anxiously were directed towards the several seamen who were bustling about the deck, with the hope of beholding their lovers; but they were doomed to disappointment, and while they were thus occupied a gun was fired, which was answered from every vessel in the harbour ; a deafening cheer from the seamen and the persons assembled on the shore rent the air, and the noble ship sailed on its way. With clasped hands and beating hearts the sisters watched it till it became little more than a speck upon the horizon ; their feelings then overpowered them, their senses left them, and they remembered no more till they arrived at home.

CHAPTER XIV

THE SEIZURE OF ALICE AND ROSE, AND DEPARTURE OF THE PIRATE SHIP BLOODHOUND.

Sir Raymond Perceval, although, as the reader is aware, it was supposed that he had left the Manor House, and it was uncertain what time he would return, was still secreted there, at least in the subterranean retreat beneath the building, and only awaited the fitting opportunity of putting his diabolical plans into effect.

All his efforts to subdue the spirit of old Maud, or to wring the secret of her real character from her breast proved ineffectual, and unable to make up his mind to follow the monstrous advice of the villain, Luke Harden, and to embrue his hands in her blood; also fearing that it would not be safe to leave her where she was when he should in all probability be far away with his destined victim, he had her at midnight secretly conveyed on board the pirate craft, which was ready to sail at a moment's notice, and where he felt convinced she would be securely in his power.

In the meantime he and Luke had fully arranged all their guilty plans for the future, and he now felt confident of their complete success.

"Yes," he observed to Luke, when they were consulting together, " all now goes well, and promises a successful issue. The suspicions of Alice and her friends are quieted by my supposed departure from the Manor House, and they little dream of the dark plot that is working to accomplish my ends. I am sanguine, Luke—most sanguine."

"And so you have a right to be, Sir Raymond," returned Luke ; " in a day or two the Spitfire will quit these shores, and Ben Bolt and Harry Helm once away, our designs may, I think, be accomplished without difficulty."

"Aye," remarked the baronet; " and I look forward to the time with the utmost impatience. The excitement caused by the attempt which we recently made has almost passed away, and everything has proceeded much better than I expected. All is prepared, I believe, for the reception of the girls on board the Bloodhound?"

"It is," answered the pirate; " and let our gallant craft get but once clear away from these shores, and, with the wind in our favour, we may then set pursuit at defiance. It must be no washing-tub to give chase to the Bloodhound on the waters of the deep, and woe to them who venture to try the mettle of her crew. They have proved their lion-hearted courage in many a bloody affray, as well you know, Sir Raymond.

"True." agreed the latter; " they are daring rascals who laugh at danger, and stick at nothing to accomplish their ends, and I place every confidence in them. We may well congratulate ourselves, Luke, on possessing such able accomplices. Alice Maitland, the man whom you have ventured to treat with such scorn will soon hold you completely at his mercy, and you will have no power to resist his will. Oh, what feelings of transport does that thought impart to my senses!"

OLD BEN CONSOLING **THE PARENTS OF ALICE AND ROSE.**

" And her beauteous sister Rose is my destined victim," observed Luke ; " nor shall all the scorn and reproaches she may heap upon me deter me from my determined purpose. Our triumph will be mutual, Sir Raymond, and henceforward our fortunes must be the same."

" Aye, they should be so ; but we perfectly understand each other upon that subject. Our friendship is of long standing, and under all the circumstances that connect us, 'tis not likely that it will easily be terminated. But enough of this at present ; as I said before, our plans are all in readiness, and we do but wait the sailing of the Spitfire to put them into operation."

" The girls will then be entirely at our mercy," added the pirate ; " unless we receive any interruption from the land-sharks."

" Ah ! we must be on our guard against them," remarked Sir Raymond ; " for no doubt, after the affray of the other day, they are on the alert. It was a fortunate job that you were enabled to elude the vigilance of the coast guard on that occasion, for, had they traced you to this secret haunt our game would have been up."

No. 10.

"You may say that," coincided the ruffian; "but come, 'tis new dark, and you promised to accompany me to the ship."

"Aye," resumed his companion, "I am ready; for I wish to see old Maud, that I may again endeavour to intimidate her into a compliance with my wishes."

"And that, depend upon it, you will find as fruitless a task as you have hitherto done. Had you thought proper to have followed my advice, she would have ceased to trouble you long since."

"No, Luke; you would urge me to that from which I must acknowledge my mind shrinks appalled. I dare not stain my hands in the blood of that mysterious woman."

"'Tis a feeling of cowardice, Sir Raymond, which is quite unworthy of you. Her threats and denunciations have alarmed you, and she exults at the influence she holds over you."

"No," returned the baronet, "while I hold her securely in my power, as she is at present, I have nothing to fear from her; her great apparent age precludes the probability of her living any length of time to annoy me, why then should I recklessly add another to the fearful crimes that so heavily press upon my soul already?"

"What bitter mockery is this," said the pirate, contemptuously; "but come—to the vessel."

Sir Raymond returned no answer to this, but motioning Luke Harden to lead the way, followed him from the cavern."

On the morning of the sailing of the Spitfire Sir Raymond Perceval and Luke, disguised, and in a convenient place where they could remain concealed from observation, watched its departure with feelings of the utmost satisfaction and delight, and then returned to the cavern to exult over the circumstances, and to consult upon their future plan of operations.

"So," exclaimed the baronet, "the vessel which contains my hated rival has now quitted these shores, and if the Fates do not conspire against me, Alice Maitland and him shall never behold each other again. Oh, what a proud gratification is this to my hopes. But a day or two, probably but a few hours only, and the scornful beauty who has excited such a powerful passion in my breast shall be mine, and all resistance to my wishes will then be vain."

"Truly spoken, Sir Raymond," said Luke; "and who will then own a fairer mistress than the pirate, Luke Harden? All is ready for the completion of our work, and therefore we will not delay a moment longer than prudence may dictate."

"Right! right!" returned his companion, "I am all impatience, and shall not rest satisfied until I see the beauteous Alice kneeling at my feet, and have the opportunity of pouring forth the impassioned language of my transported soul in her ears. Did you notice with what pale and anxious looks Alice and her sister watched the receding vessel, Luke?"

"I did," replied the latter; "'twas right that they should do so, for it was but an ominous prelude to the fate which awaits them."

"Aye, if fortune fail us not.'

"Let no misgivings cross your mind, for all is sure. The coast is now clear before us, and they cannot escape the net we have laid to ensnare them."

"Then let to-morrow night see the completion of our designs. There is no necessity, I conceive, for any further delay, and my eager impatience can wait no longer."

"Be it sure,' said Luke Harden; "as soon as darkness shall have set in, we may make the attempt with safety. The cottagers retire early to rest from their daily toil, and there will be no one to obstruct us."

"True," said Sir Raymond; "but we must watch well our time, and be sure that there is no one on the alert; for should their cries reach the ears of the coast-guard—"

"Oh," interrupted his companion, "we must take effectual means to stifle their cries, should not their terror deprive them of their senses. From the village we shall have, comparatively, but a short distance to go to the place of our destination; and it must be our care to avoid the most frequented route."

"Yes," said the baronet, "we have only to use all proper precaution, and we have nothing to fear. But mark me, Harden; I would have this business accomplished without bloodshed, if possible."

"Bah! how particular you have become of late."

"And why should we recklessly sacrifice human life to achieve our ends, if it can be avoided?"

" Well," observed the ruffian, "I have no particular disinclination to comply with your wishes, if it can be done with safety; but should any one be daring enough to offer to resist us, why, they must take the consequences, that's all about it. And so, Sir Raymond, you are fully prepared for a cruise in the Bloodhound ? and for all the dangers we may have to encounter ?"

" Certainly. It will not be the first voyage I have made in her, and on occasions equally as important as the present. You remember the time, many years ago, when we—but we will not talk upon that subject now. 'Twill be as well not to recall the past to my memory."

" True, but to look forward to the future with firmness and determination. Once more afloat, I shall feel myself again in my native element. The spirit and daring of Luke Harden and his crew are as undaunted as ever, and the black flag of the bold Bloodhound shall still strike terror and dismay into the breasts of all who behold it. But the Manor House, and your affairs here, during your absence—what of them, Sir Raymond ?"

" That is all arranged," he replied; " I have left everything to the care of an old and confidential servant, on whom I can place every dependence. To-night I will also have conveyed on board, property sufficient to provide against any emergency that may arise; so that everything promises to turn out as well as we could wish."

" Even so," observed Luke; " to-morrow night then—"

" If no cursed accident occurs to obstruct our deep laid schemes, Alice Maitland and her sister will be safe on board the pirate craft; and, with a favouring gale before many hours have elapsed, the wide ocean will be bearing us bravely on, far away from the reach of pursuit."

" Aye," coincided the pirate; " and then to triumph o'er the rich prize our courage and determination will have won. Oh, Sir Raymond, does not your very soul rebound with rapture at the thought ?"

" It does—it does !" replied the guilty man; " to obtain possession of one so lovely as Alice Maitland, methinks it would not be too much even to sacrifice a fortune. But should we be disappointed—"

" Fear nothing of the sort," interrupted Harden; " for I feel confident of success. Oh, did their lovers but know the dark plot which is working against them, and they not at hand to prevent it, how great would be the agony of their feelings !"

" It would," returned the baronet; " but my satisfaction is the more complete to know that I have got rid of that hated boy, whose features ever struck a feeling of terror and remorse to my soul which I could not conquer. Oh, may my eyes never more encounter him, to rekindle the horrors of the past in my breast !"

" Oh, fear not," said Luke; " the ball of the enemy or the tempestuous waves will cut short his career; he will never again cross your path. But, come; we must to other and more important business, for we have no time to lose."

They now changed the topic of conversation, and here we will leave them to the concoction of their guilty plot, and return to the cottage.

A day of misery and anxiety was this to our heroine and her sister, and in vain did their parents and old Ben Bolt seek to console them, and to banish the dismal thoughts that had taken possession of their minds. Again and again were their fervent prayers offered up to heaven for the preservation of their lovers from the many dangers and vicissitudes it would doubtless be their lot to encounter; but still they could not divest themselves of the dismal forebodings that haunted their imagination, and pictured the future in the blackest colours.

" Alas !" sighed Alice; " dear Ben, little did I anticipate that we should so soon be again torn asunder, and that I should once more be tortured by the doubts and fears that now fill my breast. Why, oh, why, should the dangerous waves thus interpose between us and happiness ?"

" Cheerly, cheerly, lass," said old Ben, " and fear not but Ben will again weather every gale, as he has often done before, and after he has helped to thrash the enemies of old England, he will be restored to you safe and sound, and with a fresh cargo of love to reward your truth and constancy."

" But may they not perish in the deadly strife ?" ejaculated Rose, with a shudder; " and then what but despair and the most insupportable misery will be left for myself and Alice ?"

" Why as for that," observed Ben, " you see the life of the hardy mariner is all a lottery. Hows'ever, Providence ever keeps watch over the side of justice ; so hope for the best, my girls, and never be taken aback by dismal forebodings.''

It was to no purpose, however, that Alice and her sister tried to arouse themselves from their state of melancholy ; and, after a time, having excused themselves, they were allowed to retire to their chamber, so that they could give full and unrestrained indulgence to their grief.

Indeed on that day a general air of melancholy pervaded the pretty little village of Mayland, which seemed to be almost deserted. Many were those of its inhabitants who mourned the departure of a friend or relation, who had sailed in the Spitfire, and whom, when they considered the danger of the expedition they had gone upon, they feared they might never behold again.

Night came, but with it no relief to the anxious minds of the fair sisters, and when they retired to their couch, and sleep descended upon their eye-lids, their imagination was haunted by the most torturing visions, which rendered their slumbers unrefreshing. The next day found them in much the same condition, and they kept themselves almost entirely secluded in their own room, for the society even of their own parents was irksome to them. Mr. and Mrs. Maitland, however, had occasion to leave home, and Alice and Rose were thus left to themselves.

How drearily the hours passed away now that they were deprived of the society of those noble-hearted youths whom they so fondly loved. But had they been aware of the misery which was in store for them, how doubly powerful would have been the anguish and horror of their minds.

Towards the evening a storm which had long been gathering portentously in the clouds broke forth with great violence, and added to their terror and misery, for their parents had not yet returned, and they wondered what could have detained them, when they knew that they were alone and would feel uneasy at their absence.

Another hour passed away, and it was quite dark, still they came not ; and they felt still more uneasy and melancholy as old Ben was also away, who, had he been present, might have served in some measure to have cheered their spirits. As they listened to the fierce voice of the tempest, which raged with increased fury, a feeling of dread came over them which made them tremble, and they could but apprehend some approaching calamity. They pictured to themselves the terrible dangers to which their lovers might at that moment be exposed in such a storm as this ; and their hearts sunk within them with a feeling of dread which was almost overwhelming.

" Would to heaven that our parents would return," ejaculated Alice, as she gazed anxiously towards the window, in at which the lightning played vividly ; " what can detain them ? Alas ! I fear that some accident has befallen them.''

" God forbid !'' fervently cried Rose ; " but no, we must not alarm ourselves thus, perhaps unnecessarily. They have probably sought shelter in the house of some friend on the road home. till the storm has abated.''

" I shudder to be alone,'' said our heroine, casting a timid glance around her ; " this tempest is a fearful one, and strange feelings come over me, for which I can scarcely account. Something terrible, I am certain, is about to happen to us. Ah ! what noise was that ?''

" I heard nothing but the wind and the pattering of the rain against the casement, dear Alice,'' replied her sister ; " come, come, arouse yourself, we must not encourage such abject terrors as these.''

" Oh, Ben ! dear Ben !'' sighed Alice, clasping her hands together ; " where are you now ?''

" Heaven will watch over them, never fear,'' returned Rose, " and guard them in the hour of danger.''

At that moment Alice started and clung to her sister, for she could almost have sworn that she had seen by the lightning's flash a pair of dark eyes glaring stedfastly in at the window, but in an instant they were gone, and she endeavoured to persuade herself that her imagination had deceived her. Still, however, their parents returned not, and naturally their apprehensions for their safety increased.

In this state of anxiety and suspense a few more minutes elapsed, and the sisters remained silent ; but they were at length aroused by hearing a knock at the door:

" Ah ! thank heaven, they have returned,'' cried Rose, and she was advancing towards the door when Alice arrested her.

"Stay! stay!" she ejaculated; "we must not be too precipitate; we know not what danger may be abroad in such a night as this, and we are alone."

"Courage," whispered Rose, "we have nothing to fear; at any rate let us question whoever it is that seeks admission."

She advanced to the door as she spoke, but our heroine kept timidly back.

"Who knocks?" demanded Rose, in a firm voice.

"A poor traveller," replied the strange voice of a man, "who seeks a temporary shelter from this fearful storm. For the love of heaven, do not refuse him."

Rose hesitated and looked at her sister, who was also half irresolute what to do.

"I have travelled far, and am wet to the skin," again ejaculated the stranger; "you have nothing to fear from a poor miserable wretch like me; so I once more earnestly beseech you, do not refuse to comply with my request."

The tone of voice in which this appeal was spoken completely disarmed the fears of our heroine, and she motioned to Rose to unbar the door, which she did, and a man clad in tattered garments, and with a most forbidding cast of features entered the room, and fixed an inquisitive and suspicious look upon the sisters, which made them shrink, and trembling cling to each other.

"You are very accommodating," said the fellow, with a malicious grin; "and it seems my visit could not have been more opportune, for you are alone. This is very fortunate."

"Oh, heaven!" exclaimed the terrified damsels, in a breath; "who are you? and what is your purpose here?"

"You will soon know that," replied the ruffian; "nay," he added, as he drew a brace of pistols from his bosom, and levelled them at them; "if you utter the faintest cry—even a whisper, it will be your last. What ho, there!"

In an instant the room was filled with armed men; a large mantle was drawn tightly over each of their heads, so as to stifle their cries, and they were then carried, fainting and helpless towards a vehicle which was in waiting close by, into which they were lifted, followed by Luke Harden and two others of the pirates, and it was then driven off with the utmost rapidity, and by an unfrequented route, towards that part of the coast where the Bloodhound, unsuspected of being anything else but a fair trader was lying at anchor.

The storm now abated, and at length entirely ceased, and Mr. and Mrs. Maitland, who had been unavoidably detained both by business and the storm, arrived at the cottage, anxious for the safety of Alice and Rose, who they knew would be greatly alarmed at their protracted absence.

We need not attempt to describe their surprise and apprehension on beholding the cottage door standing wide open, though the light still glimmered in the window. But their alarm was increased beyond all bounds on entering the cottage, and finding that they were not there; while the marks of several footsteps on the floor, showed that a desperate struggle had taken place.

For a moment or two, the poor old people stared around them aghast; and then in accents of frenzy and despair, they simultaneously exclaimed:

"Our children—our dear children! Oh, God! where are they? What wretches have robbed us of our offspring? Alice! Rose!—oh, misery!—oh, despair!"

They were so distracted that, for a minute or two they knew not what they were about, but at length, uttering loud cries of anguish, they rushed from the cottage, and hastened to that of old Ben, who was quickly aroused, and on hearing what had taken place, his agitation was scarcely less than that of the unhappy parents.

"The villains!" he cried; "they have taken advantage of the departure of their lovers, to hoist the black flag again and bear down upon their innocent and defenceless victims. Poor girls! poor girls! you have indeed got into a sea of trouble now. But there is not a moment to be lost. We must alarm our neighbours, and see if we can't get upon the right tack to give chase to them."

"Oh, it was most thoughtless of us to leave them alone and unprotected," said Mr. Maitland; "our poor children, they are lost to us for ever, and what may not at this moment be their fate? I shall go mad—I shall go mad!"

"Be calm, my friend," said Ben; "it may not yet be too late to rescue them. But we have no time to waste."

"Oh, whither can we go in search of them?" cried Mrs. Maitland, wringing her hands; "the miscreants have succeeded too well in their fiendish designs. Who are the wretches who have committed this inhuman and diabolical outrage?"

"Why the same infernal rascals who made the former attempt, no doubt," replied Ben; "but only let me arm myself, and arouse a few of the neighbours, then we will spread every inch of canvass, and navigate the whole country but we will find them. Poor girls! poor girls! but cheer up, my good old friends, Providence will watch over them and protect them from the fate which now seems to threaten them."

Thus saying, honest old Ben left the distracted parents for a moment, and entered his cottage, but quickly returned armed with a huge stick, and a brace of pistols.

The inhabitants of the village were alarmed, and the excitement which prevailed on its being made known what had taken place, may be readily imagined. Several of the men armed themselves in the best manner they could, and the whole party then set forth on their important expedition.

An officer of the coast-guard was also informed of the monstrous outrage, and a number of men were despatched in various directions, to endeavour to discover the villains, and to rescue the unfortunate girls. But so well had the nefarious plot been planned, and so secretly executed, that this was a task of the greatest difficulty, if not entirely hopeless, and the wretched parents and old Ben, after wandering about for several hours, without being able to discover any traces of them, or to hear the least tidings of them, returned home—heart-broken, and in a state of the utmost despair.

"Lost! lost for ever!" groaned Mr. Maitland, striking his forehead in the greatest agony of mind; "oh, wretched parents that we are to experience such an awful bereavement as this. Alice! Rose! beloved, innocent children, what dreadful fate has now befallen ye? Oh, may the avenging curses of heaven light upon the heads of the inhuman wretches who have perpetrated this frightful deed! Ben, Harry, what feelings of agony would now lacerate your manly hearts, did you but know the awful catastrophe which has taken place!"

"And oh, why did we thus leave them unprotected?" sighed Mrs. Maitland; "indeed, indeed, we are much to blame. Oh, agony most insupportable!"

The poor old woman wrung her hands and wept bitterly as she thus spoke, and it seemed impossible to impart the least degree of consolation to either her or her husband.

"Come, come, my good friends," remonstrated the old seaman, soothingly; "you must not reproach yourselves thus bitterly, for you are not to blame. Who could have thought that the pirates had been cruising so near, and so soon after their late daring attempt, for no doubt they are the same. But shiver my timbers, if I ain't taken all aback; regularly capsized as it were, with rudder and compass both gone. Now I would give a trifle to know who it is that has done this. There is some lubber at the bottom of it, I'll be bound, who has the means of hiring assistance; and if it was not that he has changed his station, damme, if I should not be half inclined to suspect Sir Raymond Perceval."

"Ah!" cried Mr. Maitland, starting; "that thought arouses all my worst suspicions. Sir Raymond Perceval I am certain is a villain, who is capable of committing any guilty act; and may not his departure from the Manor House, be merely a subterfuge to deceive us, and the better to enable him to carry his infamous projects into effect?"

"Too true—too true," ejaculated his wife; "and if our poor children have fallen into his power, heaven help them, for they will indeed be lost for ever, their destruction is inevitable!"

"He must be discovered!" exclaimed Mr. Maitland; "there must not be the least delay in this important and painful business, and should he prove to be the guilty party who has committed this monstrous outrage, not all his wealth or station shall shield him from our vengeance."

"Aye," remarked old Ben, "he shall pay most dearly for his villany. But come, my friends, try to compose yourselves, and—"

"Compose ourselves!" interrupted Mr. Maitland, impatiently, and with emotion. "Oh, is it not sheer madness to talk to us of composure under such dreadful circumstances as these? My brain is distracted, and I scarcely know what I say. My poor innocent children, to be thus cruelly deprived of ye, and left in uncertainty as to the fate which has befallen ye! Oh, it must be a fiend who could even for a moment contemplate such a cruise as this!"

"Aye," replied Ben; "that it must. But if he escapes from being overhauled and punished for his villany, it is a strange thing to me."

Mr. Maitland and his wife groaned, in the bitter anguish and despair of their feelings, and Ben finding that it was useless to interrupt them, or to attempt to console them, suffered them for a time to give free indulgence to them.

In the meantime, the unfortunate Alice and her sister, after their seizure, remained in a complete state of insensibility, and the vehicle pursued its way, without attracting any notice, until it had arrived at the place of its destination, when they were lifted out, and conveyed to a boat which was moored close by, and then rowed in the darkness of the night to the pirate ship, which was lying at anchor at no great distance off; and the storm which had recently raged so violently, had now entirely ceased.

Sir Raymond Perceval had been on board some hours, and awaited in a state of the greatest suspense the result of his guilty plot; though he entertained but little doubt of its success, and already anticipated the triumph which was in store for him, in the possession of the beauteous Alice.

With folded arms he traversed the deck, notwithstanding the violence of the storm, and, as his restless eye penetrated through the darkness of the night, his impatience increased, and mingled feelings of doubt and apprehension occupied his breast. He heeded not the tempest—the roar of the thunder—the lightning's fire, as it flashed around, and the rough billows, as they dashed against the sides of the vessel, alike he regarded not, so completely were his thoughts absorbed by the subject which engrossed them, and rendered everything else indifferent to him.

"They cannot surely fail," he ejaculated; "no, now that everything is so well prepared, Fortune, that fickle jade, will not, must not, frown upon my hopes. Luke Harden has as much to stimulate him as myself, in the possession of Rose Maitland, and it will be no fault of his, I am certain, if he does not succeed. I place the firmest reliance on his skill and intrepidity. And yet how tedious seems the time that elapses previous to the gratification of my wishes," he added, after a pause. "Oh, Alice, how does my soul pant to enfold your beauteous form in my arms; to gloat upon those surpassing charms that have ravished my senses; to sip the honey from thy ruby lips, and as I clasp thee to my throbbing heart, to be able to utter the exulting cry—'Thou art mine! mine; and no earthly power can ever again wrest thee from me!'"

A fearful expression passed over the features of the guilty baronet as he gave utterance to these words, and his whole soul was wrought up to a pitch of fierce determination. Still his mind wavered between doubt and sanguine expectation.

At one time he regretted that he had not accompanied Luke and the other ruffians on their daring and diabolical expedition. But then, he considered, upon more mature deliberation, that it would have been an act of the greatest imprudence and danger for him to have done so, while his presence could not at all have accelerated the success of his plans.

In this state of suspense he was kept for nearly a couple of hours, and every moment of delay appeared an age to him. The storm had greatly abated, and the atmosphere became clearer; but still for some time longer his eyes wandered in vain to meet with any gratification to his hopes and wishes.

"They tarry," he once more soliloquised; "this delay is most torturing, and fills me with strange apprehensions that I would fain banish from my mind. It would be a sad disappointment, when all is so well prepared, should they meet with a defeat. But no; let me not encourage such thoughts, Luke and his companions are determined, and they must succeed. Ah!" he suddenly exclaimed, as his eyes still more eagerly gazed towards the shore; "a boat has just now quitted the land, and is making hither! This must be them. Oh, fate! be not thou against me, and my triumph is close at hand!"

Nearer and nearer the boat approached the pirate ship, and so great was the anxiety and impatience of Sir Raymond, that he could almost have leaped into the ocean and swam to meet them.

But in a few minutes the boat approached so near that he was enabled to distinguish the objects within it clearly, and he then perceived that it only contained a portion of the pirates who had accompanied the expedition, and that her whom he so anxiously expected was not there.

The hopes that had arisen in his breast were annihilated, and he growled a fearful oath between his teeth.

The boat now came alongside, and the pirates sprang on deck.

"How now, fellows?" sternly and hastily demanded the baronet; "why have ye thus returned? Where are the girls? Where is Luke Harden? Answer me, Hal Redford, and keep me not in suspense."

"I will, Sir Raymond," replied the man whom he had addressed; "and that probably to your satisfaction, if you will only have a little patience. We have proceeded hither first, to apprise you of the result of our adventure. Luke and the others w''' be here anon."

"Ah! but the girls?"

"Fortune smiled upon us," answered the ruffian; "we met with no obstruction. Alice Maitland and her sister are secured."

"Secured!" reiterated Sir Raymond, and his eyes flashed with an expression of savage delight; is it indeed so? By all the infernal host, then, at last I triumph! Oh, what a gratification is this to my thirsting soul! But quick, quick, the particulars?"

Redford related them in a few words, and the baronet, grasping his hand with fervour, exclaimed:

"Thanks! thanks! for this glad news, which has set my doubts at rest, and even exceeds my fondest expectations. All praise is due to Luke and his daring associates; they have performed their task well, and deserve my lasting gratitude. Now, Alice—proud and scornful Alice—thou must yield to him whom I know thy soul abhors, and he to whom thine heart's fondest affections are devoted, is indeed lost to thee for ever."

A smile of triumph again passed over the libertine's features as he thus spoke, and for a moment or two he paced the deck, indulging in the thoughts that occupied his mind.

"But," he said, suddenly turning to Redford, "had you not better put off again in the boat to the shore in order to receive them."

"True," replied the pirate; "and probably they will arrive as soon as we reach it."

Redford, and another of his companions, then re-entered the boat, and Sir Raymond watched them depart with the most eager impatience. The darkness soon hid them from his view, and the noise of the tempest having subsided, he listened with breathless attention to catch the sound of the oars from the boat on its return. He had not to wait long; the sound he so anxiously listened for saluted his ears, and in a minute or two he distinguished through the darkness the boat rapidly approaching. In a few seconds more the boat had gained the vessel, and the insensible forms of poor Alice and her sister were handed on deck, and were quickly followed by Luke Harden and the other pirates.

It would, indeed, be a difficult task to do adequate justice to the feelings of the guilty Sir Raymond at this moment. With the most unspeakable transport he clasped the form of our heroine in his arms; gazed triumphantly in her pale but beauteous countenance, and dared to pollute her lips with his unhallowed kisses, while the ruffian Harden held the unconscious Rose to his guilty breast, and his feelings of exultation were equal to those of the baronet.

"Luke," at length said Sir Raymond; "you have performed your task well, and I owe you a debt of gratitude which I can never repay. The prize we have so long thirsted to obtain, at last is ours, and what power can now tear it from our grasp!"

"Not heaven nor hell shall oppose the gratification of our wishes," answered the miscreant; "the hour of our triumph has arrived; the fair sisters are safe on board the pirate barque, the eye of suspicion rests not on us, the storm has subsided—the darkness of the night favours us, and before the first blush of day shall appear on the eastern horizon, the Bloodhound will be far beyond the reach of pursuit. But see; they revive."

A sigh at that moment simultaneously escaped the bosoms of Alice and her sister, and opening their eyes, and beholding themselves in the loathsome embraces of Sir Raymond and Luke Harden, they uttered a cry of horror, and struggled to disengage themselves.

"Gracious heaven!" exclaimed our heroine, as she fixed her eyes upon him with an expression of terror, loathing, and disgust; "Sir Raymond Perceval! Miscreant; is it then you who are the author of this monstrous outrage? Oh, villain, villain!"

"Milder terms will best become those pretty lips, my scornful beauty," he returned, and he fixed upon her a look which called the blushes of shame and indignation to her cheeks; "kind fate has at last crowned my wishes; you are mine, I press you with

BEN AND HARRY ON BOARD THE SPITFIRE.

rapture to my throbbing bosom; there is no one here to thwart or obstruct me, and my happiness is complete!"

"Oh, God! where are we?" cried both the distracted sisters in a breath.

"On board the pirate ship, the Bloodhound!" answered Luke Harden, triumphantly, "which, ere many hours have elapsed, will have borne you far away upon the surging billows."

"Oh, horror! horror!" shrieked the unfortunate girls; a deadly faintness came over them, their brains turned giddy, and quite overpowered by their emotions, they once more became insensible.

Again Sir Raymond and Luke Harden contaminated their hapless victims with their bold and odious caresses, and, as they gazed upon them, their feelings of exultation increased.

"Enough of this," said Luke at length; "we have other business at present which calls for our prompt attention, and there will be another time for us to give free indulgence to our wishes. We must set about sailing while the darkness favours us, and we have thus an opportunity of giving our enemies the slip. Let us convey the girls below, where Madge Redford will attend to them, and see to their recovery."

They did so, and left Alice and her sister in the care of the old woman mentioned by Luke, and who had been for many years connected with the villains; they returned on deck.

All was now bustle and activity on board the pirate ship, and Sir Raymond Perceval, with folded arms, stood and watched the proceedings with feelings of the deepest

No. 11.

interest and satisfaction.   Not a moment was to be lost, all hands exerted themselves with alacrity, and in less than an hour from the time of Alice and her sister being brought on board, the anchor was weighed, and with the utmost secresy the Bloodhound sailed from the place where she had so long laid moored, in the character of a fair trader, and in the name of the Water Nymph.

Providence seemed to have deserted them, and the fate of the unfortunate sisters appeared to be inevitable.

CHAPTER XV.

ON BOARD THE SPITFIRE—SATURDAY NIGHT AT SEA—A DISCOVERY.

The reader must now suppose a month to have elapsed since the departure of the Spitfire, and the occurrence of the events recorded in the foregoing chapter.

It was Saturday night at sea, and the gallant crew were enjoying themselves to their content.   The grog went freely round; the yarn was spun, and the joke, the song, and the dance were, by turns, called into requisition.

But although our hero tried to be as cheerful as the rest—and, generally speaking, there was not a merrier fellow on board the Spitfire than Ben Bolt—on this occasion a feeling of melancholy at times came over him which he could not conquer, but from which his friend Harry Helm sought to arouse him.

There was another individual who stood silently by, and watched the proceedings of the gallant crew with a heavy heart and a sad expression of countenance, which showed that the cankerworm of care and sorrow preyed upon his mind, and that the cause of his secret grief had its origin in years long past, but which time had failed to eradicate.

This was Lieutenant Morton, a man of mystery and reserved habits, but as brave an officer as the British navy could boast of, and who was held in the highest respect by the captain, and all the crew.

He was a man evidently verging upon the age of sixty, of tall and commanding form, and features that had once been handsome, and even now had that noble expression which could not fail to create a feeling of veneration in all who looked upon them. For a few minutes he stood and listened to the mirth of the sailors in the same melancholy attitude; then, as some intense pang seemed to flash upon his brain, he sighed deeply, pressed his hand upon his forehead, and abruptly retired.

The appearance of our old friend Jemmy Jingle, who was present on the occasion, was as grotesque as could well be imagined.   The manner in which he was dressed gave him the character of a sort of amphibious animal, neither sailor nor landsman. He was sitting apart from the rest, attended by Sally, his better half, and the paleness and woe-begone expression of his features plainly showed that his " inward man," was sadly out of order.

" Come, Ben, my friend," said Harry; " you seem as dull to-night as if you had just shipped a heavy sea of trouble.   Rouse ye, lad, rouse ye."

' The truth is, Harry,' replied our hero, " I do not feel exactly in good sailing trim to-night.   I cannot help thinking of my dear Alice, and the sad forebodings that haunted her mind at our parting.   Should the villains who attempted to tear her and her sister from us take advantage of our absence to —"

" Avast! avast, Ben!" interrupted Harry, " where are you steering to now?   Providence will protect them never fear.   My pretty, merry little Rose too, how I wish I was alongside of her now.   No doubt, poor girl, she has made up her mind never to see me again, but that I shall be food for the sharks, as sure as my name's Harry Helm."

" Aye, Harry, and you was very near being so the other day, when you was washed overboard in the gale."

" And was rescued by you, my friend," said Henry, gratefully.   " Yes, Ben, I have had many narrow escapes; struck upon many a rock; but, thank heaven! my vessel's safe and sound—I have not foundered yet, and here I am, as merry as a grig, alongside my old messmate Ben Bolt, one of the bravest fellows that ever trod the deck.   Give us your flipper, my hearty.   Well, Jemmy, what about poetry now?"

"Poetry be blowed!" replied Jemmy, with a doleful countenance. "Oh, I am seriously ill. Oh! oh!"

"Heave too, Jemmy," cried Harry, smacking him on the back.

"Heave two!" repeated the barber; "oh, don't! I'm so ill, and my Sally's gone to get me a cordial. Heave two! I've heaved enough for two dozen, I'm sure. Oh; my precious internals"

The sailors laughed heartily, and the poor barber could obtain no sympathy.

"There's a set of sea monsters," he said; "they've no bowels of compassion, or they'd pity my poor bowels. Oh, dear! there was a twist! My inside's all out. I shall die."

"What, my worthy poet of the deep, die?" said Ben; "oh no, you must not talk about slipping your cable till you have experienced all the pleasures of the sea, the battle and the breeze—the cat and the catastrophe. You've come in search of the sublime and beautiful, and that's the way you'll find it."

"Oh, don't talk to me about the sublime and beautiful, Master Bolt," returned Jingle, "for I've had enough of them. As for lines of poetry, a pretty line you got me into in crossing the line. Such barbarous barbers as you sailors hair I never knew; why you haven't left enough flesh upon my face to bait a mousetrap, and such a pickling you gave me in the salt water that my carcase is little better than a lump of old junk."

"Cheer up, Jemmy," said Harry Helm, "and you'll live to be an admiral yet. But come, my lads; what say you to a dance?"

"Aye, a dance—a dance!" shouted the sailors unanimously; and the black fiddler scraped a hornpipe, and they all footed it merrily for some time.

"Well done, my lads," said the captain, as he made his appearance among them; "it glads me to see you so merry. But you must now on deck; pleasure must always yield to duty."

"Aye, aye, your honour,' cried the seamen, as they prepared to obey his orders, and pushing Jemmy before them. Our hero was about to follow them, when Lieutenant Morton suddenly made his appearance, and detained him.

"Stay, Ben," he said, "a word with you."

"With me, your honour," said Ben. "I—I hope I've done nothing wrong, and that you are not going to overhaul me."

The lieutenant looked at him intently, and an expression of emotion passed over his features.

"No, no, my brave fellow,' he replied; "you misunderstand me. You are too good a seaman ever to disgrace the jacket you wear."

"Oh, your honour's too kind," said Ben; "to receive the praise of such a gallant officer as you, sir, is so flattering that I'm taken all aback."

"I would again express to you my admiration of your noble conduct in the late storm," said the lieutenant; "when, at the risk of your own life, you not only rescued your old friend and shipmate Harry Helm, but likewise two more of the crew, and—'

"Avast, avast, your honour,' interrupted our hero, "though I ask pardon. But I feel almost as queer as if I was in the bilboes, to stand here and listen to nothing but yarns about my good conduct. I did no more than my duty as a man, and if I had shrunk from it I should have deserved to be strung up to the yard-arm as a scarecrow to the sea-gulls."

"You are a brave lad, Ben, and I honour you for it. Oh, how proud ought your parents to be of such a son."

"Ah, your honour," returned Ben, "that's where it is, you see, that I'm all adrift; because your honour, I never had any parents."

"How?"

"That is, sir, I mean I never knew my parents. I am what they call an innocent foundling. Old Father Neptune was my nurse; salt water was my mother's milk; the only cradle I was ever rocked in was the cradle of the deep, and the blustering wind, as it swept o'er the heaving billows, was my lullaby."

"Your observations move me strongly," remarked Lieutenant Morton; "pray explain yourself."

"Why, you see, your honour," answered our hero, "I might say that poor old Ben Bolt, from whom I take my name, has been both father and mother to me. He picked me up when an infant clasped to my mother's breast, from a crazy boat, about twenty years ago, and—"

"Strange coincidence !" ejaculated the lieutenant, in an agitated voice; "what means this powerful emotion ?   Should it be !"

"Why, your honour's sprung a leak," said Ben; "you've shipped a heavy sea, and—"

"Proceed !—proceed—the name of the vessel to which that boat belonged ?"

"Ah ! that they never knew, and my mother couldn't tell them, because, you see, she was dead; murdered, poor soul !"

"Dead ! murdered !' repeated Lieutenant Morton, and his agitation increased; "oh, my heart !   But tell me, was there nothing found upon her which might lead to a discovery of who she was?"

"Yes,' replied Ben; "a locket, containing the miniature likeness of a gentleman, was found suspended from her neck."

"Ah ! and that locket !" cried the lieutenant, eagerly.

"Is here !" replied our hero, producing it.

Lieutenant Morton snatched it impatiently from his hand, and as he gazed upon it, a groan escaped his breast, and his limbs trembled with a powerful and most indescribable emotion.

"Gracious heaven !" he exclaimed; "can I believe my senses?   It is—it is the very locket I gave to my wife, my deeply wronged Emeline !   The promptings of nature are now explained.   My son ! my son !"

And with these words he embraced the astonished Ben frantically, and hysterical sobs, for the present choked his further utterance.

CHAPTER XVI.

THE TALE OF SORROW—THE SUSPICIOUS VESSEL.

It was some minutes before our hero could sufficiently recover from his amazement to speak, but at length gently disengaging himself from the arms of the lieutenant, he said :

"Ah ! what ! son ! am I dreaming ?   Your honour—my gallant officer—sir, I—I—oh, damme, my upper-works must be out of order !"

"No, no,' hastily ejaculated his companion; "the tale you have told me—the period at which you were saved—this locket—your features, all convince me of the truth.   You are indeed that son whom I had thought was lost to me for ever.   Oh, my Emeline, that you should have met with such a dreadful fate !   May heaven's curses light upon the head of the inhuman miscreant who perpetrated the hellish deed !   Yet, boy, in me you behold the unfortunate author of your being.   No longer Lieut. Morton, but Lord Alfred Sidney !"

"Lord Alfred Sid—" faltered our astounded hero; "and my father !   Oh, have I indeed one whom I can hail by that dear, that sacred name ?   And that father too, one of the bravest officers in his Majesty's navy !   I—I—oh, I'm taken all aback !   I know not where I'm steering to ; yet there is a yearning feeling at my heart which convinces me of the truth.   I—I—no, no, my scuppers are not running over ; father ! father !"

Overpowered by his feelings, the young seaman sunk at the feet of his parent and sobbed aloud.   Lord Alfred raised him, and once more embracing him, for a few minutes in silence they gave free indulgence to their emotions.

"I can scarce believe my senses," said Ben, at last; "your honour—your lordship, the father of such a poor fellow as me !"

"'Tis true; but," he added, "you say that your unfortunate mother was murdered; how know you that."

"Alas !" replied Ben, with emotion; "poor dear soul, it was too evident; she was fastened to the bottom of the boat, when she was found—quite dead, and a ghastly wound in her side showed too plainly by what foul means she had perished."

"Bloodthirsty monster !" exclaimed Lord Alfred, with a shudder ; "could not her innocence arrest his remorseless hand ?"

"Who ? who ?   Oh, tell me how is this ?" eagerly interrogated our hero.

"Alas! it is a fearful tale," replied his father; "and I almost tremble to reveal it. But I will be as brief as I can, and at another time you shall be made acquainted with the whole particulars. I was once the happy husband of one of the most amiable and lovely of women; and who, to complete my bliss, presented me with one smiling babe, and oh, how bright was the sunshine of our hopes, till a fiend in human form stepped in, and at one fell blow destroyed them all for ever."

"Ah! his name?"

"He called himself Roland Sommerton; but I have reason to believe that name was only an assumed one. But hear me out. At the death of my father it was necessary for me to go Granada in the West Indies, where I had large and valuable property. My wife and my mother accompanied me; and for some time nothing occurred to interrupt our happiness. It was accident that introduced me to Roland; he did me a great service, and that established a friendship between us, which, heaven knows, was most sincere and fervent on my part. At that time he was a young man of the most prepossessing appearance and insinuating address. He stated that family matters had called him to Granada, and that his father was a gentleman of considerable property residing in England. I believed him, for what reason had I to doubt his statement? I admitted him to my house on terms of the greatest intimacy, and treated him with the regard as if he had been my own brother. The heartless, the unprincipled miscreant, what was the return he made to me for my kindness? He dared to raise his unholy thoughts to my wife—your mother, boy. Aye! well may you start and shudder, while the glow of indignation mantles in your cheeks. Watching his opportunity when business called me from my home, he made a midnight attack upon the house, and forcibly conveyed my beloved Emeline and yourself on board a strange vessel, which had been anchored for a few days near the coast. It immediately set sail, and left me to misery and despair!"

"Oh, villain! villain!" exclaimed our hero; "poor unfortunate mother!"

"The next day," continued his lordship, after a brief pause to recover himself; "the next day I returned to hear the awful tale from the lips of my mother, whom he had secured in the house. Oh! my son! judge my feelings! I immediately gave chase in one of my own vessels, but could hear no tidings of her, and it was afterwards supposed that the ship, which it was discovered was a pirate, was destroyed in some engagement and that all on board had perished."

"But your mother?"

"When I returned I found that she had disappeared in a most mysterious manner, and from that time to this I have never been able to learn anything of her. Broken hearted, I scarcely knew what I was about, and I became disgusted with everything. I sold off my property in Granada, and having been brought up to the sea, I assumed the name of Morton and entered once more into the service. From that hour I have lived alone for revenge, for I cannot help thinking that the false destroyer of my happiness is still in existence, but Fate has hitherto not permitted me to meet him."

"What a horrible tale is this," said our hero.

"Yes, it was indeed a dreadful blow, and I often wonder that I did not go mad. But, my son, for the present let all that I have told you remain a secret confined to your own breast; and —"

He was interrupted by the hasty entrance of one of the seamen.

"How now, Hawser?" he demanded.

"Sail a-head, your honour," replied Hawser.

"Have you made her out?" demanded the lieutenant.

"A black-looking craft, your honour, and she flies before the wind like a bird."

"Ah! she seeks to shun us, then; that looks suspicious. Is the captain on deck?"

"He is, sir."

"We must crowd all sail in pursuit of this craft, and see what she is made of. On deck, Ben—my —, follow me!"

"I'm astounded!" said Ben, when Lord Alfred was gone; "the gallant lieutenant my father, and a great lord! Who would ever have thought Ben Bolt would arrive at such a dignity? Oh, won't my pretty Alice be astonished? But I'm not going to desert her because I turn out to be a first class ship instead of a bum-boat. No! no! I should despise myself if I could harbour such a thought. Ah!" he added, as the report of a gun sounded in his ears, "we have saluted the stranger. We shall have some sport presently."

He was going when Jemmy Jingle made his appearance, in a state of great consternation.

"Oh, Mr. Bolt," he said, "you don't think there'll be any fighting, do you?"

"Fighting!" repeated Ben; "aye, or else I shall be greatly disappointed."

"Oh, dear! oh, dear! I shall faint," gasped forth Jingle. "There! Oh! but I won't fight! I can't fight! I didn't engage to fight, and if I'm killed I'll bring an action against the captain and all the officers for damages, as sure as my name is Jingle."

"Heave a-head, you swab!" cried Ben, "or, damme, I'll pour a broadside into you presently."

Loud shouts were now heard on deck, and poor Jingle trembled more than he had done before.

"Oh, dear! oh, dear! Jemmy Jingle," he said; "your poetical *exasperations* will be the death of you to a certainty."

"Sheer off! sheer off, you lily-hearted son of a land-lubber!" cried Ben, hurrying him away.

CHAPTER XVII.

CABIN IN THE BLOODHOUND—PERILOUS SITUATION OF ALICE—THE CHASE.

We will pass over the sufferings to which Alice and her sister had been exposed from the persecutions of Sir Raymond and Luke Harden; but hitherto they had been able to resist all their importunities, and to bear up against their trials with much greater fortitude than might have been expected. For some days past they had been separated, and Alice was thus left to her own melancholy reflections. Thus was she situated on the evening when the Spitfire was seen bearing down upon them, and most anxiously did she await the result.

"How my heart trembles with doubt and fear," she ejaculated; "and yet there may still be some hope of rescue from the power of these merciless wretches, who have torn me from my home and all I held most dear. My heart sinks with horror and dread. Weeks have now elapsed since that fatal night when the villain Sir Raymond Perceval forced me and my poor sister on board this fearful vessel, and what horrors have we not had to endure? Oh, Ben, dear Ben, how awfully have the dismal forebodings that haunted my imagination when cruel Fate tore us asunder been realised. We shall never meet again."

The sounds of loud laughter from the pirates on deck now reached her ears.

"Oh, how I shudder," she said, "as I listen to the rude and boisterous mirth of these hardened wretches, and my disordered fancy pictures to me, in still more vivid and torturing colours, the fate which is probably in store for me."

She now heard the voice of Luke Harden without, and shuddered with fear.

"See to my orders, Redford," he said; "I will be with you on deck again anon.'

"Ah! the pirate captain comes this way," she said; "oh, heaven protect me."

Luke Harden entered the cabin as she spoke.

"The wind is in our favour," he muttered to himself, "and we shall yet outstrip them. Now Alice," he added aloud; "still hoisting signals of distress. Thinking of your lubber, I suppose. However, Sir Raymond will be here presently, and perhaps he will be able to arouse you from this gloomy mood."

"Oh, villain!" cried our heroine, with a look of disgust.

"Villain!' repeated Luke; "humph! not very complimentary, at any rate. However, I do not disdain the title, for I think my daring deeds upon the dark blue waters have fairly won it. Oh, it was a glorious triumph for myself and Sir Raymond, when we succeeded in capturing such fair craft as the pretty Alice Maitland and her sister Rose."

"Cowardly ruffian!" she replied, firmly, "you bear the outward form of man, and yet can delight to taunt and triumph over the weak and defenceless. But though you and the guilty Sir Raymond hold myself and my sister in your power and threaten our destruction, we will still defy you. We are armed so strong by virtue and justice, that we may boldly laugh your base designs to scorn."

"Ha! ha! ha!" laughed the ruffian, triumphantly; "very pretty and heroic. But, hark ye, my proud beauty, the time for forbearance is nearly past; in a few hours we shall arrive at one of my secret haunts among the rocks near the Devil's Creek, and then the triumph of myself and the baronet will be complete."

"Oh, never! never!" exclaimed Alice; "heaven will not permit so monstrous a sacrifice!"

"Indeed," said Luke; "but you will find that you will be disappointed. Ha what's in the wind now?" he demand, as Redford hastily entered the cabin.

"The ship is gaining rapidly upon us," replied Redford, "I do not think it is possible to avoid her."

"Then we must prepare to give her a hearty welcome," remarked Luke. "She will find the Bloodhound no easy conquest."

"I know not, captain," returned Redford; "I do not like the look of her build, and I'm afraid she might prove more than a match for us."

"On deck—on deck!" said Harden; "we have the wind in our favour, the Bloodhound is a clipper, and if I like not her appearance, we must endeavour to give her the slip. Away!"

And they both hastily departed, and again left our heroine to herself. They were scarcely gone, however, when Sir Raymond Perceval entered, and advanced boldly towards her.

"Beauteous Alice," he said, "even at this moment when danger seems to threaten us, I cannot resist the temptation to visit you, and once more pour into your ears the impassioned sentiments of my soul."

"Hold, villain!" she cried; "nor dare to shock my ears with your odious vows."

"Nay," he returned; "this obstinate and scornful resistance shall avail you not. You are mine, Alice, and by this fond embrace I seal the compact."

"Forbear, miscreant!" exclaimed the damsel, retreating; "dare not to approach me; your sight is odious to me, and your very touch would freeze my blood with horror!"

"Alice," replied Sir Raymond; "this is no time for trifling, and thus do I seal my happiness on your lips."

He seized her in his arms as he spoke and endeavoured to put his threats into execution; but she struggled violently.

"Unhand me, ruffian!" she cried; "release your hold! Oh, help—help!"

Suddenly she snatched a pistol from his belt, and rushing from his arms, levelled it at him, and he started back alarmed.

"Villain!" she cried, resolutely; "move but a step—advance but an inch, and my woman's arm, strong in the defence of honour, shall deal you death!"

"Confusion!" exclaimed the baronet; "thus foiled and defeated; Alice, I—"

"Nay." she said; "dare me not, for I am resolute; offer not to obstruct me, or you die!"

Before he could make any reply the door was thrown open and Luke entered followed by Rose, who rushed to her sister's arms, and she dropped the pistol, which Sir Raymond regained possession of.

"Come, Sir Raymond," said Luke, "we have other business to look to just now. Follow me on deck; the girls will be safe enough here."

Redford now appeared.

"All I fear is lost," he said; "the vessel skims the ocean like a water-witch. She is nearly within gun-shot of us!"

"Have you made her out?" demanded Luke.

"Yes; it is the Spitfire."

"The Spitfire!" exclaimed Sir Raymond, "'sdeath

"The Spitfire!" cried our heroine and Rose, in a breath; "thank heaven, we shall yet be saved."

"What is to be done in this emergency?" said Sir Raymond, with a look of alarm.

"There is no time to be lost," remarked Luke; "secure the girls in the hold," he added, speaking to the pirates.

"Oh, mercy, mercy!" shrieked the terrified sisters, in a breath; but it was useless for them to offer any resistance, and they were forced away.

"What a cursed misfortune is this," cried the baronet, passionately; "we shall never be able to resist a foe of such superior power as the Spitfire."

"No," returned Luke Harden; "we must not risk an engagement with her, if possible. We must part with some of our heavy metal, and lighten our vessel all that we can. The Bloodhound never failed yet. Quick, quick!—on deck—on deck!"

Luke, Sir Raymond, and the others, now hurried away, and soon all was bustle and activity on board the pirate ship.

Two or three of the heaviest guns were thrown overboard, which lightened her considerably; but it was soon evident that it would be impossible for them to avoid her, and they therefore made every preparation for the action which must inevitably take place

With folded arms and disordered steps Sir Raymond Perceval paced the deck and watched the approach of the dreaded enemy, which every moment gained more and more upon them, with anxious looks, and in a state of mind which it is unnecessary for us to attempt to describe.

"And shall all my hopes be thus blasted, and at the moment when my triumph seemed so secure?" he ejaculated. "Curses light on this misfortune! Why did I not remain with the girl on shore? She would have been safe from discovery in the secret cavern beneath the Manor House; but now—"

"Psha!" interrupted Harden, impatiently; "this is not the time for idle fears and useless regrets. Have I not as much at stake as yourself? The daring crew of the Bloodhound will fight like tigers to the last, and, in spite of her superiority, the Spitfire will obtain no easy conquest, depend upon it. But should we suffer defeat, we shall still have the means of revenge; nor must we shrink from it."

"Ah!" exclaimed Sir Raymond, eagerly, "what mean you?"

'Sooner than the girls shall again be restored to their lovers," answered the miscreant, "we will scuttle the ship, and all perish together!"

"Horrible thought!" cried the baronet, with a shudder; "what fiend of hell could suggest it to you?"

"No matter," replied Harden; "this is not the time to discuss the subject. We shall have our full work to do presently."

"But old Maud?"

"Why trouble yourself about her at such a moment as this? She is safe enough, and should a ball happen to reach her it will be all the better. 'Tis a confounded job, however, to think that we should be compelled to part with some of our heaviest guns. They would have done good service. Ah! see! she is just within gunshot of us, and we must therefore prepare ourselves for the sport. Hark! she salutes us! Return the compliment, and when we have heard the sound of our voices we shall understand each other better."

A gun had been fired from the Spitfire, a signal for the pirate to heave to, and this was quickly answered by one of defiance from the Bloodhound, and the pirates prepared with the greatest coolness and determination for the deadly strife which was about to ensue. A few minutes more and the two vessels were alongside each other, and the conflict then commenced.

The chase had been a rapid one, and the captain and crew of the Spitfire never anticipated for a moment that a vessel of such inferiority in size and the number of guns she carried would offer any resistance.

Just before the Spitfire approached the pirate ship, Lieutenant Morton, as we will still continue to call him, drew our hero aside, and in accents of emotion addressed him:

"My son, should the crew of this vessel give us battle, there is no knowing what the result to any of us may be. I may perish, and—"

'You perish, my noble father," interrupted Ben, with a look of affection, and grasping his hand—"Heaven forbid!"

"Nay, if it is the will of heaven, it must be so," remarked the lieutenant. "Should I happen to fall, I repeat," he continued, as he took a small packet of papers from his pocket, "these documents will be indispensable to you to establish your rights, and to see that justice is done. Take them, my brave boy, and should Fate ever bring you to a knowledge of the monster from whom I date all my sorrows, and those of your

THE ATTACK ON THE PIRATES.

murdered mother, do not forget that the wrongs of your parents call aloud for retribution on his guilty head."

"If I do," replied Ben, vehemently, " may the curses of the Commander aloft pursue me. But fear not, my father; all will go well. We have nothing to fear from this piratical craft. If they are bold enough to offer to resist, which it would almost be madness for them to do, no doubt they will soon be glad to cry peccavi, and strike to a foe whom they must know they can't have the least chance to conquer."

"True, Ben, my friend," said Harry Helm, who at that moment joined him; " no doubt this business will be settled off hand. I ask your honour's pardon, I didn't see you."

"My brave fellow," replied the lieutenant, you are the friend of— of— Ben Bolt, and I honour you for it. At some future time I may have a better opportunity of convincing you of the sentiments of friendship I entertain towards you."

"Oh, your honour's too kind and condescending," said Harry; " but see, we are now nearly alongside the pirate, and no doubt we shall be yard-arm and yard-arm with em presently. So we must bear a hand, Ben; for it appears after all that they are

No. 12.

resolved not to yield without an effort. Ah! why shiver my timbers! don't you see? If it ain't the very vessel that was lying in the port at the same time as the Spitfire, and which they called the Water Nymph.'

"It is," cried our hero, gazing with a look of astonishment towards the ship. "I could swear to her. So she has been sailing under false colours after all. Well, it strikes me that we shall soon make her humble herself, or the Spitfire will never plough the salt waters again. Dear Alice, may heaven watch over your safety in this moment."

"And my faithful Rose, too," said Harry, "But I trust they are both secure from all danger."

They had not time for any further observations; the pirates had been called upon to yield, and having replied by boldly opening fire upon the Spitfire, the combat commenced in real earnest.

The scene which now ensued was of the most exciting description. The pirates fought with the most determined courage; but it was quite evident that they could not long resist their powerful antagonist, and that if they remained obstinate to the last, the destruction of human life which must inevitably take place would be dreadful. In a short time after the commencement of the engagement the pirate vessel, which was greatly shattered from the heavy guns of the Spitfire, was boarded, and then the combat was continued with redoubled courage on both sides.

Our hero and Harry, in the confusion of the strife, became separated from Lieut. Morton, and the rest of the sailors who had rushed with them on board the Bloodhound, and fought their way below, while those on deck continued the fight with the most fierce determination. The pirate ship, however, was so much damaged that it was rapidly filling, and must shortly sink, so that the lieutenant gave the word to fight their way back to the Spitfire, and leave the wretches to their fate; when turning round suddenly, his eyes encountered the form and features of Sir Raymond Perceval, who was fiercely engaged by the side of Luke Harden.

He started back a few paces, and gave utterance to a mingled exclamation of surprise and horror, while the baronet, who recognised him at the same instant, evinced as much emotion and terror as if he had encountered some ghastly phantom.

"Powers of mercy!" cried Morton; "it is Roland—the monster whom I have so long sought in vain!"

"Aye," replied Sir Raymond, recovering himself; "at last we meet, Lord Alfred."

"Miscreant! villain! murderer of my Emeline! revenge! revenge!" exclaimed the infuriated nobleman, as he rushed upon him, and the struggle which ensued was frightful. But the danger that threatened every instant became more imminent, and the lieutenant and the sailors were at length compelled to retreat to their own vessel, after leaving many dead and wounded behind them.

"All is lost!" said Luke Harden, now advancing to Sir Raymond, who was standing gazing at the scene around him with mingled feelings of fear and disappointment; "all is lost! they have regained their vessel. Our battered vessel is fast sinking—there is not a moment to be lost, if we would save our lives. Ah!'

Loud shrieks were heard, and the next moment our hero and Harry appeared upon deck with Alice and her sister in their arms, and followed by two or three others of the crew of the Spitfire.

"By the infernal host!" exclaimed Luke, exultingly; "we have yet the means of vengeance."

"Aye,' cried the baronet, fiercely; "at any rate they must not live to triumph at our defeat."

"Ah! outnumbered!" ejaculated Ben; "heaven then aid our arms!"

Ben and Harry now defended themselves with a bravery which could not be surpassed; but overpowered by numbers, they were quickly disarmed, and the pirates were about to sacrifice them to their fury, when Alice and Rose, with a loud shriek, interposed between them.

"Hold!" exclaimed the miscreant Luke; "his destruction and that of his companion is inevitable; but I have a more exquisite revenge. Bind them to the mast, and leave them to perish in the sinking vessel?"

"Ah! but the girls!" demanded Sir Raymond, hastily.

"They shall not escape us," replied Luke; "not an instant is to be lost!"

"Monster! fiend!" cried Ben, struggling violently in the arms of the pirates.

"Oh, horror! horror!" exclaimed our heroine and her sister, in a breath; "Mercy! mercy!"

"Heed not their cries," said the ruffian Luke Harden; "but obey my orders—quick!"

Immediately, in spite of all their resistance, they were secured to the mast, and the unfortunate sisters, overpowered by the horror of their feelings, again screamed and fainted.

"Revenge! revenge!" shouted Luke, as he and the baronet seized the insensible forms of the damsels in their arms; "at least thou art ours. To the boats! to the boats!"

In an instant they were gone, and the young seamen were left to their apparently inevitable fate.

"Oh, Ben, my poor friend," sighed Harry, "after all the dangers we have hitherto so successfully braved together, shall we be permitted to perish thus? And those fair creatures so dear to us! Alas! what will be their terrible fate?"

"Despair! despair!" groaned Ben; "the battered hulk is filling more rapidly every instant; in a short time it must go to pieces, and there is no help at hand to rescue us! Oh, Alice! beloved Alice! farewell for ever in this world!"

Again they struggled desperately, but in vain, to release themselves from the cords that bound them, and the deck of the vessel was now almost brought to the water's edge. It was a moment of intense horror, and the hearts of the poor fellows were fast sinking within them, when suddenly they heard the sound of hasty approaching footsteps, and Maud of the Ruins, having forced her way from the place in which she had been confined, stood before them.

CHAPTER XIX.

A MOMENT OF EXCITEMENT—THE PIRATES AND THEIR VICTIMS—THE RESCUE.

"It is not yet too late to save ourselves," said the old woman; "the miscreants even now make their way to the nearest shore with their unfortunate victims. But there is still another boat in which we may, with the aid of Providence, reach the Spitfire, if we do not delay. So, quick! quick!"

"But Alice! Rose!" cried our hero and his companion, in accents of agony and despair.

"They also may yet be rescued from the power of the miscreants," replied Maud; "but this is not the time for talking, but for action; a few minutes more and the deep waters of the ocean will form our grave."

Instantly she severed the cords that bound them, and then, without waiting to hear another word they might have to say, and hurrying them away, the next moment they had entered the boat and dashed from the wreck, and scarcely had they done so when it went to pieces, leaving scarcely a vestige on the breast of the billows.

With frantic and eager looks Ben and his companion cast their eyes around, and beheld in the distance the boats that contained the pirates and the hapless sisters, but almost immediately they disappeared behind a rock, and clasping their hands together, and uttering a groan of despair and agony, the young men almost became insensible.

Maud worked with almost superhuman strength and fortitude to guide the boat, for little was the assistance which Ben or Harry could render. From the Spitfire, however, they had evidently beheld the perilous situation in which they were placed, and boats were put off to their rescue. Just as their boat was fast filling and likely to sink, they reached them; all were conveyed in safety on board the Spitfire, and our hero was clasped in the arms of his father, the captain and crew gathering round them with mingled feelings of astonishment and emotion.

"Saved! saved!" exclaimed Lord Alfred, in a voice of the greatest agitation; "oh, heaven be thanked for this. My son! my son!"

"Son!" repeated the astonished captain; "what is the meaning of this? Do you rave, Mr. Morton?"

"No, no, I rave not!" he said; "the time for further concealment is past; in m you behold not Mr. Morton, but the deeply wronged and heart-broken Lord Alfred Sidney, and this—that son whom the most black-hearted villany so long deprived me of!"

At that moment a strange cry startled them all, and Maud rushing into the midst of them, gazed earnestly at his lordship, as she exclaimed :

"Gracious heaven! the hour I have so long panted for has arrived at last! Alfred, dear, long-lost Alfred! look closely in these care-worn, haggard features, and say, oh, say, do you not recognise them ?"

Lord Alfred did indeed look narrowly into the countenance of the unfortunate woman, and then with a frantic cry of mingled astonishment and incredulity he exclaimed :

"Good God! do my eyes deceive me; or have my senses left me ? No! no—my throbbing heart convinces me that it is no delusion! That voice—those features so fondly remembered. Mother! mother!"

In an instant they were clasped in each other's arms, and our hero knelt at their feet, overpowered by emotions of the most exquisite and indescribable nature!

A few words will explain all ; that mysterious woman who has hitherto only been known as Maud of the Ruins, was no other than the mother of Lord Alfred, the Dowager Lady Sidney !

We cannot paint in adequate colours the scene which followed, and great was the curiosity of the captain and the others to learn the particulars ; but after the first emotions of this extraordinary and unexpected meeting were over, Lord Alfred said :

"There is no time for further explanation now ; shall the monster who has been the cause of all this crime and suffering be permitted to escape that terrible retribution he has so justly merited ?"

"And the innocent Alice Maitland and her sister are in his power," cried our hero ; "shall they be left to fall the victims of their atrocious persecutors ?"

"No," replied the captain ; "they have doubtless landed on some adjacent island, where we must immediately pursue them, rescue the unfortunate girls, if possible, and secure the villains. It was behind yonder rocks that the boats containing them disappeared, and to that point we must make with all speed."

The order was given without delay, and in a short time the vessel arrived at what appeared to be a small island, and our hero and his father, Harry Helm, Lady Geraldine, and a number of the crew of the Spitfire landed, and proceeded on their search.

We will now return to Alice and her sister, and the wretches in whose power they were. It was some time before the poor girls recovered their senses, and when they did so, to their horror they found themselves clasped in the arms of Sir Raymond and Luke, while the scene around them was wild and frightful in the extreme. They tried to speak, but overcome by the terror and agitation of their feelings, they uttered a faint cry, and again became insensible.

"Our situation is a perilous one," said the baronet; "our vessel destroyed, and ourselves, with only a remnant of our crew, driven to this wild place. Fool that I was ever to quit England with my prize ; I should long ere now have accomplished all my wishes, and without exposing myself to all these dangers. Our destruction is inevitable."

"It is no use regretting now," replied Luke; "curses light on the lubbers who rescued our rivals."

"Yes," remarked the baronet; "they have put off from the ship in pursuit, and should they discover us, our game is up."

"We waste time in talking here," observed Harden. Distant voices now sounded on the air.

"Ah !" cried Luke Harden; "they are upon our track. Quick—quick! or all is lost !"

In a moment they rushed away in a different direction to that of their pursuers, and they had not been gone many minutes when our hero and his companions arrived at the spot, and looked anxiously around them.

"Hitherto our search has been vain," said Ben; "oh, my poor Alice! But kind heaven, in its mercy, will surely restore her to me. By the foot-marks in the earth, it is evident they have taken this way, and if we do not delay, the villains cannot escape us."

His father was about to return some answer, when the sound of distant shrieks was borne upon the air.

" Ah! those cries!" exclaimed his lordship; "thank heaven we are on the right track. Quick! quick!"

They departed in the direction of the cries with the greatest precipitation.

Night had now set in, and a violent storm had commenced, so that everything was against them, and they almost began to despair of success.

Alice and her sister, on again recovering their senses, found themselves in a wild rocky place, with a view of the sea, and Sir Raymond and Luke Harden hanging over them, while the other ruffians who had escaped from the ship, were standing with sullen and disappointed looks around.

They shuddered, and averted their looks from those of their cruel oppressors, and the howling voice of the tempest added to the terror of their feelings.

" For the present," remarked Harden; " we have eluded our pursuers, and probably this storm may induce them to return to the ship."

" Ah, no !" ejaculated our heroine; " they surely will not thus abandon us to our fate. Oh, Sir Raymond, if your heart is not entirely insensible to every feeling of pity, you will have mercy on me and my unfortunate sister."

" Oh, forbear, forbear," ejaculated Rose; " or rest assured that the vengeance of offended heaven will overtake you, and that, too, when you least expect it."

" Bah !" exclaimed the ruffian, Luke; " you appeal to us in vain. Our situation is a desperate one, but, at any rate, a woman's tears, entreaties, or threat, shall not move us from our purpose. Rose Maitland, and you proud, scornful Alice, will find myself and Sir Raymond determined; this night, nay, this very hour seals your fate."

" Miscreants !" cried Alice; " you will not, you dare not put your diabolical threats into execution."

" And think you," said the baronet; " think you that, after having thus far proceeded we will now retrace our steps? No, by all the infernal host I swear that nothing whatever shall induce me to relent. Already have I acted with too much forbearance, and which has brought ruin upon me. You have treated me with scorn and opprobrium, and now am I determined to have sweet revenge. You have called me murderer, I admit that I deserve the title, and it will be my greatest triumph to know that you must yield to the wishes of the assassin !"

" Oh, horrible! horrible !" gasped forth our heroine; " almighty God! You will not surely permit this heartless miscreant to put his monstrous designs into effect !"

" Ha! ha! ha !" laughed Sir Raymond, triumphantly; " your fears and anguish are food to my soul; but how will that terror increase when I inform you that it was this hand which shed the blood of the mother of him you love so fondly !"

" Gracious heaven ! can this be true?" gasped forth our heroine.

" It is, it is," replied the inhuman baronet; listen to the tale, which perhaps may serve to interest you. Lady Emeline Sidney, for that was the title of the mother of the young sailor whom you have loved as Ben Bolt, raised a passion in my breast, which I was resolved should at all hazards be gratified; secretly, carefully I watched my opportunity, and when her lord, who looked upon me as his dearest friend, was absent from his home, I attacked his house at midnight, aided by Luke Harden and his daring crew, and conveyed her and her infant on board the pirate ship, which immediately set sail, without suspicion, and was soon out of the reach of pursuit. What could her resistance then avail against me? Nothing, and I triumphed—yes, triumphed over the honour of the parent of your lover."

" Good God!" cried the shocked and trembling Alice; " what a frightful disclosure is this!"

" Nay, girl," said the villain; " you have not yet heard all. The Lady Emeline dared to threaten me, and to heap her heaviest curses and reproaches on my head; my desires were gratified, and the sight of her now became hateful to me. One night she was even more reproachful and vindictive than usual, and unable any longer to control my rage, I plunged my knife deep into her side, and she fell, bleeding and dying, at my feet. Her body, with her infant at her breast, was then placed in a crazy boat and consigned to the mercy of the waves ! You know the rest."

" Fiend !" exclaimed Alice; " for after this dreadful avowal I cannot call you by any other name--and dare you think for ever to escape the vengeance of outraged heaven for this awful deed? Approach me not, for your very touch would freeze my blood with horror."

"We do but delay, Sir Raymond;" said Luke; "let this moment witness our triumph."

"Aye!" replied the baronet, as he advanced towards our heroine; "be it so—now, beauteous Alice, thou art mine! No earthly power can save you!"

Alice and her sister struggled violently, and rent the air with their cries; at that moment the sound of many footsteps were heard approaching, and they felt startled and confused. A sudden panic seemed to seize the villain, Sir Raymond, and he fled from the spot among the intricacies of the rocks.

"Cowardly knave!" cried Luke Harden, fiercely, as he held Rose Maitland still more resolutely in his arms; "but be firm, and we may yet be able to defeat them."

The words had scarcely escaped his lips, when the loud report of a pistol was heard, and the pirate, with a fearful oath, bounded slightly into the air, and then fell a ghastly corpse upon the earth. Maud, followed by the others, now arrived at the place, and Alice and her sister, with an exclamation of mingled joy and gratitude, rushed to the arms of their lovers.

The pirates were thrown into such confusion by the death of Luke and the cowardly flight of Sir Raymond, that they became an easy conquest, and the combat that ensued did not last long. Two or three of them were slain, several others taken prisoners, and the rest fled in dismay, in all directions.

The lovers embraced fervently, and sincerely returned their thanks to heaven; and then Lord Sidney, looking eagerly around him, said :

"But the inhuman wretch who has been the cause of all this; oh, where is he?"

A loud laugh of defiance drew their attention towards one of the rocks, on the extreme point of which, and which overhung the sea, with folded arms and a countenance expressive of fiendish malice, stood Sir Raymond Perceval.

"He is here!" he cried aloud; "here, to laugh ye all to scorn, and to invoke the curses of perdition on your heads!"

"Murderer of my unfortunate Emeline, mother of your rival," cried Lord Alfred; "at least you shall not escape my avenging arm. Die!"

He discharged the contents of a pistol at him as he spoke; a loud laugh of scorn followed, and throwing his arms above his head, the murderer leaped from the rock into the sea. But whether the contents of the pistol had reached him or not, they had no means of ascertaining.

"The monster must not be suffered to escape," observed Lord Alfred; "follow me, my friends."

They did so, towards that part of the beach beneath the rock from which the guilty Sir Raymond had taken his leap; but not the least sign of him could be seen.

"He has doubtless perished," said his lordship; "and if so, may heaven grant more mercy to his black and guilty soul than he awarded to others. The murder of my unfortunate Emeline is avenged, and henceforth my mind will be more at peace."

"Ah! my son," said Lady Geraldine; "and thank heaven I have lived to see this day. The object of my soul is gratified; the designs of the bloodthirsty Sir Raymond Perceval have been frustrated; my brave and noble-hearted grandson will be restored to his rights and to his proper position in society, and I am now satisfied, and can die in peace. Maud of the Ruins has not suffered in vain."

"Oh, my honoured mother!" exclaimed Lord Alfred; "how can I express my feelings on this occasion? The ways of Providence are wonderful indeed. But this is no time to enter into further explanations. This storm is threatening; the night, too, advances, and we had better at once return to the ship. Come, we do but tarry."

No one opposed any objection to this, and with feelings such as the imagination of the reader may well conceive, they departed from the gloomy scene in which such important events had recently taken place, and made their way towards the boats, and were all soon again safe on board the Spitfire.

The storm abated much sooner than had been anticipated, and at length subsided altogether, and the Spitfire was quickly again steering on her cruise over the boundless waters of the deep, and with many a grateful heart on board, which had lately palpitated with emotions of fear and anguish.

CHAPTER XX.

JOYFUL PROSPECTS—THE TALE OF LADY GERALDINE.

It was not for some time after their arrival on board the vessel that the fair sisters retired to the cabin allotted to them, but not to sleep, for the wonderful events of the last few hours occupied their minds, and completely superseded every other thought. They were, indeed, so extraordinary that they could with difficulty persuade themselves as to their reality, and they could never be sufficiently grateful for their miraculous escape from the terrible dangers that had threatened them.

But the strange discovery as to the origin of our hero astonished them more than all, and the mind of Alice was tortured by a variety of doubts and apprehensions.

"Alas!" she sighed; "may it not cause the destruction of all those bright hopes I have hitherto so fondly formed?"

"And can you doubt the fidelity of your lover, Alice?" said Rose; "indeed I am convinced that you do him an injustice if you can. He can never cease to view you with the same sentiments of affection that he does now."

"Alas!" replied our heroine; "but dare the humble Alice Maitland dare aspire to the hand of one so noble, and elevated so far above her in rank and station? His father will never give his consent, and I see that there is yet the greatest misery in store for me."

"Come, dear Alice," ejaculated her sister; "you must not torture yourself with any such gloomy ideas that will, depend upon it, turn out to be erroneous. If Lord Sidney sincerely loves his son, he will not for a moment seek to crush his hopes or to thwart his wishes, and you will yet be happy."

"Heaven grant that your wishes may be gratified and your predictions verified, dear Rose," returned Alice, most sincerely; "but our poor parents—oh, what may not have happened to them since our cruel and mysterious separation from them? How could they ever support so awful a bereavement."

"I do, indeed, tremble to think of that," replied Rose; "poor dear parents, what must have been your sufferings. Oh, what a villain must Sir Raymond Perceval have been to perpetrate so monstrous an outrage."

"He must indeed," said Alice; "but what crime is there that the murderer—the cowardly murderer of an innocent woman—would hesitate to commit? Poor Lady Sidney; her's was, indeed, a dreadful fate."

"It was; and how providential and miraculous was the preservation of her son; and the manner in which those wonderful discoveries have been brought about."

"True; and that the very vessel in which our lovers were should happen to overtake that of the pirates, and rescue us from the destruction with which we were threatened. We can never be sufficiently grateful to Omnipotence. But all danger is not yet an end."

"What mean you?" interrogated Rose.

"Alas!" replied Alice; "will not those we so fondly love yet be exposed to all the horrors of the deadly strife; and should they fall!"

"Oh, banish such apprehensions from your breast, my dear sister," returned Rose; "and endeavour to anticipate the best. But come, it is late, let us therefore seek that repose of which we stand so much in need after the excitement and fatigue we have undergone."

Alice returned no answer to this, and, as the night was far advanced, they did as Rose suggested.

The novelty of their situation, however, kept them long waking, and our heroine pondered in her mind the many and extraordinary events that had lately taken place; and which had produced such a wonderful change in the circumstances of her lover; and which might be the means, she could not still help fearing, of annihilating those hopes she had so long cherished.

"How dare I," she reflected; "how dare I presume to hope that his noble father will ever consent to the marriage of his son to one of my lowly condition? Lord Alfred appears amiable and generous; but yet may not family pride, so inherent in aristocratic breasts, prevent him from making what he might consider so great a sacrifice? Oh, Ben, much as I rejoice at the change in your fortune, I could almost regret it, when I think that it may be the cause of separating us for ever."

A pang of intense emotion shot through her heart as those ideas occurred to her, and it was several minutes before she could regain her composure.

"But no," she ejaculated, after a pause, and fresh hope and confidence animating her breast; "why should I encourage such vague doubts and fears as these? For by them I'm certain I do an injustice to the faithful and manly heart of my dear Ben (for by that name I must still continue to call him). No change of circumstances, I am satisfied, can ever alter the sentiments he entertains towards me; and, if his father regards him with that affection it is only natural he should, he will raise no obstacle to the accomplishment of his wishes, and, in the gratification of which his hopes of happiness depend."

These thoughts relieved her mind of a heavy weight of anxiety, and she endeavoured to await the result with patience and fortitude.

But the doubtful situation of her parents at the present time, and when they were probably in such a dreadful state of doubt and uncertainty as to the fate which had befallen herself and her sister, was a source of the greatest uneasiness to her, and various, and most torturing and conflicting, were the different conjectures which she formed upon the subject. She was afraid that so fearful a bereavement would be more than the poor old people could find strength and fortitude sufficient to bear; and that reflection dampened the ardour of her feelings at her anticipated restoration to England.

There was another subject, too, on which her mind experienced the greatest anxiety and uneasiness; and this was the many dangers to which her lover might yet be exposed, especially should the Spitfire be brought into action with the enemy, which was more than probable. Should he perish in the deadly strife, what charms would life any longer possess for her? Her heart sickened at the thought, which she tried to banish from her mind, and at length partially succeeded, and having mentally, but fervently, invoked the blessing and protection of the Supreme, she composed herself to sleep.

It is not to be supposed that Lord Alfred had failed to observe the warm feelings of admiration with which our hero regarded Alice, nor had her personal and intrinsic merits passed unnoticed or unappreciated by him. He saw plainly that she was a damsel whose bosom was the dwelling of every virtuous sentiment, calculated to adorn any station, and to make the man supremely happy who might be worthy of her, and such he fondly believed his son to be. Pride or sordidness were no part of his nature. He had experienced too much of the world to encourage any such feelings, and he was resolved that he would form no obstacle to the gratification of the hopes of the youthful lovers.

When his lordship, therefore, found himself alone with our hero, he availed himself of the opportunity to question him upon the subject.

"I cannot but acknowledge, my son," he remarked, "that I am much charmed with the manners and appearance of the fair sisters, Alice and Rose Maitland. They seem to be deserving of every respect and admiration."

"Oh, my lord," replied the young seaman, his fine eyes sparkling with delight; "how it glads my very soul to hear you say so; indeed you do them no more than justice by the opinion you have just been pleased to express of them; heaven bless you for it! Two lovelier or more innocent beings than the sisters do not breathe, and that must be a wretch indeed—a rascally shark, who could harbour a single thought to their injury. As for the pretty Alice—"

"You love her, my son?" interrupted his lordship, and fixing an earnest look upon him.

"Love her!" repeated Ben, and his cheeks glowed with the warmth of his excited feelings; "oh, my lord, that is by far too weak a term to apply to the sentiment which inspires my soul towards that beauteous girl. She is the object of my heart's fondest devotion, nay adoration; and my every hope is centered in her love, which I know that I possess. When thousands of miles have separated us from each other, her beloved form has never for a moment been absent from my mind's eye; and the thought of her has strengthened me and urged me on in the hour of danger. Love her! oh, how feeble is my tongue to give expression to my feelings. Alice, dear Alice! with

JACK TAFFRAIL BRINGS NEWS OF THE SPITFIRE.

what fond and anxious hope do I look forward to the time when our fates will be united in the happy bonds of matrimony."

"But you forget, my son," observed his lordship, in a serious tone; "you forget that Alice Maitland is poor and humble, and that the world would expect that the son of Lord Alfred Sidney should aspire to something more distinguished than—"

"The world must think me an execrable scoundrel if I could desert the lovely girl who has devoted all her affections to me, and proved so faithful to me," interrupted Ben, warmly; "pardon me, my lord, but if I am expected to purchase my new raised dignity by the sacrifice of my pretty Alice, rather let me remain the humble and simple Ben Bolt for the remainder of my days. What! turn mutineer, and cast the girl of my heart adrift to the mercy of the rude and unfeeling world! No, no; pardon me, my lord, but I must speak plainly and resolutely, if I do, may I be d—d!"

"You are too much excited, my dear boy," said Lord Alfred, who could hardly help smiling at the warmth and vehemence of his manner.

"Probably I am," returned Ben; "but, oh, my lord—father, surely you possess too
No. 18.

noble and generous a spirit to wish to deprive me of the very sheet anchor of my hopes, and to send me afloat a mere hulk on the ocean of life?"

"No, no," replied his lordship, fervently, and affectionately taking his hand; "heaven forbid that I should do so. I admire the candour and honest expression of your feelings, the true character of which I merely wished to elicit from you; and I cordially approve of the choice you have made. The consent of your father shall not be wanting to complete your happiness. Take the fair and virtuous Alice Maitland for your wife, and may heaven shower its choicest blessings on your head!"

"Eh! what!" cried our delighted hero; "do I hear aright? You then approve of my love, my lord—you consent to the lovely Alice becoming my wife, and—and—oh, bless you! bless you for this!"

Overpowered by his emotions, the young man sunk at the feet of his father, who again invoked a benediction on his head.

"Enough, my son," he said; "this explanation will no doubt afford you every satisfaction, and serve to convince you that I have your happiness at heart. We will talk further on this interesting subject on a future occasion."

"Oh, my good lord," ejaculated Ben, "what a happy man you have made me to be sure. Heaven bless you for it. Alice then will be mine, in spite of all the storms that have arisen to separate us. And she will be a lady, too; oh dear! oh dear—what joy there is in store for us to be sure. And then there's my old friend and shipmate, Harry Helm, too; he has been the companion of all my dangers, he is a noble fellow, a brave fellow, and shall he not be the partaker of my happiness?"

"Fear not," replied Lord Alfred; "I will see to his future welfare and advancement in life, for I am convinced that he is deserving of it."

"He is indeed," coincided our hero; "oh, thank you for this, my lord; Harry Helm is worthy of all that Fortune can bestow upon him, and I hope to see him one day an admiral. Besides, he will become the husband of my Alice's sister, and, of course, I must then esteem him as my brother; though, for the matter of that, I have ever done so."

After some further observations of an equally congratulatory and satisfactory nature, our hero and his father separated and the former, whose feelings were excited to the utmost pitch of delight, retired with a cheerful heart to his hammock.

At an early hour the following morning our hero and Harry Helm sought the presence of their lovers, and the meeting was all that might have been expected. Harry and Rose, however, having retired, our hero and Alice were left to the free indulgence of their own feelings.

"Dear Alice," said Ben, "how can I express the fond emotions that throb my breast at this moment? But how is this? You look sad, and why that sigh? when I expected to see nothing but joy and hope sparkling in those lovely eyes?"

"'Tis nothing, Ben," replied Alice, evasively, and in a faltering voice; "but—, but—"

"But—, but—," repeated her lover; "nay, now, this is not like my own sweet Alice. Why do you hesitate, my lass? I am certain that your spirits are labouring under some heavy depression which requires an explanation. Surely we have nothing now left but for congratulation?"

"I would fain think so, Ben," she returned; "but, alas! my heart forebodes some fresh trouble in store for us; and probably the annihilation of all our hopes."

"Avast heaving there, my pretty one," said the young seaman; "whither are you steering now? Though I have a notion I can form a pretty shrewd guess as to what point of the compass the wind is blowing from. As for our hopes being capsized, I can tell you, Alice, there is not much fear of that; for you see, it appears most probable that our old enemy, Sir Raymond Perceval, is sent to old Davy, and will never trouble us again. You are safe now under my protection; in a short time we shall return to old England, and then, my dear girl, won't the village bells soon be ringing a merry peal on the morning of our wedding?"

"Oh, Ben," said our heroine, "that's where it is that my breast is the abode of many doubts and apprehensions. I fear that happy time is now never destined to arrive.'

"What! not arrive? Do you then doubt my faithfulness, Alice?"

"Oh, no, Ben, heaven forbid that I should, for I know your heart too well. But recent events have worked a great change in our position, and created obstacles to the consummation of our hopes and wishes, which I have too much reason to fear we shall not be able to surmount."

" Explain yourself, Alice ?"

" Dear Ben," she replied, and tears trembled in her eyes as she spoke, " as the simple, but honest sailor, the friend and companion of my childhood, I own you won my heart's warmest affections, and I dared to encourage the hope that I might look upon you as my future husband. But—, but— now—that your origin is discovered to be noble— the humble Alice Maitland must no longer presume to cherish such fond ideas, and—"

" Hold, Alice," interrupted her lover; " and think you that any change in my cir- cumstances could alter my sentiments, or that I would value title or wealth if they were not shared with you ? Fie, Alice, I did not believe that you could ever think so meanly of me."

" But remember, Ben, that you have now the will of a father to consult."

" Away with all your doubts and fears, Alice," cried our hero, joyfully; " the will of that noble parent, generous as he is noble, is already known. He approves of our love, and—"

" And is here to acknowledge the fair Alice as his future daughter, the wife of that beloved son who, after the lapse of so many years, has been so miraculously restored to him," said his lordship, who, accompanied by Lady Geraldine, had unobserved entered the cabin, and listened to the conversation of the lovers. " My boy—Alice," he added, taking their hands, and joining them together, " be all your doubts and fears at once removed. You are worthy of each other; be happy, and may heaven shower its bless- ings on your future union."

It would be impossible to describe as they deserve, the emotions that filled the bosom of Alice and her lover; they knelt at the feet of Lord Sidney, who once more invoked a blessing on their heads, and in which he was fervently joined by Lady Geraldine. A heavy weight was now removed from the heart of our heroine, and her looks suffi- ciently evinced the gratitude she felt towards the generous-minded nobleman.

Harry Helm and Rose now returned to the cabin, and after mutual congratulations had been exchanged, the conversation became general.

" But, my dear mother," observed Lord Alfred, addressing himself to Lady Geraldine, " you have not yet informed me how it was that you disappeared in so mysterious a manner from our house in Granada; and by what singular means we have been for so many years separated from each other, and without being able to obtain any clue to the fate which had befallen us."

" It is a sad tale, Alfred," replied Lady Geraldine ; " but a few brief words will suffice to relate it. Being seized with a strange frenzy at the abduction of the unfor- tunate Lady Emeline and her infant, and fearing that, in your despair, you had laid violent hands on yourself, I secretly, at night, fled the house, and wandered I knew not whither, until I found myself in a deep forest, and amidst the raging of a fearful storm. Madness was upon my brain, and I rushed about calling wildly upon your name and that of Emeline, until I sunk exhausted on the earth, and became uncon- scious to all around me.

" What followed I know not; but I have a dreamy recollection of wandering for weeks, if not months, through almost impenetrable forests, and the wildest of places, flying terrified at the approach of human beings, and subsisting on berries and wild fruits.

" At length I was caught by the crew of an English vessel, who had come ashore for fresh water, and accidentally seen me. Taking compassion on me, and probably in- fluenced in a great measure by curiosity, they, in spite of my determined resistance, conveyed me on board their ship, where I was treated with every kindness, but they could elicit nothing from me; I remained absorbed in sullen silence, and cared not what became of me.

" The vessel was homeward bound, and in a short time resumed her voyage, while I remained in the same melancholy and deplorable state, scarcely conscious of what had taken place, or where I was.

" In due time we arrived in England, and notwithstanding the captain and crew kept a strict watch over me. I contrived to escape, and wandered about the country for weeks, subsisting on the charity of strangers. At length accident led me to that neighbourhood where I was for so many years, and took up my wretched abode in the old castle ruins. My mind was now alive to all my past sorrows, although I assumed that wild and mysterious character I ever appeared in, the better to forward my future designs, for something convinced me that I should yet some time or other meet with the villain who had been the cause of all this misery, and have my revenge. I also cherished the hope that you, Alfred, would some day or other be restored to me, although I had tried in vain to obtain any intelligence of you.

" How shall I describe my feelings the first time I beheld the youth who has hitherto been called Ben Bolt? The striking resemblance he bore to the unfortunate Emeline, struck me, and filled my breast with the most powerful emotions; but when I heard his history, I was at once convinced that he was no other than my grandson, and the awful and untimely fate of his mother was revealed to me. It was with difficulty that I could refrain from disclosing the truth to him, but the same hope of full and ample justice, which I had so long cherished, silenced my tongue, and I awaited the issue with patience and confidence.

" Years passed away; and Sir Raymond Perceval, on the death of his father, came to reside at the Manor House. I saw him, and immediately recognised in him the guilty miscreant who had been the author of such accumulated atrocities. How fearful was the torrent of passions which swelled my bosom at that moment; but he seemed not to have the least recollection of me. I could have sprang upon him like an enfuriated tigress, and torn his remorseless heart from his breast; but the hope of a more deliberate and exquisite revenge restrained me, and I contented myself by annoying him at every opportunity, and reminding him of the diabolical crimes he had formerly perpetrated, and thus keeping him in a constant state of fear and mystery.

" Thank heaven, the hour I had so long panted for, came at last; retribution has overtaken the guilty wretch, and I am restored to you, my son, and that beloved youth, who, in his infancy was so miraculously preserved from an untimely fate."

Thus Lady Geraldine concluded her extraordinary narrative, which her auditors, who were rivetted in profound attention, had never offered to interrupt.

" Oh, my dear mother," said Lord Alfred; " how wonderful have been the ways of Providence in bringing these events about. But how great must have been your sufferings during so many years."

" Yes," replied Lady Geraldine; " they were severe, indeed; but it was the hope of justice and revenge that sustained me, and though many an hour of bitter; nay, almost insupportable anguish, it was my lot to endure, and contumely, insult, and derision were constantly heaped upon me by the vulgar and the ignorant, I seldom murmured, but bore my assumed character with increased determination. It was my chief source of consolation to watch the noble and generous character of your offspring, the brave young seaman, who was esteemed and admired by all who knew him; and I pictured to my imagination that eventful day when all might be revealed, and be restored to his rights. Thank God, I have not been disappointed, and now I can die in peace."

" Long, my venerable relative, may you be preserved to bless us!" said our hero, fervently, and raising the hand of Lady Geraldine to his lips; " how can I, a poor simple mariner as I am, properly express to you the feelings of regard I bear towards you. But believe me, it is as sincere as it is fervent."

" Excellent youth," said her ladyship, " I know it; I know it full well, for the sentiments of your soul speak in your eyes. May heaven bless you, and the fair maiden to whom your heart is devoted, and who is so worthy of you!"

Our heroine, with an air of becoming modesty but sincerity, heartily returned her thanks for this compliment, and the conversation became more general, and in which Harry Helm and Rose did not fail most cordially to participate.

CHAPTER XXI.

THE CHANGE IN THE VILLAGE OF MAYLAND—DESPAIR OF MR. MAITLAND—SIR RAYMOND PERCEVAL STILL ALIVE—GOOD NEWS.

Many months had elapsed, and sad was the change which had come over many of the inhabitants of the village of Mayland, since the events that have been recorded in the previous chapters. In fact, an air of melancholy seemed to pervade the whole neighbourhood, which made it appear anything but like the same place. In the old church-yard, a plain marble slab, marked the spot where rested the remains of the mother of Alice and her sister, the poor old woman having gradually sunk under the painful bereavement, and died of a broken heart; and her aged partner wandered about the village a melancholy man, scarcely conscious of what he was doing, and deeply sympathised with by all who knew him.

Old Ben Bolt, too, was a much altered man, and deeply mourned the loss of the sisters; while at the same time he almost dreaded the return of his adopted son and Harry, to whom he feared that the dreadful intelligence of the mysterious loss and probable fate of those whom they so fondly loved, would prove almost a death blow.

The continued absence of Sir Raymond Perceval from the Manor House also created the utmost surprise, and various were the conjectures that were formed upon the subject. Then there was the singular and unaccountable disappearance of Maud of the Ruins, who had not been seen or heard of for so many months, and altogether there was ample food for the most perplexing surmises.

Old Ben was seated outside the Jolly Topers, on a fine afternoon, in deep conversation with old Matty Muggins, when a man enveloped in a cloak, and with his hat slouched over his eyes, appeared at the back, but observing them he hastily retired to a spot where he might remain concealed and see and hear all that passed.

"Ah! Matty," observed old Ben, "you may well say that the village only looks like a wreck of what it formerly was, since my poor Ben and Harry Helm departed. and some rascally pirates or other bore off pretty Alice and her sister. My old hulk has received a shock from which it will not easily recover, and as for Ben and Harry, should they return, what a shock it will be to their feelings, poor lads? I tremble to think of it. May the wretches who have been guilty of this crime split upon the rock of adversity and founder in the sea of despair!"

"Ah! my old friend,' returned Matty, ' so I say; and it strikes me that Sir Raymond Perceval had something to do with it."

"Ay, his continued absence from the Manor House certainly looks suspicious. Whoever it is, they have certainly much to answer for, for they have broken the heart of one parent, and nearly robbed the other of his intellect."

"Yes; it is quite painful to see poor old Ralph Maitland wander about as if he was lost, and from which state of mind it is impossible to arouse him. Should no tidings of his daughters reach him, I fear he is not long for this side of the grave."

"Eight months have elapsed since the fatal occurrence," said Ben; "but yet at times I cannot help thinking that the poor girls will be restored to us. As to the Spitfire, we have heard good news of her. The British flag has again triumphed, and it is expected she will shortly return with a portion of the fleet. But I must weigh anchor, and pay another visit to my poor old friend. So good day, Matty."

"Good day, Master Bolt," said Muggins; and the former was about to depart when he was arrested in his intention by a familiar voice, and directly afterwards a bluff-looking seaman made his appearance, and hurrying up to him grasped him cordially by the hand as he exclaimed:

"What, Ben, my old hearty, what cheer?"

"Eh, what?' cried Ben; "do my old eyes deceive me? No; may I never go aloft if it ain't my old particular friend Jack Taffrail of the Thunderer."

"The very same," said the latter; "only arrived yesterday, and so, crowding sail, I made with all speed for this port, and here I am. I've news for you.

"News for me?" repeated Ben; "good or bad?"

"Good to be sure," replied Taffrail; "the gallant Spitfire!"

"Ah! what of her?" eagerly interrogated the old man.

"Fell in with her on her voyage home," said the sailor; "went on board, saw your boy, Ben, and Harry; well and hearty, and merry as grigs."

"Hurrah!" shouted Ben; "splice my timbers! this is good news. But proceed, Jack, proceed."

"Well," returned Taffrail, "Ben had only time just to scribble a bit of a note, which he axed me to deliver to you, and here it is."

"A letter from my boy," cried the old man, in high glee; "oh, let me overhaul it directly."

Hastily he tore open the letter, and read the following words:

"Dear father that used to be, for I have found a real earnest father at last; I hope this will find your gallant old craft all sound and trim, which this leaves me and Harry at present. Such rare good news for you—my pretty Alice, God bless her! and her sister are both safe and under our protection. Rescued them from an infernal pirate, after a severe struggle. Give all our loves to the poor old people, and tell them, with the favour of Providence, they may expect to see their daughters in a few days. Such glorious news, but have not time to tell you now. Heaven bless you all! BEN."

The old man read this epistle aloud, and could scarcely keep his joy within the bounds of reason.

"Can I believe my precious old eyes!" he exclaimed. "Alice! Rose! safe! and my dear Ben found a real earnest father! My eyes, this is news, indeed! Jack, we have not time to splice the main-brace now, but you shall swim in grog presently. I must crowd all sail for my old friend Ralph, and you just tow yourself alongside of me, that you may convince the poor old man that I am not spinning a yarn. Alice, Rose, safe, and moored alongside their lovers! Damme! if this news does not almost drive me crazy. Come along, Taffrail, my old Commodore, heave-a-head, and let us make all speed for the Woodbine."

"Ay! ay! Master Bolt!" replied Taffrail, and they hurried away.

"Well," remarked Matty Muggins, when they were gone; "this is indeed wonderful and glorious news, and I can scarcely credit it. Poor Ralph Maitland, it will be almost too much for him; but I am as heartily glad of it, as if it were my own case. I must go and tell my dame, and all my customers about it."

The worthy host then retired into the house, and the man before mentioned, came forward from the place of his concealment, where he had been an attentive listener to all that had passed, and the reader will be astonished to hear that, on raising his hat from his brow, he revealed the features of the villain, Sir Raymond Perceval!

Yes! it was indeed him; he had, by some miraculous means that will have to be explained, escaped the fate which had been intended for him, and found his way once more to the immediate scene of his former villany. But so altered indeed was his personal appearance, that it would have been almost impossible at first sight, to have recognised him.

"So," he said, "I have returned safe once more to this spot, and what is this I have just now overheard? The girls still secure on board the Spitfire, which it is expected will arrive here in a few days. Be it so; they flatter themselves that I am dead, but they shall find to their cost, I still live for revenge. It is fortunate that Ben did not mention my name in the letter, for it will give me time to act. My accursed enemies shall yet have cause to tremble at Sir Raymond Perceval. But I must away from hence, for it might be dangerous for me to be seen lurking about."

He was about to depart accordingly, when he was met by a ruffianly-looking man, who having stared at him full in the face, started back in amazement, exclaiming:

"Can I believe my eyes? Yes; it is Sir Raymond Perceval!"

"Hush, Blackthorn!" said the baronet, in a low and cautious voice, and at the same time laying his hand on the arm of the pirate; "it is dangerous for you to mention my name here, where there might be listeners. Where are your comrades, whom we left behind at the retreat under the Manor House?"

"They are at present away on business," replied Blackthorn; "but you may in safety accompany me to the cavern. It has hitherto escaped discovery."

"Ah!" returned Sir Raymond; "that is fortunate; lead on, and there we may converse in safety."

They now quitted the spot, and although the curiosity of the pirate was excited to the utmost pitch, the guilty baronet firmly declined to answer any questions until they should have arrived at the secret cavern in which so many of their nefarious transactions had taken place, and which had hitherto remained undiscovered, the mind of Sir Raymond occupied by various and conflicted feelings.

CHAPTER XXII.

THE INTERVIEW OF SIR RAYMOND AND THE PIRATE, WILL BLACKTHORN—EXPLANATIONS.
THE VOW OF VENGEANCE.

Scarcely exchanging a word with each other, Sir Raymond and his ruffianly companion hurried on their way, and soon came in sight of the Manor House, which looked gloomy, lonely and deserted; and here the baronet paused, and folding his arms upon his chest, contemplated the building with mingled feelings.

"So," he muttered, in sullen accents; "proud home of my ancestors, once more I behold your ancient walls, after all the reverses of fortune, perils, and disappointments I have encountered. But oh, under what different circumstances do I retrace my footsteps hither. Curses light upon that wayward fate which has attended me, and those who have frustrated my deep-laid schemes, and crushed my hopes. But let me not despair; most miraculously I have escaped the fate which was intended me, and may not revenge, deep and deadly revenge yet be mine? Yes, by all the infernal host I swear, that, though I perish, I will immolate those whom I hate in my fate."

"We tarry, Sir Raymond," observed Blackthorn, "and I need not remind you of the danger we run in remaining here."

"True," agreed the former, looking round in order to ascertain whether or not they were observed; "let us proceed."

They did so, and, in a short time afterwards arrived at the entrance to the secret cavern, where they shortly found themselves. It bore much the same aspect as it had done some months before, and Sir Raymond surveyed it for a minute or two in gloomy silence.

"And now, Sir Raymond," said Blackthorn at last; "I pray you explain to me by what strange circumstance do I again behold you here?"

"Aye," he replied; "you may well be surprised, and you will be more so, when you hear the particulars—I am like one risen from the dead."

"We have already been made acquainted with the destruction of our gallant vessel by the Spitfire," said Blackthorn; "the death of Luke Harden, the rescue of Alice Maitland and her sister by their lovers, and—"

"How!" interrupted the astonished Sir Raymond; "by what means could you possibly obtain this information?"

"From Redford," replied Blackthorn, "who was the only one of the crew of the Bloodhound who managed to reach England."

"Ah! then he has probably made you acquainted with the discovery of Lord Alfred Sidney, whom I had hoped was long since dead; his recognition of Ben Bolt as his son, and what's more, that her whom we have hitherto known as old Maud of the Ruins, is no other than the mother of Lord Alfred, the Dowager Lady Sidney."

"No," cried the astonished Blackthorn; "is it indeed so!"

"'Tis true," answered Sir Raymond; "and may eternal curses light upon the accident, which at the very time when I thought success was mine, has brought about those events. I have, however, heard that within the last hour which leads me to hope that I may yet have the means of gratifying my revenge."

"What mean you, Sir Raymond?"

"The Spitfire is on her way to England, and a seaman belonging to the Thunderer has brought a letter from my rival to old Ben Bolt, apprising him of that fact, and also of the safety of the sisters."

"How know you this?"

Sir Raymond related what he had overheard while secreted outside the Jolly Topers.

"That is satisfactory enough," observed Blackthorn; "but it is fortunate that Ben did not mention your name, or it might have been productive of the most unpleasant and dangerous consequences."

"True," coincided the baronet; "but they believe me dead, so that I may yet have an opportunity of secretly accomplishing my wishes."

"You have not yet explained that Sir Raymond."

"I will do so in a few brief words. The principal portion of the crew of the Spitfire, finding that the Bloodhound was so battered that it was fast sinking, hastily retired to their ship; but Ben and Harry Helm remained behind, with the hope of being able to rescue their lovers. Of course, they were soon overpowered, and binding them to the mast, we left them to perish with the sinking vessel, while with the girls in our power, we made for the nearest land in the boats, which we reached in safety. The young seamen, were, however, by some means or other which I know not, rescued, and a number of the crew of the Spitfire, with Lord Alfred, his son, and Maud, came in pursuit of us. For a time we managed to elude them, but at the very moment when myself and Harden were about to carry our designs against Alice and her sister into effect, they surprised us. Luke was shot dead, and seeing that the game was up, (for, overpowered by numbers, our comrades were flying in all direction) in the confusion, I escaped. I rushed up a rock; Lord Alfred saw me, fired, but missed me, and I leaped into the sea, and swam to another part of the shore, from which I viewed them return to the ship, no doubt concluding that I was slain.

"Exhausted by the extraordinary fatigue I had undergone, I sank upon the barren earth in a state of insensibility.

"I did not revive to consciousness till the morning, and then I looked around me with rage and despair. The ship was gone; I was left alone, and as far as my eyes could stretch all was desolate, wild, and dreary. Nothing could possibly be more fearful than my situation, the place I was in, was evidently uninhabited; a frightful lingering death stared me in the face, and bitter were the curses that escaped my lips. One moment I was half resolved to plunge into the sea, and thus at once end my existence. But still the hope of rescue and future vengeance, arrested me in my deadly purpose, and I endeavoured to become more calm.

"The principal portion of my property was lost in the Bloodhound, but still I had a large sum of money secured about my person, and I hoped that it might yet prove of service to me.

"I now made an excursion into the island, with the hope of finding some inhabitants, or meeting with those of the pirates who had made their escape, but without success, and I returned in the evening, tired, hungry, and half mad, to the spot from whence I had started.

"That night, and a portion of the following day, I passed in the same state of misery, and I will leave you to judge what was the state of my mind. But in the afternoon, I espied a vessel at a distance, and half frantic with sudden joy, and the prospect of deliverance, I shouted aloud, and played all the antics of a lunatic. I stood on the very verge of the rock, and waved my handkerchief as high as I could in the air, with the hope of its attracting their observation; but at present the ship was too far off for those on board to notice my signal, and I began to fear that I should again be doomed to disappointment. However, the wind bore her swiftly on, and at length she had arrived so near, that I felt satisfied my signal must be seen, which supposition was soon confirmed, for I saw a boat put off from the ship, and make towards the rock on which I was standing. What a relief was this to my mind, and again I shouted with delight.

"The boat arrived, and I was released from my perilous and awful situation, and received with every kindness on board the ship, which was an English merchant vessel on her passage home.

"To the questions that were naturally put to me by the captain, I replied that I was an India merchant, and was on my way to England in a ship called the Enterprise, which was wrecked in the storm which had occurred three days before. That every soul on board but myself had perished. and I had succeeded with great difficulty in reaching the barren rock on which they had found me.

"My story was a plausible one, and of course, I was believed, and much sympathy was expressed for me. Two days since the Enterprise arrived at her destined port, and I immediately quitted it, and, having disguised myself as you see me now, I made my way once more to this neighbourhood, which I had never expected to see again."

"Well, Sir Raymond," observed Blackthorn, when he had concluded, "you have certainly encountered some extraordinary perils, and had some narrow escapes; but you may thank your lucky stars that you have been able to brave them, and arrived here safe."

"Aye," returned the baronet; "but I have still a desperate game to play. When

RALPH MAITLAND RECEIVING THE LETTER FROM OLD BEN BOLT.

tne Spitfire arrives in harbour from her voyage, then all my guilt will be made known, and—"

"But you are supposed to be dead," interrupted Blackthorn; "what then have you to fear?"

"I dare not again show my face in the light of day, for should I be discovered, what else awaits me but an ignominious death? I must wander about a wretched outcast from society, while I shall have the tenfold torture to know that those whom I so mortally detest have triumphed, and that all my plans are defeated. Oh, curses light on my foolish tardiness, or it would never have come to this."

" Be calm," said Blackthorn; "and let us discuss this matter coolly and deliberately. It may turn out much better than you now anticipate. The girl Alice may yet again fall into your power, and revenge will still be your's."

"Ah !" exclaimed Sir Raymond; "that thought again inspires me with confidence, and I will be firm and determined. I live now alone for revenge, and by hell ! it must and shall be mine, let the consequences to myself be whatever they may."

"Spoken like yourself, Sir Raymond," said his companion; "and I do not fear but

No. 14.

that you will yet triumph. The destruction of our gallant craft, however, was a bad job, and has placed us in difficulties of no trifling character."

"Those difficulties may be surmounted," said the baronet; "notwithstanding the severe loss I sustained in the Bloodhound, I have still more than ample means left for every purpose, and I will take good care to draw largely upon my banker's without delay, in case of any emergency; as for the Manor House, of course, as I shall not be able to occupy it when my guilt is known, I am undecided how to dispose of that, but must endeavour to make up my mind before the return of the Spitfire."

"Aye," observed Blackthorn; "it will be necessary to act with all due promptitude. As to the old Manor House, it has lately become deserted by nearly all the servants you left behind in it; in fact, old Andrew, the steward, is the only one who now remains."

"So much the better," returned his guilty companion; "they would only have been in my way. As for old Andrew, I can depend upon his secresy and silence; he is the creature of my will, and is in my confidence. All may yet go well—and yet at times fearful misgivings torture my mind, and shake my soul with terror. Frightful visions have of late haunted my imagination, and but last night the ghastly phantom of the murdered Emeline appeared to me in my sleep, and—"

"Psha! Sir Raymond," interrupted the pirate; "I am surprised to hear you talk thus. Is it possible that a man of your stamp can suffer mere idle dreams to disturb you even for a moment? You have already braved the severest ordeal, and need but firmness and determination yet to triumph completely."

"I will endeavour to think so. But how fares the number of your comrades, Blackthorn?"

"A dozen of as daring fellows as ever drew blade or cocked a pistol," replied Blackthorn.

"And are they to be depended upon?"

"Depended upon, aye; you will find no mutineers among them, I'll warrant. Nor are we quite so destitute as you may probably imagine. We have an excellent smugling vessel, safely moored farther along the coast, which may be found useful should the girl, Alice Maitland, again fall in your power."

"'Tis well," remarked Sir Raymond, approvingly; "this intelligence encourages me to hope."

"You have every reason to do so," said Blackthorn. "But come, Sir Raymond, you must need some refreshment. I have nothing better to offer you than some capital Hollands, which no doubt will serve to raise your spirits."

Blackthorn filled the baronet and himself a bumper, and then raising the glass he said:

"A toast, Sir Raymond; here's confusion to our enemies, and complete success to all our future schemes."

The baronet cordially responded to this toast, and then seating himself at the table, he partook heartily of the rude but plentiful repast which was spread thereon.

The pirates soon afterwards returned, and were not a little astonished at beholding Sir Raymond; but they welcomed him with the utmost enthusiasm. Several hours were passed in discussing their future projects, when Sir Raymond left the cavern by the secret way, and traced his steps to the Manor House, in order to make Andrew acquainted with his return, and to instruct him how to act.

This old man, who was acquainted with all his secrets, and who, for the sake of gain, not only applauded but abetted him in his crimes, was not a little surprised and gratified at his return; and he expressed himself accordingly. The baronet having again enjoined him to secresy, and urged him to act with due precaution, was lighted by him to a chamber, and for the first time for many months the guilty man slept in the mansion of his ancestors.

But could he sleep? Ah! no, that troubled mind, that guilty conscience, could know no rest; and he tossed about on his pillow with mingled feelings of doubt and dread, till the morning's light beamed in at the windows of his chamber. He then arose, and after a brief interview with old Andrew, he once more sought the presence of Blackthorn and the other pirates in the cavern, and remained with them in consultation for some time.

There was one who viewed the marked preference and partiality shown by Sir Raymond towards Blackthorn, with feelings of hatred and jealousy—and this was the pirate Redford.

"So," he soliloquised, when he was alone; "Blackthorn is to be honoured with the particular notice and confidence of Sir Raymond, in preference to I, who have had to share all the dangers and terrors that we lately encounter.d. Be it so; but they may both of them have cause to repent of the neglect shown to Redford, before many days have elapsed. Sir Raymond Perceval, make not too sure that you will not be disappointed in your fancied security; for, although you know it not, you are playing a game at present which may bring you to destruction. Blackthorn, you have thwarted me in my desires on more than one occasion; but 'twill be well for you if you do not try my patience too far. I will have revenge; and such a revenge too, as you can but little dream of."

An expression of fierce determination clothed the ruffian's features, as he thus gave utterance to his feelings, and he stalked gloomily from the place.

CHAPTER XXIII.

OLD BEN BOLT COMMUNICATES THE JOYFUL INTELLIGENCE TO MR. MAITLAND—ARRIVAL OF THE SPITFIRE, AND MEETING OF THE FRIENDS.

With an elated heart old Ben and his companion made their way to Woodbine Cottage, in order to impart the welcome news to Ralph Maitland; and on the road the former consulted with himself in what way it would be best to act, for in the present state of the poor old man's mind, any abrupt disclosure might be productive of the most serious consequences.

On arriving at the cottage they found Ralph Maitland seated in melancholy meditation, and so deeply was he absorbed in thought that he did not notice their entrance till Ben addressed him, when he arose, and started slightly and in some confusion on beholding Taffrail.

"I ax pardon, my old friend," said Ben, "for bringing my mate with me, but I dare say you will hail him with pleasure when you know all. This is honest Jack Taffrail of the Thunderer, and as good a seaman as ever mounted aloft."

"Alas!" replied Maitland, in a melancholy voice; "I make but a sorry host now; nevertheless, any friend of yours, Ben, you know must at all times be welcome to me. I greet you, sir."

"And the same to you, my old hearty," replied Taffrail; "and I'm only sorry to find you tossing about in rough weather, when you ought to be moored in the harbour of peace."

"I thank you, sir," returned Ralph, in the same tones of sadness; "I thank you for your kind wishes. I am a poor, care-worn, broken-hearted man, and—, but why should I obtrude my sorrows on a stranger? But a little longer—but a little longer let me bear with it. I must not murmur at the will of the Almighty."

"Out with it, Ben," said Taffrail, in a whisper; "why keep the poor old man in suspense?"

"Ben," said Mr. Maitland, and he looked at him stedfastly, "I cannot help thinking that something of moment has brought you here to-day. Strange thoughts have occupied my mind all the night, and when I slumbered, dreams, alas! too blissful to be realised arose to my busy imagination."

"Why you see," said Ben, "my friend Taffrail here is only just ashore, and— and—, oh, damn it, what's the use of tacking about from one to the other? It must out sooner or later, so the sooner the better. You see, Taffrail fell in with the Spitfire on the voyage home, and— and— saw Ben and Harry; and—and— Ben sent a bit of a letter which is worth a whole cargo of guineas, for the joyful news it contains; and—, oh, splice my timbers! I shall choke if I endeavour to explain; so you had better take the letter and read for yourself."

Poor old Ralph Maitland took the letter from Ben's hand eagerly, and opening it, commenced reading the contents with anxious haste but he had scarcely glanced at it a moment, when an exclamation of joy escaped him, and sinking on his knees and clasping his hands together, in a voice of the most powerful emotion, he cried :

"Almighty God! who in thine infinite mercy hath listened to the prayers of the poor bereaved parent, receive, oh! receive my soul's eternal gratitude! My beloved children, and shall I indeed be permitted again to behold ye, ere the silent grave shall inclose my cold remains? Shall I once more clasp ye to a fond father's doating heart? Shall I—"

He could say no more; his emotions choked his utterance, and the big tears rolled rapidly down his furrowed cheeks.

Ben and his companion were much affected, and turned away their heads to conceal the manly tears that also trembled in their eyes. It was some time before either of them could recover sufficiently to speak, and then Ralph Maitland rising slowly from his knees, and grasping the hand of Ben, in tones of mingled gratitude and joy, exclaimed :

"Oh, Ben, Ben, what transporting news is this; it is true—my heart assures me that it is true. I cannot doubt it. My dear children, oh, what must have been your sufferings? My heart bleeds for you. May the maledictions of outraged heaven descend upon the head of the diabolical miscreant who has been the cause of this! But to you, sir," he added, turning to Taffrail, and warmly taking his hand, "what a debt of gratitude do I owe for thus imparting hope and sunshine to my seared heart!"

"Avast there, my good friend," replied the honest seaman; "I am sure I am not deserving all these thanks; but I have been the means of drifting your vessel from the rock on which it was likely to split, why, all I can say is, that I feel myself one of the happiest fellows on deck."

Ralph Maitland grasped his hand with more warmth than before, and looked what his tongue could not speak :

"Well said, Jack," observed Ben, "and I honour you for the sentiment. Cheer up, Ralph, my old Trojan, for the storm is nearly over, and I see fair weather approaching. Oh, only to think now that the gallant Spitfire should have the good luck to come athwart this infernal buccaneer, and that the poor girls should come under the immediate protection of their lovers."

"Ah!" ejaculated Mr. Maitland, "how wonderfully and how wisely was it ordained by Providence. But should anything yet happen to prevent the restoration of my dear children; should storms assail the gallant vessel which bears them!"

"Oh, belay your fears, Ralph," interrupted Ben; 'for that same Providence which has already rescued them from so many imminent perils, will not fail to watch over and protect them till they are safely moored in your arms."

"God grant that it may be so," cried Mr. Maitland, fervently; "alas! my poor old dame, that you did not live to see that happy day! How great will be the anguish of my beloved children when they find that that fond mother, who ever guarded them with such indulgent, affectionate, maternal care, now sleeps within the old churchyard."

"Ah! poor old dame," said Ben, feelingly, "may heaven rest her soul! But come, Ralph, let us banish these gloomy thoughts; oh, won't everybody in the neighbourhood be delighted when they hear the news?"

"But," said Mr. Maitland, "who can have been the principal actors in this monstrous outrage?"

"Why," answered Ben, "that it is impossible to say. But fear not; if they still live, they are detected and will be brought to justice. I only wish I had the hanging of the scoundrels, I would do it with the same pleasure that I chew this quid of baccy."

"Aye," observed Taffrail, "and well they deserve it, too; but I say, shipmate, I must be for sailing, for I've many calls to make, and I dare say you can dispense with my company. Good day; I will take the liberty of coming alongside of you again before long."

Mr. Maitland again grasped the hand of the generous sailor cordially, and once more returning his heartfelt thanks, Jack Taffrail departed from the cottage.

Ralph again and again perused the letter, and gave free vent to his emotions; which his companion did not offer to interrupt.

"Oh, Ben," said the former, at last, "what joyful news is this. I can scarcely persuade myself that I am not labouring under the delusion of some deceitful dream. But no, the well-known handwriting of Ben convinces me of the truth; and my heart o'erflows with gratitude to the Supreme. Never, oh, never did I expect to see my dear children again. Oh, with what anxious impatience shall I await the arrival of the vessel which contains them.''

" Aye," returned Ben, " and so shall I my poor boy; my gallant-hearted son, for such I shall ever regard him, though he says that he has discovered a real earnest parent. Now, that's a point at which I am taken all aback, and cannot make it out anyhow.''

" Yes,'' said Ralph, " it is, indeed, a mystery; but I hope, for his own sake, that he has done so, and that that parent, whoever he may be, may prove worthy of such a son.''

" Oh," replied Ben, " there can be but little doubt of that. Lor! lor! how I do long to see the dear boy! What a story he will have to tell us! Won't it be a meeting! All the village will be out that day to meet and welcome 'em; but I say, my old friend, there's one thing I've got to say to you.''

" And what is that, Ben?''

" Why, when they return, just to complete their happiness, and bring their hearts to an anchor at once; let there be no more delay, but splice them off-hand.''

" You know my feelings upon that point, Ben," answered Mr. Maitland; " and may be sure that I will offer no objection to what you suggest.''

" Bravo!'' shouted the veteran; " it delights me to hear you say so; where can you find two more worthy captains for such fair craft as Alice and Rose Maitland, than Ben Bolt and Harry Helm ?''

" True," coincided Ralph, " they have honourably won the hearts of my daughters, and heaven knows the happiness I shall feel in bestowing their hands upon them. May no other calamity arise to prevent the consummation of our wishes!''

" Oh, fear not," said Ben, confidently; " all will now be as fair and as prosperous as we could wish it. My eyes! methinks I see that joyous day already, and I know I shall grow young again on the occasion. There will be Alice and Rose, all blushes, beauty, and modesty; and Ben and Harry, all smiles, and love, and happiness! And who is there who will not sail forth to honour them? Young and old, rich and poor, married and single. And I say, Ralph, what if this newly-discovered father of Ben's should turn out to be some great man—some rich man ?''

" Ah! my friend," suggested Ralph, " and should he do so, may he not object to his son becoming the husband of the humble Alice Maitland, the poor cottager's daughter ?''

" Wheugh!'' cried Ben, with a whistle; " there may be something in that, sure enough. But he must be a surly and unreasonable old grampus, if he could do so. And think you that Ben would obey orders ? 'Think you that he would abandon his pretty Alice; her whom he loves dearer than his own life? Oh, no, I know his heart too well for that. He would turn mutineer directly. So overboard with all such doubts and fears, and let us look forward to the best!''

In this strain Ben and Mr. Maitland continued to converse for some time longer, until the former seeing that his companion wished to be alone, took his leave, and poor old Ralph was left to his own reflections.

What the nature of these were may be easily imagined; oh, how different to what they had been only a few hours previously, then he was overwhelmed with anguish and despair, but now his heart was elate with hope.

His bosom overflowed with gratitude to Omnipotence; and yet there was something so wonderful in the event, that at times he was half inclined to doubt it's reality. But no, the truth was so palpable that he could no longer remain incredulous, and tears of joy again trickled down his aged cheeks.

Once more he returned his thanks to heaven, and most earnestly he implored that nothing might occur to disappoint the fond hopes that were excited in his breast, for that he was certain would at once prove his death blow.

He pictured to himself all the troubles and suffering that Alice and her sister had probably undergone, and he could not but admire the wonderful ways of Providence that had so miraculously preserved them throughout so many difficulties.

It was indeed a busy night for the mind of Ralph Maitland, and such was the anxiety of his thoughts, that sleep was almost banished from his pillow. Yet at times he could not help entertaining some misgivings that greatly diminished the ardour of his joy at the unexpected intelligence he had received. Should anything happen to the vessel where those fondly precious to him were on board, they might never more be suffered to reach their native shores, and then how terrible, how overwhelming would be the disappointment to his hopes. He could not help shuddering at the thought, and again the poor old man most fervently prayed to heaven to avert any such calamity. And then he reflected on the grief which Alice and her sister would naturally feel at the death of their mother; and that was a source of fresh anxiety and uneasiness to his mind.

"My poor old dame," he sighed; "oh, why did cruel death deprive me of thee, at the very time when, borne down by affliction I most needed thy consolation and advice? But the wretches that tore our children from our arms, and thus robbed us of the only support of our declining years, were the sole cause of thine untimely death, and the just retribution of offended heaven, cannot fail to pursue them for it. Alas! God only knows how I have been able at all to bear up against such accumulated misfortunes; though at times, indeed, madness has almost seized upon my brain, and—may heaven pardon me for the dreadful thought! I have been half tempted to lay violent hands upon myself, and thus at once to terminate my wretched existence. But, oh, my beloved children, should ye indeed again be restored in safety to my arms, methinks, notwithstanding the severe bereavement I have experienced by the death of your excellent mother, I could find sweet consolation."

Ralph felt somewhat comforted by these reflections, and sought to await patiently and confidently the happy time which he anticipated. Again and again he perused the letter of our hero, and every time he did so, although he could have wished Ben had been a little more explicit, his conviction of its being the truth became the more firm.

And thus passed the night away, and when Mr. Maitland arose from his couch on the following morning, his mind felt more calm and tranquil than it had done for many a month before. He was soon afterwards joined by old Ben Bolt who, when he had left him on the previous day, had been round to all his neighbours to make them acquainted with the joyful news, and we need not say that, respected as the fair sisters and their lovers were, it created universal satisfaction, while every one deprecated in the most unmeasured terms, the miscreants who had been the cause of so much misery.

"But it is all over now, my old friend," observed Ben; "the infernal rascals, if we may believe what Ben has set down in his log, have had to pay dearly for their villany and we have nothing more to fear from them. I only wish I had had the overhauling of one or two of them; old as I am I fancy they would have thought the devil had hold of them, if I had once laid my grappling irons upon them. Oh, how I do long for the time to arrive when the dear boys will be here to explain to us all about the business."

"Ah! my old friend," returned Ralph, "and need I say that my impatience is at least equal to yours. The whole affair is so extraordinary that it appears to be almost incredible."

"Aye, that the gallant Spitfire should happen to bear down upon the very pirate craft which held in the bilboes the pretty Alice and her sister. It was a fortunate circumstance, and it seems that the brave lads of the Spitfire did not fail to make good use of it. Lor! lor! what a meeting it must have been between the lovers!"

"It must, indeed," coincided Ralph, "and it makes my heart throb to think of it. May kind heaven guard them from every future danger, and favouring breezes waft the noble vessel which contains them once again in safety to these shores."

"Well said, my old hearty," returned Ben; "but fear not, our hopes will not founder, and the storms to which the poor girls and their sweethearts have hitherto been exposed, will be succeeded by a happy calm. What puzzles me more than all is, the father that Ben has discovered. Hows'ever, I know his heart too well to suppose that he will ever turn his back on the old pilot who has for so many years guided him through the ocean of life."

"True, Ben," observed his companion; "he is too noble and generous ever to harbour within his breast such a despicable feeling as ingratitude."

"Ingratitude!" repeated Ben; "I should like to see the lubber who would dare to accuse him of it. My boy, my Ben, would sooner be strung up to the yard-arm, or blown to mincemeat at the mouth of the cannon, than he would ever strike the flag of honour to any one in existence. The brave boy! how it glads my old heart to think upon the glorious career he has hitherto pursued; and I trust that I shall yet live to see the day when he will be promoted to one of the highest ranks in the service. Ralph, my old Trojan, won't that be a happy day which sees him and Harry spliced to the girls of their hearts?"

"Yes," agreed Ralph Maitland, "and God grant that nothing may occur to prevent it."

"Prevent it," reiterated Ben, "what can occur to do that? Fear not but Ben and Harry will remain as faithful to their lovers as the needle to the pole."

"I do not doubt their fidelity," observed Mr. Maitland; "but, as I have before said, should this newly-discovered parent of Ben's turn out to be a person in a superior station of life, he might refuse to unite his son to the humble Alice Maitland."

"Then he will prove himself unworthy of such a son," replied Ben; "but avast with such thoughts, and do not be meeting squalls half way. You do him wrong if you suppose that anything whatever could induce Ben to abandon his beloved Alice, and much as I regard him, I should consider that he deserved to be flogged through the fleet if he could do so. But come, Ralph, you must tack about, and not give way to any of the doubts and suspicions you have just now expressed."

"Well," remarked the latter, ' I most sincerely hope that they may prove to be erroneous, and that no obstacle will be thrown in the way of the complete happiness of those who are so worthy of each other."

"And I will stake my life," said Ben; "that there is not. If the father of my boy (for I shall always call him such), could wish his son to have a fairer craft to sail alongside of than the pretty Alice, why, it will prove that he knows no more about such matters than a newly-fledged marine. Take my word for it that the lovers have only to be safely anchored in this port, to be made the happiest beings in existence. As for you and I, my old friend, we shall ship such a cargo of joy that we shall hardly know how to dispose of it. Come, Ralph, my tar, let us slip the cable of dull care, and keeping a sharp look out, fear not that the enemy will get the weather-guage of us in future."

"Well," returned Mr. Maitland, "I will endeavour to follow your advice, Ben, though I should like to know who is the real author of these atrocious outrages."

"That we shall discover ere long, I dare say; though no doubt it will be put out of his power to harm us again."

"Is it not strange," observed Ralph, after a minute or two's reflection, "that Sir Raymond Perceval should remain so long absent from the Manor House, and that no one should know what has become of him?"

"It is," agreed Ben, "and old Maud of the Ruins, too—to what port can she have sailed, and to weigh anchor in such a mysterious manner."

"I have often thought of that," replied Mr. Maitland, "and it is a mystery which I hope will some time or other be solved. Maud was no ordinary individual depend upon it; and when I think of her denunciations against Sir Raymond, and the evident alarm with which he viewed her, I cannot help strongly suspecting that there has been some foul work to get rid of her."

"Well," said the old seaman; "that may be, but a short time I hope will explain all. But oh, Ralph, who'd have thought after the lapse of so many months, and we had nearly abandoned ourselves to despair, that matters would have turned out as they have?"

"True, true, Ben, and need I tell you how my heart o'erflows with gratitude to the Supreme, for the infinite mercy that's shown towards me? Deprived of all that was valuable to me in life; children, wife, everything, what an insupportable burthen to me had existence become, and hourly did I pray that it might please the Almighty to rid me of it, and thus put a period to my misery. But now the dark clouds that obscured the horizon of my happiness are partially dispersed, and fond visions of future peace and tranquillity burst upon my imagination."

"Well spoken, Ralph, and they will be realised too, as sure as my name's Ben Bolt, and I have helped to give the enemies of my country a sound drubbing, on more than one occasion. I have been on a cruise since I left you yesterday, and made all our neighbours acquainted with the joyful news, and you should only have witnessed their satisfaction when they heard it. I shall respect my old shipmate, Jack Taffrail more, than ever for having been the first to bear down to our assistance when we were cast upon a lee shore."

"Aye," responded Mr. Maitland; "I feel myself greatly indebted to him. He seems to be an honest-hearted man."

"Honest!" repeated Ben; "you may say that; a better seaman than Jack Taffrail never faced the enemy; and as for his heart, it has always a cargo of good feelings on board, which he is ready and willing to divide among his fellow-creatures. Jack and I were shipmates together the very last voyage I made; and on one occasion in a a storm, when I was washed from the rigging, and was very near going to old Davy, who was it that, at the hazard of his own life, plunged into the angry ocean and saved me? Why, Jack Taffrail, to be sure; and have I not, therefore, a right to look upon him as one of my best friends?"

"True, true," agreed Ralph; "the brave fellow is worthy of your warmest gratitude. But come, Ben, let us take a walk down to the coast, and, perhaps, we may hear some more tidings of the expected ship."

"With all my heart," replied Ben; "so just tow yourself alongside of me, and I'll pilot you there in gallant style."

Ralph Maitland took his arm, and they then departed from the cottage.

In the mean time the Spitfire, impelled by favouring breezes, was rapidly proceeding on the passage home, all hearts on board elate with hope and joy at the prospect of once more being restored to those dear friends and relations who no doubt, so anxiously looked for their return; and none more so than those who have been the principal actors in our little drama.

The lovers and their friends passed as much of their time together as possible, and Lord Alfred hourly saw more and more to admire and esteem in the beauteous and gentle sisters, and to approve of the love which his son had encouraged for his pretty and innocent Alice.

"She is worthy of you, my dear son, she is every way worthy of you;" he would say, when they were conversing together; "and with what feelings of unfeigned delight do I anticipate the happiness which is in store for you, when heaven shall have united your hands as well as your hearts!"

"Thanks, thanks, my noble parent," replied our hero, his looks sufficiently testifying the sincerity of his observations; "I am but a poor simple seaman, unused to the lingo of polite life; so you will pardon me I know, if I cannot find proper language to express to you those feelings of gratitude that my heart prompts me to do. My sweet Alice worthy of me! Oh, she is worthy to become an empress, let alone such a poor sailor as me. Throughout all the storms and troubles it has been her lot to encounter, has she not ever remained faithful to me? Yes, and sooner could she forfeit her life, I know, than cease to love the poor, and once unknown sailor, the friend and companion of her childhood."

"I do believe you, my son," said his lordship; "for truth and innocence are depicted in every lineament of her countenance, and renders her an object that no one can see without admiring.'

Our hero raised the hand of his father to his lips in respectful acknowledgment of the flattering eulogium he had passed upon the lovely mistress of his affections, and they being at that moment joined by Lady Geraldine, the conversation dropped.

Various and conflicting were the thoughts that occupied the bosoms of Alice and her sister, as the vessel proceeded on its way. Hope and fear alternately predominated, and their joy was not unmingled with some powerful misgivings, which, in spite of all their efforts, and those of their lovers, they found it impossible entirely to subdue. 'Twas true the generous assent of Lord Alfred to the union of herself and his newly-discovered son, had removed a weight of anxiety from the mind of Alice, which had been almost insupportable; but still how should she find her beloved parents on her return home; or was it not more than probable that they had sunk under the dreadful bereavement they had experienced, and that the silent now grave inclosed their cold remains? If so, what a sad drawback would it be upon the joy which would otherwise be her's and her sister's!

This thought was most torturing, and kept her in an almost constant state of dread and uneasiness.

Rose, who was far more calm and confident than her sister, endeavoured to banish such gloomy ideas from her mind, whenever she gave utterance to them, but seldom with any degree of success, such was the strong hold they had taken of her.

"Oh, remember, my dear sister" she observed, "how merciful Providence has

THE MEETING OF THE FRIENDS.

hitherto been to us, in preserving us throughout so many dangers; and fear not but the same Almighty Power has watched over our beloved parents in the midst of their troubles, and enabled them to bear up against them. We shall be restored to their arms and happiness will once more be ours."

"I would fain endeavour to think so," replied our heroine; "but be not too sanguine in your expectations, Rose, lest they should be doomed to a bitter disappointment. Oh, I shudder to think upon what the anguish of our parents must have been at our mysterious disappearance, and the uncertainty of the fate which had befallen us. The blow was a terrible one, and I fear that they could never find strength to survive it. Anxious as I am once more to tread our native shores, I yet feel a dread of approaching them, which I am unable to conquer."

"Persevere, my dear Alice," said her sister, "and depend upon it your fears will turn out to be erroneous."

Alice was about to make some reply, when they were suddenly joined by Ben and Harry, who embraced them with the utmost affection.

No. 15.

"But Alice, my sweet lass," said our hero; "why do you look so sad? Tears, too, in your eyes, what is the meaning of this?"

"Oh, Ben, forgive me," replied Alice; "if I appear unmindful of the kind fortune which attended me and Rose in our preservation from the awful fate which threatened us, and our restoration to you and Harry. I am all joy and gratitude in one sense of the word, while at the same time a sad presentiment distracts my mind that our troubles are not yet at an end."

"Nay, Alice," said her lover, "you take me all aback, and I am at a loss to understand you. What have you now to fear? Our enemies are destroyed; our gallant vessel nears the shores of old England; my father approves of our love, and—"

"True, true," interrupted the damsel; "but my beloved parents; my anxiety is for them."

"The poor old people are alive and well, I hope," returned her lover; "and good old Ben, too. Come, come, do not give way to these fears, my love, and depend upon it all will go well."

Our heroine appeared to be satisfied, attempted to be more composed, and the topic of conversation was changed.

*   *   *   *   *   *   *   *

At length the white cliffs of Albion appeared in sight, and all was joy and gladness on board the Spitfire. How the hearts of the sisters and their lovers throbbed with hope and expectation as their eyes rested on the distant outlines of their native shores, and they thought of the many dangers from which they had escaped. It would be a matter of impossibility to give anything like an adequate description of their feelings, and we must therefore leave it to the imagination of the reader.

At an early hour the following morning, the Spitfire cast anchor in Portsmouth Harbour, and was received with a welcome salute by the other vessels that was moored there.

It was agreed that Lord Alfred and Lady Geraldine should remain on board for the present, and that Ben and Harry should accompany the sisters alone, but so great was the agitation of Alice, that it was not without the greatest difficulty she could support herself.

Notice of the approach of the Spitfire had been communicated on shore on the previous evening, and soon reached the ears of Mr. Maitland and old Ben Bolt, and the agitation of their feelings, especially those of the former, may be easily imagined. To sleep that night was, of course, impossible; and before daylight the following morning Ralph and his friend were on the spot, and witnessed the arrival of the Spitfire.

They waited some time in the greatest suspense, when a couple of boats put off from the ship, and they strained their eyes in vain to distinguish the objects they contained.

A few minutes more and one of the boats reached the shore; there was a loud and simultaneous exclamation of delight, and Ralph Maitland once more clasped the beloved forms of his beauteous daughters in his arms, while old Ben shook the hands of his adopted son and Harry alternately, and big tears chased each other down the furrowed cheeks of the kind-hearted veteran.

And here we must leave the scene which followed to the imagination of the reader.

At length our heroine and Rose gently disengaging themselves from the arms of their father, and looking anxiously around, ejaculated, in a breath:

"But mother, dear mother, oh, where is she?"

"Alas! alas!" sighed Mr. Maitland, and his voice and looks sufficiently told the melancholy tale. The sisters understood him, and uttering a cry of anguish, they fainted, and with the assistance of Ben and Harry were conveyed to the cottage.

It was some time ere either of the party could calm their feelings, but when they were enabled to do so, our hero briefly entered into the particulars that have been already related, and to which Ralph and old Ben listened with the most unbounded astonishment and almost incredulity.

"What!" exclaimed the old seaman, when our hero had concluded, "my Ben the son of a lord! Shiver my timbers! here's a pretty go!"

"But still your son also," said the young man, fervently grasping his hand; "still your son also, my best earthly friend, nor can any change in circumstances possibly alter my feelings of gratitude and veneration towards you. My dear Alice, too, her Ben is now the same to her that he ever was, and thank heaven, my father approves of our love, and will freely give his consent to our union."

"Bravo!" shouted old Ben, and his ruddy countenance was lighted up with redoubled pleasure; "bravo! true blue for ever, and damn the fellow who flinches."

"But is it possible," said Ralph, "that Sir Raymond Perceval can have been the author of all these miseries?"

"'Tis true!" answered our hero; "but he has paid the penalty of his crimes, so there is an end of him."

"The infernal shark!" added old Ben.

"And her whom we knew as Maud of the Ruins?" interrogated Ralph.

"Is no other than the Dowager Lady Geraldine Sidney, the mother of my parent," replied the young seaman.

"Wonderful!" cried Ralph; "I can scarcely believe the evidence of my senses but—"

He was interrupted by a knock at the cottage door, which, being opened, Mr. and Mrs. Jingle entered.

"Ah! my old friend," said the former; "here we are, all arrived once more safe in happy old England, (from which I will never more depart, while my name is Mr. James Jingle) and after all the perils and dangers which only bold and enterprising spirits, like mine, dare encounter."

"What, my worthy poet," said old Ben; "I'm glad to come within hail of you once more; give us your flipper; have you found the—the—what d'ye call it?"

"The sublime and beautiful," replied our hero.

"Oh, yes," answered Jingle; "and what's more I've greatly *extinguished* myself, as your friend Ben, or rather, I beg his pardon, the Honorable Lord Alfred Sidney, can testify."

"True, true," said our hero; "but what of his lordship and Lady Geraldine, Mr. Jingle?"

"They have left the ship, and are on their way here," answered the latter, "they sent me and my Sally forward, to announce the same to you."

"Then I will hasten to meet them and conduct them hither," said Ben, and he quitted the cottage accordingly.

"Shiver my timbers!" cried old Ben, when he was gone; "here's wonders for you! My boy, my Ben, the Hon—hon—hon—oh, damn it, I should dislocate my jaw if I was to utter that word, so I won't try. Old Maud of the Ruins—not old Maud of the Ruins—but a right down earnest lady of title, and the grandmother of my Ben! Oh, that I should ever live to see such a day as this!"

"It is indeed most wonderful," said Mr. Maitland; "but, oh, my dear children, that you should at last be rescued from the awful fate with which you were threatened; and that I should once more press ye to my bosom, when I never expected to behold ye again! May heaven receive an old man's thanks, an old man's boundless gratitude, for the infinite mercies extended to him!"

Before Alice or Rose could make any reply, the cottage door was thrown open, and our hero returned, introducing his father and Lady Geraldine.

The meeting was one of the most gratifying description; Lord Alfred was evidently much prepossessed in favour of Mr. Maitland and old Ben, greeted them with the greatest affability and warmth of feeling, and they were soon on the same easy and familiar terms, as if their stations in life had been equal, and they had been acquainted for many years.

"To you, my respected old friend," said his lordship, taking the hand of the veteran seaman, "I owe a debt of gratitude, which I fear it will never be in my power to repay. You saved the life of my son, and brought him up with the same care and affection as if he had been your own, and it shall be my constant study to reward and—"

"Oh, your honour, your lordship, I ax pardon," interrupted Ben; "you hurt the feelings of old Ben by talking of rewarding him for doing that which has been one of the chief pleasures and comforts of his life. But if your honour's lordship will only permit me to call him my boy, as I have always done, you will make me one of the happiest old fellows in the world."

"Take your wish, my good old man," said Lord Alfred, "and with it a father's blessing for the inestimable service you have rendered him!"

Old Ben could not speak, for his heart was too full, and he was about to kneel at the feet of his lordship, when the latter presented him; and smiling graciously upon him conducted him to a seat by his side, where he entered into familiar conversation with him.

The day passed most agreeably away, and, at an early hour in the evening, Lord Alfred and Lady Geraldine retired to The Jolly Topers, where apartments had been engaged for their accommodation.

CHAPTER XXIV.

AN IMPORTANT ONE—PLOTS AND COUNTER-PLOTS—REDFORD'S REVENGE.

The news of the expected arrival of the Spitfire, had reached the ears of Sir Raymond Perceval, and greatly excited him; and he immediately sought an interview with Blackthorn, to advise with him what was best to be done.

"Immediately on their arrival it will be known that I was the author of the abduction of Alice and Rose Maitland," he remarked, "and the whole of my guilt will be divulged."

"And what of that?" demanded Blackthorn. "You are supposed to have perished, and have, therefore, nothing to fear from discovery. You have only to act promptly, and according as I shall advise you, and you will not only have the full gratification of your revenge, but get the girl Alice again in your power."

"Ah! say you so?" said Sir Raymond, eagerly.

"I do," replied Blackthorn, "and feel confident of the success of my designs."

"Blackthorn," observed the baronet, "your words reassure me. Could I but again get possession of Alice, my revenge would indeed be gratified."

"I promise you that it shall be so, if you will leave everything to me," said Blackthorn.

"Enough," returned Sir Raymond; "I will be guided alone by your advice. But there must be no delay in the business."

"There is no necessity for any, and the sooner it is accomplished the better."

"Could I destroy the hated Lady Geraldine and her son, Lord Alfred, my revenge would be doubly satiated," said the guilty Sir Raymond.

"That also may be accomplished," replied his companion.

"Your hand; your promises prove you to be my best friend, and I will not fail to reward you amply for your services."

"Well, we can talk about that some other time."

"But will it be safe for me to remain here?"

"Yes; in this cavern for the present," answered Blackthorn, "though not in the Manor House. I repeat, you are supposed to have perished, and so it is not likely that they will trouble themselves any more about you."

"True," said Sir Raymond; "and everything seems most favourable to the accomplishment of my designs."

"Nothing can be more so."

"Oh, Alice, proud beauty," cried the baronet, "should I again get you into my power, what a glorious triumph it will be for me. Little do you dream that he whom you have so much cause to dread still lives to persecute you."

"Aye, Sir Raymond," said his guilty companion, "you will indeed have ample cause for exultation. To-morrow night then, should the Spitfire arrive in time, we will put our designs into execution."

"Be it so," said Sir Raymond; "I am all impatience for their accomplishment, at any risk."

"Oh, fear not," observed Blackthorn; "I will arrange it so that we need not fear detection."

"Do this, Blackthorn, and you will doubly secure my favour."

The villain again promised to do his best to forward the nefarious wishes of his guilty employer, and they sat conversing for some time, arranging their future plans and having settled that Blackthorn should go in the morning and await the arrival of the Spitfire, Sir Raymond Perceval retired to rest in the secret haunt.

Redford had been a secret and attentive listener to this conversation, and as he retired, with a malicious expression of countenance he muttered to himself:

" 'Tis well, you may flatter yourselves with the hope of success; but if I fail not in my designs, methinks you will be most wofully disappointed. You have aroused the hatred and jealousy of Redford, by treating him with undue neglect, and he will not rest until he has had an ample and signal revenge for the same. Beware, Sir Raymond Perceval, for the crisis of your fate may be nearer at hand than you imagine."

As the ruffian thus spoke, he walked away from the place where he had concealed himself, with fierce determination in his looks.

At an early hour the following morning, Sir Raymond left his rude couch, and after exchanging a few observations with Blackthorn, the latter, in disguise, departed from the cavern to watch the arrival of the Spitfire.

Sir Raymond paced the cavern after his departure, indulging in a variety of conflicting thoughts, and, notwithstanding all that had passed between them, and the confidence which Blackthorn had expressed as to the ultimate success of their diabolical designs, in spite of all his efforts to the contrary, doubts and misgivings would at times disturb his mind, and he could not but forbode some disappointment to his wishes. On the arrival of the Spitfire the whole of his guilt would be exposed, and the subterranean; haunt beneath the old Manor House would be revealed by Lady Geraldine, which might lead to the worst consequences.

"But psha!" he ejaculated, endeavouring to arouse himself; " let me not give way to these idle apprehensions, that after all may turn out to be quite erroneous. Do not my enemies believe me dead? They do, and that, of course, will quiet all their suspicions, and prevent them from taking any further trouble in the business, at least for the present, and I have only to act with promptitude and determination to accomplish my designs. A few hours shall decide all, and I am resolved to triumph or perish in the attempt."

The guilty baronet felt more firm and confident as he gave utterance to these words, and he awaited the return of Blackthorn with the most eager impatience.

In this manner two hours elapsed, when his suspense was terminated by the reappearance of Blackthorn with the intelligence of the arrival of the Spitfire, and the disembarkation of our hero and Harry Helm and their lovers, and their meeting with old Ben and Mr. Maitland.

'But Lord Alfred and Lady Geraldine?" eagerly demanded Sir Raymond. "Saw you nothing of them?"

"No," answered Blackthorn. "They did not come ashore with the others."

"Ah!" exclaimed the baronet, "what can be the meaning of that? Can anything have happened to them on the voyage?"

"I know not," returned his companion; "but probably they may have deferred their landing till after the excitement of the lovers and their friends was over."

"True, true," observed Sir Raymond. "I did not think of that. But you watched the meeting of the fair sisters and their parents, Blackthorn?"

"Secretly I did so," answered the latter, "and well may you judge the nature of it. The beauteous sisters were overwhelmed with emotion, and joy and exultation were expressed in the countenances of your rival and Harry Helm."

"Curses light upon them!" cried the baronet, in a fierce voice, and with a malicious frown; "but their joy may be turned to sorrow, and they may be compelled to acknowledge the triumph of Sir Raymond Perceval."

"Aye," coincided the ruffian, "if fortune abandon us not. To-morrow night, when darkness reigns around, and no one can have any suspicion of the danger which threatens, we may make an attack upon the cottage, and the result is all but certain."

"Ah! to-morrow night be it then; it would not be prudent to delay it longer, and most anxiously shall I await the arrival of the time. But think you that it would be safe to convey Alice here?"

"No, I have already made arrangements with respect to that, and by which, with the girl in our power, we may make our escape without delay to one of the smuggling vessels I have before mentioned, and, covered by the darkness of the night, soon be beyond the reach of pursuit."

"And must the Manor House, and its contents be abandoned to our enemies?" said Sir Raymond.

"There is no other alternative," replied Blackthorn.

"It will be a dear price at which to purchase my revenge," observed the baronet, in a dissatisfied tone ; "but no matter, as it will no longer be safe for me to remain here, or to return hither, having secured all the portable property that I can, I must e'en submit to the sacrifice."

"And who is to reward us for all this risk and trouble?" demanded Redford, who now came forward, having been a silent but attentive listener to this conversation ; "why should we expose ourselves to such danger, when our services are likely to be so badly requited?"

"How now," demanded Sir Raymond, suspiciously ; "grumbling, Redford?"

"Aye," replied the latter ; "have I not cause to be dissatisfied, when, after I have shared so largely in all the dangers of the former adventures, I find myself now neglected, and my advice neither sought after or valued."

"Psha!" exclaimed Blackthorn ; "I am surprised to hear you talk so, Redford. You misunderstand Sir Raymond, I am certain ; he fully appreciates your services, and I have no doubt, will amply reward them."

"Redford should know me better than to doubt that for a moment," replied the baronet ; "I have ample means still at my command, notwithstanding what has taken place, and I will not fail to pay all those liberally who assist me in my designs. Let me but get Alice Maitland in my power, banished from the society of the world as I now am, henceforth a rover's life must be mine, both from choice as well as compulsion. Are you satisfied, Redford?"

"Well," returned Redford, thinking it prudent to disguise his real feelings, lest it should counteract his designs, "I probably was too hasty in my observations ; your promise is enough, Sir Raymond, and I am satisfied."

"And you are willing to render your assistance in the furtherance of the designs we have in contemplation?"

"I am," answered the pirate, in a tone of sincerity.

"Aye, Redford will keep his word, I have no doubt of it," remarked Blackthorn.

"You have always found him do so, I believe," replied the other ; "and I dare say he will not fail to do so on the present occasion."

He then retired.

"I do not half like the jealous and dissatisfied feeling in which Redford spoke," observed Sir Raymond ; "think you that we may still trust him, Blackthorn?"

"Yes," answered the latter ; "it was only a momentary feeling of envy on his part ; but after the assurances you judiciously gave him, I have no doubt that he is satisfied."

"I would, however, that a strict watch be set upon him, during the interval which must elapse before we attempt to put our designs into execution," said the baronet.

"That shall be done," said Blackthorn ; "but depend upon it you have nothing to fear from him."

"Well," remarked the baronet, "I only trust that it will turn out as you say. To-morrow night, then, at all hazards, we will perform the task we have allotted to ourselves."

"True; and I am much deceived if success does not this time crown our efforts. In the meantime, I will see that every preparation is made for our reception on board the craft."

"Ah!" ejaculated Sir Raymond, "that is important, for our departure from this coast must take place as speedily as possible. I feel myself worked up to a pitch of determination, and am fully prepared to encounter any risk to secure the gratification of my wishes."

"We so said, Sir Raymond," remarked Blackthorn, "and I must state this time you will not be doomed to disappointment. You have said truly that it will not be safe for you to remain here, as circumstances have turned out ; for it may be discovered that you still live, and I need not remind you what the consequences may be."

"True," agreed the baronet, "but only let me obtain the darling object of my desires, and I care not."

Blackthorn still endeavoured to encourage his hopes, and they passed two or three more hours together in arranging their nefarious designs, which they at length did to their mutual satisfaction. Blackthorn then departed to give the necessary instructions to those on board the smuggling vessel, after having cautioned his lawless associates to keep a strict watch upon the movements of Redford, and to see that he did not quit the cavern.

"So," said Redford, on retiring from the presence of Sir Raymond and Blackthorn, "you flatter yourselves with the idea that your designs will meet with success, and that you will escape detection. Fools! you little dream of that which awaits you, if I fail not, and the terrible retribution which awaits you Redford's jealousy and revenge were never yet aroused without their being gratified. To-morrow night, Sir Raymond Perceval, your fate shall be decided."

It was not, however, till the following day had far advanced that Redford could find an opportunity of secretly leaving the cavern, so narrowly was he watched, and he then made his way towards Woodbine Cottage, fully determined at all hazards to put into effect the accomplishment of his intentions. Tired of the life he had hitherto led, he was anxious to escape from it, and thought that no better opportunity of doing so than the present could not be afforded him.

On knocking at the door of the cottage he was instantly admitted, and on entering found Lord Alfred, Lady Geraldine, and all those whom he expected to see assembled.

They started back in amazement on beholding him, and our heroine and her sister turned very pale, and clung to their lovers, for they immediately recognised the features of Redford, and knew him to have been one of the pirate crew of the Bloodhound.

"How now, fellow?" demanded our hero, who also knew him. "Is it possible that you are still afloat? I thought that you had slipped your cable long ago. What brings you here?"

"I come to save you," replied Redford, "and to thwart the villainous designs that are formed against you."

"What!" exclaimed our hero; "another mutiny? Explain yourself—what mean you? But, hark ye, do not seek to sail under false colours, for if you do, you shall be strung up to the yard-arm, as sure as you're a living man."

"If you mean truth and honesty," remarked Lord Alfred, "speak plainly, and fear not."

"Believe me," said Redford, "that I seek not to deceive you; but, on the contrary, as I said before, I would render you a service. I admit that I have been a villain, and that my life is forfeited to the offended laws of my country, but I would fain abandon the guilty course I have hitherto pursued, if mercy should haply be extended towards me."

"Should your penitence be sincere," said Lord Alfred, "I may possibly possess influence sufficient to save you from the punishment your offences have incurred. Speak plainly and fearlessly what it is you have to communicate."

"That which, no doubt, will excite your utmost astonishment," answered Redford. "I come to warn you of the villain, Sir Raymond Perceval."

"Sir Raymond Perceval!" they all exclaimed, with looks of unfeigned amazement and incredulity."

"Hold!" exclaimed Lady Geraldine, what erroneous tale would you attempt to foist upon us? Sir Raymond Perceval perished by the hand of Lord Alfred Sidney, my son, months ago."

"No," returned Redford; "fate preserved him to endeavour to add to the dark catalogue of crimes he has already perpetrated. I repeat that Sir Raymond Perceval still lives."

"Is it possible?" cried Lord Alfred. "But where?"

"In this very neighbourhood, and is now concealed in the secret cavern beneath the Manor House, which Lady Geraldine has too much reason to know well."

"Wonderful!" exclaimed Lady Geraldine. "By what extraordinary means did the heartless miscreant contrive to escape from the fate which we all thought had befallen him?"

"That there is not time to explain at present," observed Redford. "This has assisted by such of the pirates who did not go on board the Bloodhound, the meditating a secret attack upon the cottage, in the hopes of once more getting Alice Maitland in his power."

"This story appears almost incredible," said our hero. "Did we not see the villain sink wounded from the summit of the rock into the ocean?"

"The contents of the pistol missed him," replied Redford, "and he was enabled to swim in safety to the shore."

"Can you speak the truth?" demanded Lord Alfred, with a look of suspicion.

"By all my hopes of mercy, I do," answered Redford.

"Ah, then," cried his lordship, "at length the monster will be brought to justice, and the cruel murder of my unfortunate Emmeline will be avenged. Come, let not a moment be lost in securing him."

"Pardon me, my lord," returned Redford, "but not so ; he does not intend to put his diabolical plot into execution till after dark, and therefore what I propose is that in the meantime application be made to the proper authorities for assistance, and the villains may then be surprised and secured before they have time to escape from their secret haunt. In order the better to prevent suspicion, I think it would be advisable for me now to return to the cavern, but I will be ready to admit you into the Manor House in secresy, and to conduct you to the place in which they will be assembled."

"Aye," remarked Lord Alfred ; "that appears to be a prudent arrangement. But can we depend upon your fidelity?"

"If you suspect me of any attempt at treachery," answered Redford, "you have me now in your power, and can deal with me as you think fit."

"Enough," said Lady Geraldine, "we will trust you. To-night, then, as soon as darkness veils the earth, you may expect us at the Manor House, accompanied by a force sufficient to accomplish our intentions."

"You will find me faithful," said Redford, "and the apprehension of the villains you may consider as certain."

Redford was allowed to depart, and it would be impossible to describe their astonishment at what he had communicated to them.

"I am completely lost in amazement," observed Lord Alfred. "The villain, Sir Raymond, one would almost be tempted to believe, possesses a charmed life."

"It is most extraordinary," said Lady Geraldine, "but the terrible hour of retribution is at hand, and if this man, Redford, has spoken the truth, the miscreant cannot now escape us "

"The daring scoundrel," observed Mr. Maitland, "still to harbour the thought of revenge. Oh, my dear Alice, if this man has spoken the truth, and we have no reason to doubt him, what shall we not owe him ? From what a terrible and revolting fate will you have escaped?"

Alice expressed her feelings in suitable language, and a messenger was then despatched to the officer of the coast guard, requesting his presence at the cottage. That gentleman quickly obeyed the summons, and upon being made acquainted with the particulars, expressed his utmost astonishment and disgust at the guilt of Sir Raymond, and his willingness to render all the assistance in his power to forward the ends of justice.

Everything being arranged, they anxiously awaited the arrival of night, which promised to be productive of such an important event.

CHAPTER XXV.

THE ATTACK ON THE PIRATES—AWFUL DEATH OF SIR RAYMOND PERCEVAL.

As Redford retraced his steps towards the cavern, he exulted in the success which had attended his designs, by which he should not only gratify his revenge, ut, in all probability, save himself from the punishment due to his former offences. he pictured to himself the horror and despair of Sir Raymond when he should discover that all his diabolical plans were frustrated, and that he was betrayed into tho hands of justice, and his feelings of triumph increased.

Redford still hurried on his way, and, as he did so, his satisfaction at what he had done, and his exultation at the anticipated gratification of his malicious feeling increased. The step he had taken was a bold one, but, at the same time, there could be no doubt that it was the most prudent one he could have adopted, under the peculiar circumstances in which he was placed ; and he argued the most favourable results from it to himself.

It must not be supposed, however, that the ruffian Redford acted from any remorse of conscience, or that he was guided by any other motives in his conduct than those of avarice and revenge. No ; he was still as hardened in guilt as ever, and he acted more from the idea of self-preservation than anything else.

He was perfectly satisfied that, even had he remained silent, now that his former guilt was so well known, and the persons whom he had so deeply injured were in the neighbourhood, it would have been almost impossible for him to remain long undetected, consequently that the career of the baronet, and also that of his infamous and guilty colleagues must be speedily brought to a termination, and that, if he had been discovered amongst them, he would most undoubtedly have shared the same fate as themselves ; so that he could not help again and again priding himself on the course he had adopted, for by betraying them he flattered himself that he should not only save his own life, but in all probability receive a handsome reward for his services from Lord Alfred Sidney, and his past offences be forgiven and forgotten. This idea was sufficient to excite his hopes, and the villain became more confident and determined every moment.

"Yes," he soliloquised, and a malicious expression of triumph overspread his forbidding features as he spoke ; "the course I have adopted is a wise and a prudent one, and by it I shall not only save my own life, but likewise gratify those feelings of revenge which the neglect of Sir Raymond, and the favoritism he has shown towards Blackthorn, have excited in my breast. Oh, how little does he dream of the ruin which is shortly about to overwhelm him, and the terrible retribution which is so shortly to descend upon his head. And how will his guilty soul quail when he finds that he is not only defeated in his guilty plans, but that he cannot escape the fate which he has incurred by the crimes he has committed ; for, in spite of his empty boasting, I know full well that he is a miserable coward at heart. Had he made a confident of me, and showered upon me his favours instead of Blackthorn, he might not only still have set his enemies at defiance, but have accomplished all his designs. As it is, be the consequences of his own folly upon his head. In a few hours, Sir Raymond Perceval, and your guilty course will be run. But I must be cautious," he added, after a pause ; "for the least act of imprudence on my part in this critical juncture, might betray me, and then my destruction would be inevitable. But psha !—what have I to fear? I must indeed be a consummate fool, if I could not fully accomplish my designs, now that I have proceeded thus far. My triumph is certain, and therefore I will not entertain any more doubts upon the subject."

With these feelings, Redford continued to pursue his way, and having arrived at the cavern, entered the presence of the baronet and the pirates with a firm determination and a bold front.

As the time approached for the proposed attack upon Sir Raymond and the pirates, the impatience and excitement of the persons at Woodbine Cottage increased ; and various were the thoughts that it engendered in their breasts.

"But should this man have deceived us," said our heroine, as a feeling of doubt and hesitation entered her bosom.

"Nay, Alice " returned Lord Alfred ; "what cause have we to suspect him ? His mann was candid, and there was a plausibility in all he stated to us, that, I think, leaves us but little, if any room to doubt. The crisis of the villain's fate is approaching : he cannot escape us this time, and at length the death of my unfortunate Emeline will be avenged."

"Aye," observed Lady Geraldine, "the hour—the terrible hour of retribution, for which I have so long panted, and which I have suffered so much to bring about, is fast approaching ; the knell of fate is sounding, and when I see the inhuman miscreant writhing in agony and despair, I shall be content."

No. 16.

"Yes," remarked Ben, "the infernal shark will have to lower his piratical flag at last, and then, Alice, we may fairly slip the cable of doubt, care, and anxiety, and sail through the voyage of life with a favourable breeze to waft us on our course, after having so fortunately and bravely cleared the rocks and the quicksands."

"Heaven grant that all may turn out as you seem to anticipate, dear Ben," ejaculated Alice, fervently, and with a look of affection.

"And can you doubt it, Alice?" said Harry Helm; "why, what is to prevent it? The many severe storms that it has been our lot to encounter have passed away; we have got the weather-gage of Fortune, who will not again shift from her moorings, and I can see nothing but calm and sunshine in the future. But what says my pretty Rose.

"Oh, Harry," replied the beauteous damsel; "how can I do otherwise than participate in your feelings? Let but our enemies be removed, and what then shall we have to fear?"

"Right! right!" coincided Mr. Maitland; "the prospect before us is most promising, and I feel most sanguine upon the subject. Oh, how grateful shall I ever feel to the Almighty, who has thus frustrated the designs of the guilty, and brought about such remarkable events. My dear children are restored to me, and that at the very moment when I feared they were lost to me for ever. They will be happy, and what more have I to hope for in this world?"

The looks of all present plainly showed that their feelings perfectly coincided with his own, and, unable to give adequate expression to the thoughts that were passing in their minds in words, they remained for a short time silent.

The hour for their departure on this momentous expedition at length approached, and all was anxiety and impatience. Several of the coast-guard now made their appearance, their comrades having already made their way towards the Manor House, and all being arranged, with a fervent prayer for success, they took their departure from the cottage. Alice and Rose, notwithstanding the persuasions of their friends to the contrary, insisting upon accompanying them.

In the meantime Blackthorn had completed all the arrangements for the execution of the nefarious plot, and he and Sir Raymond awaited impatiently for the time to arrive which they had fixed upon to start on their daring expedition.

"But should it fail?" said the guilty baronet, as a feeling of doubt crossed his mind.

"Fail!" repeated Blackthorn; "psha! there is no fear of that. We shall take them by surprise, and need not apprehend any resistance. All is ready on board the vessel, and you may reckon Alice Maitland as secure as if she were already in your power."

"And yet," observed Sir Raymond, "in spite of all that you have said, and my own efforts, I cannot acquire that confidence I would wish."

"I'm surprised to hear you talk so, Sir Raymond," returned his companion; "when everything goes on so well. Come, come, you must arouse yourself, and before many hours have elapsed, depend upon it, Sir Raymond Perceval, your triumph will be complete."

"Well," said Sir Raymond; "I only trust that your predictions may be verified. But where is Redford? I have not seen him for some time."

"He is here," said Redford, stepping forward, he having just returned from the cottage; "do you want me?"

"Where have you been?" demanded Blackthorn.

"No further than the beach," replied Redford, calmly; "I suppose I am not a prisoner?"

"No," returned Blackthorn; "but your services will be required by Sir Raymond anon, so it is necessary that you should not again absent yourself from your comrades in the cavern."

"Be it so," returned Redford, "I shall be at hand whenever you may require my services."

Blackthorn returned no answer, so Redford retired back, and entered into conversation with two or three of the pirates; and, after some time passed in this manner, he watched his opportunity, and stole secretly away.

The impatience of Sir Raymond increased every moment, and strange doubts and misgivings disturbed his mind. Night came at length, and darkness overspread the earth.

"The time has now arrived," remarked Sir Raymond; "there is no necessity for any more delay."

"True," said Blackthorn; "all is ready, and so the sooner we depart on our expedition the better. Where is Redford?"

No one could answer that question, and Blackthorn was about to give instructions to seek him, when the well known signal was heard at the secret entrance to the cavern, and one of the pirates, who had been for some time absent, entered breathless, and evidently in a state of the greatest excitement.

"How now, Stanton?" hastily demanded Blackthorn, "why do you look so agitated and alarmed?"

"Danger threatens us," replied Stanton; "a large number of the coast-guard, accompanied by the friends and lover of Alice Maitland and her sister are approaching this way."

"Ah! betrayed!" exclaimed Sir Raymond; "infernal curses light upon the head of him who has done this."

"Confusion!" cried Blackthorn, with an oath; "how can this have occurred? Ah! Redford! Oh, villain! traitor! There is nothing left for us then, but a determined resistance. Secure the secret entrance, and be every man prepared!—Quick!"

Two or three of the men prepared hastily to execute these orders, but before they could do so, a number of the coast-guard leaped into the cavern, and attacked the pirates determinedly.

Hastily concealing his face in his cloak, and muttering curses to himself, Sir Raymond Perceval seized the opportunity in the confusion which prevailed, and retreated from the cavern into the subterranean passage.

Desperate and bloody was the combat which ensued—the pirates offering the most resolute resistance; but unable to stand against such an overwhelming force as that by which they were surrounded, and Blackthorn and several more being slain, the others were compelled to yield themselves prisoners.

In the meantime Sir Raymond, in a state of alarm which may easily be imagined, pursued his way along the subterranean passage, hoping to make his escape by the Manor House. He had nearly reached the extremity, when he was startled by hearing the sound of many approaching footsteps, which to his horror convinced him that his retreat was cut off, and that a portion of the assailants were advancing in that direction.

The wretched, guilty man trembled with terror and knew not what to do, but there was not a moment to be lost. Fortunately for him he discovered a deep recess in the wall near which he was standing, and he hastily concealed himself there, and crouched down in one corner of it, scarcely venturing to breathe, just as a number of the coast-guard entered the passage, led on by Redford. Oh, how willingly could Sir Raymond have discharged a bullet at his head, had it not been for the fear of betraying himself. They passed hastily by the recess, without observing him, and the wretched baronet breathed again. Hastily he resumed his flight, and succeeded in reaching an apartment in the Manor House, where again the sound of many footsteps ascending the stairs smote his ears, and filled him with dismay.

"Lost! lost!" he groaned; "they hem me in on every side; I cannot escape!— Ah!—they come! Still will I make one more determined effort to save myself from them!"

With the speed of lightning he hurried from the room, and dashed up the stairs towards the top of the house, but their shouts convinced him that they were upon his track, and the frenzy of despair was on his brain.

And now, scarcely knowing what he did, the wretched man rushed through a trapdoor on to the roof of the building, and was hailed by the shouts and execrations of the persons assembled below.

With folded arms, and ghastly looks of despair, he paced backwards and forwards, not knowing what course to pursue.

Only for a few moments, however, was he suffered to remain so uninterrupted. His pursuers rushed upon the roof, and the crisis of his fate approached.

"Yield!" exclaimed the officer in command; "for further resistance is now useless!"

"Yield!" repeated Sir Raymond, in a hoarse voice, and with bloodshot eyes ; " never but with life !"

" Fire then," ordered the officer.

A dozen muskets were immediately discharged at the guilty baronet, who bounding n the air, fell, a bleeding and frightfully-mangled corpse, from the lofty roof of the Manor House to the earth below !

For a few minutes the whole of the persons present were completely paralyzed and appalled by this awful event, and stood gazing with feelings of horror at the mangled mass before them ; whilst Alice and Rose, unable to endure the revolting spectacle, averted their looks, and, with a shuddering sensation of horror, covered their faces with their hands.

" Justice has at last overtaken the guilty," cried Lord Alfred, at length ; " the mis-creant is summoned to answer for his diabolical crimes, before the awful tribunal of God, and the blood of the ill-fated Emeline is now avenged."

" Aye," observed Lady Geraldine, and an expression of triumph animated her features ; " the murderer has met with his doom, and the soul of his unfortunate and innocent victim will be at rest."

A solemn pause ensued ; then the remains of Sir Raymond Perceval were removed into the Manor House, the spectators of this exciting scene were aroused from their lethargy, and, deeply ruminating on the tragical events of the evening, they slowly left the spot.

Every danger was now removed ; the bitter enemy to their peace was no more, and their fears were at an end.

And such was the fate of Sir Raymond Perceval! such the awful termination to his long career of crime!

CHAPTER XXVI.

CONCLUSION.

Solemnly impressed with the thrilling scene which they had just witnessed, the principal actors in our little drama slowly retraced their steps towards home, and so completely were their feelings excited and absorbed by the startling events that had taken place that, but little conversation passed between them.

Alice and her sister were much shocked at the awful fate of Sir Raymond Perceval ; but now that their bitter enemy was no more, their minds were relieved of a weight of care, dread, and anxiety, which had before been almost insupportable, and mentally they returned their heartfelt thanks to that Supreme who had so mercifully watched over them in the hour of adversity, and rescued them from all the terrible dangers that had formerly surrounded them, and that, too, at the very moment when they thought all hope was at an end.

The manner in which these events had been brought about was so extraordinary, that they appeared to be almost incredulous, and they could scarcely believe but that it was all a dream.

" So," observed Ben, when they had returned to Woodbine Cottage, and were sitting discussing the important subject ; " after many a tough engagement with the enemy, the victory is at length our's, and all the squalls that we formerly had to encounter are at an end."

" Yes," returned Mr. Maitland ; " thank heaven, the vindictive enemy our peace can no more disturb us, and I trust that I shall yet live to see my dear children com-pletely happy, and to be able to bury the gloomy past in oblivion. The ways of Pro-vidence are wonderful and just, and ever must our hearts rise in boundless gratitude to heaven for the mercy shown us."

" True," coincided Lord Alfred ; " a terrible retribution has at last overtaken the guilty, and my heart is relieved of the heavy burthen which before oppressed it. But you, my noble parent," he added, turning to Lady Geraldine, "how can I ever sufficiently express my wonder and admiration at the remarkable energy, patience, and fortitude with which, for so many years you have been enabled to bear up against an accummulation of misery and misfortune, the bare contemplation of which is sufficient to appal even the stoutest heart."

"Ah! my son," replied her ladyship; "terrible indeed were the trials to which I was subjected, and at times my spirits drooped before the dreadful ordeal. Scorned, and shunned by the low and vulgar; looked upon as a thing of hate, and doomed to pass my days and nights in a state of solitude even more awful than the grave, what could possibly be more wretched than my fate? But still the hope of vengeance, and of one day being restored to you, sustained me; and I braved everything with a moral and physical courage which it is impossible for me now to look back upon without the most indescribable feelings of wonder and incredulity. But, thank heaven, my hopes are realized; the blood-stained miscreant who was the cause of all those miseries has at length met with that fate which his diabolical crimes so justly merited. I am again surrounded by those beloved beings who are far more precious to me than my own existence. My every wish is accomplished, and I am satisfied."

"Aye," remarked old Ben; "I knew the infernal sharks must at length strike to an enemy who had justice on their side. But now we have cleared the rocks of misfortune, let us toss all dull thoughts overboard, and look forward to the future with the same glad feelings as the toilworn mariner views the white cliffs of old England after his return from a long cruise."

With the feelings of honest old Ben, which he so simply, but heartily expressed, every person present coincided, and they continued to converse for some time longer in the same strain.

It was several days ere the excitement caused by these startling events at all abated in the neighbourhood, and when the manifold crimes he had committed were taken into consideration, there was no one who pitied the awful fate of the guilty Sir Raymond Perceval. As for Alice Maitland and her lover, they could never be sufficiently grateful to heaven for their preservation from so many dangers.

A peaceful calm having succeeded these fearful storms of misfortune, Lord Alfred proposed without any further delay to reward the love and constancy of our hero and his "sweet Alice," by uniting their fates together.

The happy day was fixed, the nuptials of Harry Helm and the beauteous Rose being appointed to take place at the same time; the ceremony was to be solemnized in the old village church of Mayland, and all was joy and expectation; while the preparations that were being made for the auspicious occasion were on the most extensive scale.

The family mansion and domains of Lord Alfred Sidney were situated in one of the most fertile and romantic parts of Yorkshire, and his lordship's disappearance, and all endeavours to ascertain what had become of him or his noble parents leading to the conclusion that they were dead, for many years the family estates had been in the possession of his lordship's nearest relation, Sir Robert Glanville, a most amiable gentleman, who was held in the highest esteem by all who had the honour of making his acquaintance.

On his arrival in England, his lordship lost no time in writing to this gentleman to make him acquainted with the same, and all the extraordinary particulars that have been related, particularly the discovery of his long-lost son.

Only two days previous to the one appointed for the union, Sir Robert arrived at Mayland, and the meeting which took place between him, his cousin, Lord Alfred, Lady Geraldine, and our hero, was of the most cordial description.

The happy morn at length arrived, and all was joy and festivity in the village of Mayland, and the surrounding neighbourhood.

Followed by the blessings of their numerous friends and acquaintances, the Hon. Alfred Sidney, alias Ben Bolt, and his long-tried friend Harry Helm, led the beauteous sisters to the altar, where the sacred ceremony was performed with all due pomp and solemnity.

The next day the happy party, of whom honest old Ben Bolt was one, departed to the mansion of Lord Alfred, in Yorkshire, where the restoration of their lord, his noble mother, and the introduction of our hero and his beauteous bride, was celebrated by the domestics, tenantry, and gentry and nobility, in the most joyous manner for a month.

We have little more to add. Our hero and Harry, blessed in the possession of the lovely Alice and her sister, forgot all past troubles, and in future enjoyed all the happiness that Providence could bestow upon them

Mr. Maitland and old Ben resided with those so dear to them for the remainder of their days, and lived to see them surrounded by a numerous family of lovely and smiling children, who as they increased in years, emulated all the virtues of their parents.